THE FATE
IN THE BOX

Also by Michelle Lovric

The Undrowned Child
The Mourning Emporium
Talina in the Tower

THE FATE
IN THE BOX

Michelle Lovric

Orion
Children's Books

First published in Great Britain in 2013
by Orion Children's Books
a division of the Orion Publishing Group Ltd
Orion House 5 Upper St Martin's Lane London
WC2H 9EA
An Hachette UK Company

1 3 5 7 9 10 8 6 4 2

ISBN 978 1 4440 0339 0

Typeset by Input Data Services Ltd, Bridgwater, Somerset

Printed in Great Britain by Clays Ltd, St Ives plc

CONTENTS

PROLOGUE
Lamb and seahorse

Sunday July 20th, 1783, the Feast of the Redentore

The girl who climbed the ramp knew that there were only two possibilities at the top of the tower.

Life, or sudden death.

Amneris climbed slowly. As well as the taper fixed to the wreath on her head, a few candles flickered in dark niches. Their light had just revealed the church's great secret to her. Everyone thought the Frari possessed just one slender bell-tower. In fact, there were two: one inside the other. The ramp wound its way in between the gigantic arches of the inner tower and the small hooded windows of the outer one.

'But what,' thought Amneris darkly, 'is the use of a secret if you're going to die before you can share it with anyone?'

A relentless dripping of some nameless liquid made the steep path slippery. Cold bricks grazed her right hand as her fingers scrabbled for a safe hold. In her left hand, she clutched her blue glass seahorse. The long cloak slithered behind her. The mechanical lamb creaked in front of her, its flagpole waving aloft, its tail flopping against its back legs.

The voices of the choir – full of heart, full of fear – echoed from the nave of the church below. 'The Lamb! The Lamb!' the congregation pleaded.

It was known as 'The Lambing', this grisly ceremony in which Amneris now played the main role. Amneris was not sure if the words of the prayers referred to the strange little automaton in front of her – or herself. After all, the mechanical lamb *always* came back down the stairs with its self-satisfied smirk unchanged. The people called it 'the Lamb who leads the Lamb'. This time, the lamb being led up the ramp was Amneris: Amneris D'Ago, a twelve-year-old seamstress from the cloth-dyers' quarter in Cannaregio.

The air grew distinctly colder and thinner the higher she climbed. Drips smeared her face like thick, chill tears.

The first few windows gave her glimpses of the glowing church interior. But soon she was looking down on the roof and the spires of the Frari. Eventually, the whole city of Venice stretched out below in a glimmer of heat.

Amneris held the glass seahorse so tightly that its fluted nose dug into her palm. She was trying with all her might to believe in its power as a good-luck charm.

The ramp wound on, seemingly without end. Ahead of her, there was nothing but blackness.

'Oh no!' Amneris held her fingers open. A trickle of blood – shiny and black as ink in the candle-light – fell from a cut in the centre of her palm. And there lay the seahorse, the one thing that should have secured her safety, cracked in two by the terrified grip of her hand. The seahorse had snapped right across its blue glass heart.

'It's a sign,' thought Amneris, despairingly.

Then she stumbled over a pigeon so dead that its mummified corpse rattled as it tumbled down the way that she had come.

Now there was more darkness below her than above. Before she was ready, the ramp ended in a steep flight of stairs. The lamb chittered imperiously, mounting the steps in stiff hops. A minute more and Amneris was bathed in the silvery sunlight pounding through the open belfry, with a dizzying view of the city below. The bronze bells, twice as tall as her, hung motionless on their chains. Her eyes fell on the hole in the floor between them, just big enough for a human body to drop through. But the lamb clicked its feet impatiently, leading her to a new set of wooden stairs. After the brightness of the belfry, darkness swallowed her again. All too soon she was entering a chamber faintly illuminated by red-paned lanterns and lined with billowing velvet curtains the colour of black plums.

Amneris stared around wildly, her heartbeat contracted to a tiny throb of fear.

What was behind those curtains? Was it a footstep that made the floorboard creak? Was that breathing she could hear? Or was it the rasp of hot wind in the belfry?

Grey ringlets of fog curled out from behind the curtains, swirled briefly around the little room and disappeared.

The mechanical lamb turned around, bowed, and skittered past her to commence its juddering descent of the stairs. Alone, Amneris faced the Box, which had been placed on a fluted pedestal carved from stone. The candle on her head cast a shimmering light over it.

It was not what she expected.

The Fate in the Box was so small that it could have fitted in her hand. Somehow that felt worse: so much evil concentrated in such a little thing. And instead of showing itself deadly and serious, the Box was gaudily decorated with harlequin shapes and circus colours.

Amneris hesitated. She glanced back towards the stairs. The singing far below in the church had risen to a crescendo

3

of anguish. But the Box emitted an impatient little creak, minutely raising its lid so that a ray of light darted into her eyes. There was nothing for it. She stepped forward into a circle of light that seemed designed to hold her in the correct position. She glanced down. Yes, there was the faint outline of the trapdoor beneath her feet.

She stretched out a trembling hand. The handle of the Box was cold and muscular like a little serpent. She began to turn it. The well-known tune tinkled out in tinny little sobs. She closed her eyes

A penny for a spool of thread,
A penny for a needle.
That's the way the money goes,
Pop! Goes the ...

The words were appropriate for a girl who earned her living by sewing, thought Amneris, her eyes still firmly shut. She'd know when the Fate in the Box opened. Any moment now, the music would suddenly stop, and the lid would snap open like a musket firing. That much she had been told by the woman down below who'd been so rough – with both words and hands – when hustling Amneris into the robes she wore now.

The woman had told her some of the rest, too.

When the Box opened, it could be the wax head of a beautiful Madonna that rose on a gilded coil, with gently smiling lips and eyes modestly cast down. That would mean that the Fate in the Box decided in Amneris's favour, and she was saved.

But there was another possibility. It could be an ivory skull that popped up on a screw of rusted wire, with ropes of matted hair and endless blackness stirring in its eye pits.

If so, it would be the last thing she'd see. If the Fate in the Box decided against Amneris, no trace of her would ever come down those stairs. And no one who loved Amneris would ever know what had happened to her.

She wound the handle round and round. Each second was a heart-heaving tussle between hope and despair. Did the winding always go on this long? It had not seemed so on previous occasions, when she had been just one of the hundreds of children safe in the church, waiting and praying, as all her friends and her family did now. Her mother would be weeping. Her father would be silent with fear. Her granny would be coughing, as she always did. The mechanical primate would be standing at the pulpit, his glass eyes glittering.

Amneris kept cranking the handle. The torture ate her composure, destroyed her dignity. She began to weep, and to plead.

'I beg you, I beg you,' she sobbed. 'Spare me.'

She could have sworn she heard a man's laugh. She spun around, scanning the curtains for bulges or movement. There was nothing but the curls and fronds of grey vapour.

The lid of the Box opened infinitesimally and then shut again.

'It's teasing me!' Amneris cried in agony.

The decision of the Fate in the Box was always known instantly. A child saved by the Madonna always ran down the ramp on light feet – but not so light that the congregation could not hear that happy foot music. Everyone roared with joy; many threw themselves to their knees in grateful prayer. When the child burst through the tower door at the left of the nave, there was a general rejoicing, cuddling, kissing, and the child was raised on the shoulders of the crowd and paraded around the square in front of the Frari.

The other result was also audible.

Back inside the church, everyone could hear the crack of

the flaps dropping on the trapdoor. And as they held their breaths, they could also hear the child's last scream.

The lid of the Box in front of Amneris opened just a little more.

Avanti la morte no se sa la sorte.
Until you die, you can't know your destiny.
Venetian proverb

1
Tockle's beastly morning

Temistocle was *already* having a beastly Monday.

His older sister had sneaked the piece of bread he'd toasted to perfection. Then his mother had reproached him for taking an extra slice and emptying the jam pot. Stella's cheeks were swollen with stolen toast and her lips were rough with crumbs as she grinned at him. She knew Tockle would never betray her.

Mamma's reproach hurt more because it was so mild. '*Two* slices, Temistocle? And the rest of the sweet-fig jam? My dearest boy, you know how many buckets of water I have to sell to keep us all fed.' Her voice rose. 'To be truthful, I don't yet know what we'll eat tomorrow. And there'll be no more jam until Christmas. If I could, I'd feed you cutlets and cake every day—'

She smothered a sigh and ruffled Tockle's straight, white-blond hair. Then she kissed the top of his head.

'I wish she'd just shout at me,' thought Tockle, miserably.

9

He was so unhappy that he could not bring himself even to apologize. And, given that it was Stella who had committed the crime, any apology would be a lie. His mother hated lies.

Mamma bent over and placed her hands on her hips, so that she looked like a two-handled teapot. Tockle could positively feel the ache in the small of his mother's back as she hoisted the curved yoke on her shoulders. The *bigolò*'s two copper buckets swung heavily on their hooks – and they were still empty. They would weigh four times as much when they were full. Stella furtively gulped down the stolen toast while coiling Mamma's rope. Tockle jumped up on a chair to place the elegant top hat on his mother's head, the way he always did. The spotless cylinder with its smart brim was a sad contrast to the shabby striped dress and the frayed shawl beneath. His mother was a beautiful woman, but her face had grown gaunt, and her eyes lacked their former lustre. Too often, they were casting about anxiously, as if she was frightened of something.

Tockle's mother was a *bigolante*, a water-seller. She was no great height herself, so her profession's traditional top hat made her visible in the crowded streets of Venice. When people called to her, she would make her way towards them, careful not to hit anyone with the swinging buckets. Boys and girls would simply tip one up to their mouths. If they had no shoes, Mamma never charged them. Housewives would decant a jug of the cool water. Mamma also had regular customers. She visited their dark kitchens daily, to fill their tall earthenware pots. Occasionally she stopped to gossip, but never for long. Each bucket of water, she'd once told Tockle, was two mouthfuls of golden polenta grain or a cup of milk for the baby: every pleasant chat wasted a meal's worth of time. When her buckets were empty, she used her rope to lower them back into the depths of the well. Then she set off again, not returning home until the streets had emptied of potential customers. At the end of each day she poured the last of her water into the scooped-out bowls in the marble base of the well at the centre of the square of San Zan Degola. This was for the cats and dogs: it was an old tradition that the *bigolanti* gave their local animals a fresh drink every evening.

His mother briefly passed her hand over her tired face. It had been a hard life since Papà went away, and this morning Tockle had made it just that bit harder.

She kissed the baby, asleep in her crib, careful to keep the buckets away from the tiny doll-like face.

Tockle watched Mamma walk slowly into the square, where she rested a hand on the stone wall for a moment, struggling to align her yoke in the least painful way with small jiggling motions of her shoulders. Tockle wished he could carry it for her. But she insisted that he go to school.

Baffi poked a furtive, wild head around the door Tockle's mother had left open. There was a new tatter to his left ear and some whiskers were missing too. The cat had been out all night again, as was his habit. Baffi's staring eyes were ringed with black; his ears stood high, tufty as a lynx's. He was mostly white with splotches of tabby that looked as if they had been flung onto his fur with a careless paintbrush. Back in the days when Baffi was a button-nosed little kitten, Tockle used to carry him round in a straw bag on his back. But now Baffi was a famous fighting cat who could roam the streets of Santa Croce without any embarrassing assistance from a human, thank you very much.

Baffi plumed his tail in a question mark, seeing his master's unhappy expression. Then he reached behind himself for something in the fig vine and strolled in.

'No!' shouted Tockle. 'Not in here!'

But it was too late. Baffi was already at his feet, where he dropped the limp rat he'd brought in. Unfortunately it

11

was only playing dead, and took the opportunity to run up the chimney that Tockle had neglected to clean. Baffi's battle-cry, the screaming of the rat, and the shower of loose bricks and ash from the chimney now woke his little sister in a most disagreeable and frightening manner. She made her eighteen-month-old feelings felt, at high volume. Meanwhile, in his pursuit of the rat, Baffi upended every one of the chipped jars that held Stella's precious fragments of coloured glass.

This enraged Stella, who had counted on a peaceful morning inserting the glass into the three kaleidoscope tubes that now lay smashed on the floor.

'He's *your* cat, the monster!' she shouted at Tockle. 'So you can clean up that mess. Every flake of ash! Every piece of glass! Every whisker! Every drop of blood!'

She thrust the three broken cylinders into his face. 'A week's work – ruined. Everything you touch, Tockle, is a disaster.'

So it was a blackened, scratched and bitten Temistocle, his ears ringing with the baby's cries and Stella's bitter words, who set off for school late, with the guilty slice of bread and jam wrapped in a handkerchief. He'd not had time to finish that last difficult sum in his homework. But at least he'd left the hearth spotless for his mother's return, and the chimney brushed and ratless. The little one was still sobbing on Stella's shoulder. And Stella was in angry tears too.

She said vindictively, 'And by the way, I believe there's another leak in your *sandolo*. It was listing when I walked past the canal last night. How will you get to Murano this evening if it's lying at the bottom of the canal? After what your cat did, I need more glass urgently.'

'Why didn't you tell me *last night*?'

Stella knew full well that there wasn't time to bail out

the boat before school. Tockle would have to spend all day worrying about it.

With a quiet howl of despair, he flung himself out of the house.

Stella called out after him, 'If Papà ever does come back, how disappointed he'll be in *you*. And that vile cat of yours – why, Papà would sell him for his meat!'

Apart from Baffi's rats, there had been nothing resembling a piece of meat in the Molin household for two years – not since Rizardo Molin had disappeared, before he could even lay eyes on his youngest child.

'Thief!' cried Amneris. 'Stop that at once!'

With his body and head hidden, the boy was visible only from the waist down. The rest of him was buried among the branches of the apricot tree that overhung the wall of her garden. The thief was standing on a cloth-dyers' barrel. His knees were grimy, his shoes gaped and knee-stockings straggled at half-mast. At the sound of her voice, his legs stiffened for a moment, but he did not stop.

Amneris tried again. 'You are not even a gentleman, to be doing that! *Clearly*, you're not a gentleman. You have a thief's legs. Anyone can see that! What dirty knees you have! And there's coal dust in the folds of your stockings!'

Perhaps her insults would not bother such a hardened criminal? Amneris racked her brains for something worse, something that would stop him immediately. She decided to appeal to his conscience – if he had one.

'We need those green apricots!' she told the legs. 'My granny bottles them for us to eat all winter. If we let every sticky-fingered boy in Venice steal them, there'd be none left for us. Do you want to leave us without a bit of something nice when the snow comes, and the *Bora* wind?'

Then she thought back to the worrying thing that had happened earlier that morning. 'We might even be forced to start *selling* those apricots soon!'

She picked up a stick and poked the back of his knees with it for emphasis. One of the legs twitched, and the boy said, 'Ouch!'

But he did not stop, and he did not climb down.

'Have you no shame?' cried Amneris. The events of the morning pressed on her temper. She had been sad and confused. It was simpler – quite refreshing, really – to be in the right, and to be angry. With someone else.

So it was anger that pushed Amneris one step closer to the boy at exactly the some moment that he finally pulled his head out of the branches and peered down at her. Their faces were suddenly just a hand's breadth apart.

In one of his hands was a baby bird. In the other, a piece of bread lightly smeared with jam and also pecked with holes.

'This,' said the boy, using the little bird to point at the bread, '*was* my lunch. And my breakfast, come to think of it. And probably *tomorrow*'s breakfast too.'

The baby bird took another healthy peck at the bread. Jam glistened on its tiny beak.

The boy continued, 'I was already late for school. So I was running to take that shortcut through the Corte Berlendis. But out of the corner of my eye, I saw this little thing fall out of its nest as I was passing. I was afraid it was dead. But then I saw that it was trying to get up. So I lifted it and climbed this barrel to return it to its nest. The mother bird has disappeared, so I decided to give the baby something to eat before I put it back.'

Amneris blushed. 'I forgot about the nest. The blackbirds

build one every year. I try to keep my cat, Grillo, indoors until the babies are ready to fly.'

She suddenly remembered one of her mother's favourite sayings: *Manners Make Ladies, not Ermine Tippets.* She had not been very mannerly with this boy, who was turning out quite different from what she had suspected.

'So, if I may just continue,' said the boy in a strained voice, 'without dog's abuse from you, I'd like to finish saving this bird's life and go to school. I wouldn't touch one of your apricots if you offered me a basket of them. Even though I myself haven't tasted an apricot since ... since I was very young.'

Amneris watched him place the baby bird back in the nest. She stood aside as he jumped off the barrel and made an ineffectual attempt to shake the coal dust out of his stockings.

'No apricots, no peaches and no cherries for two years,' he said pointedly. 'Nothing but bread and sweet-fig jam and polenta. And not enough of that either.'

His voice trembled, and he passed an elbow over his face, raising his white-blond hair in a comical crest. Then he blanched, looking around sharply.

'Don't worry, there are no ears in this wall!' Amneris reassured him. 'Just a garden behind it. No Anagrammaticular. I swear.'

'How do you know?' he whispered. 'They hide the mechanisms so well. It would be just my luck ...'

Amneris thought, 'He's actually going to cry. What have I done?'

'Don't worry,' he said gruffly, 'I'm not a blubber. It's just that the sun's hardly up and it's already been such a beastly day. And I'm heading straight for a beating at school because I didn't finish my arithmetic homework, because my cat Baffi killed a rat all over our kitchen, and—'

15

Amneris stood on tiptoe to pluck a green apricot from the tree. She pushed it into his pocket. 'Please help yourself from now on, whenever you are passing. Thank you for saving the bird. I'd like to return the favour. So let's have a look at that sum, shall we?' she said.

Things might be looking bad – but she could spare an apricot for this thin boy with his straight pale hair and look of desperation.

He looked into her large brown eyes, also taking in the pale heart-shaped face and the rich chestnut hair that clustered in waves around her shoulders. Amneris smiled when she saw the doubting twitch of his lips.

'I'm a seamstress by trade, and I know I don't look like a girl who would be fond of arithmetic,' she said. 'But I assure you I am ferociously good at it.'

And that was how Amneris D'Ago met Temistocle Molin, otherwise known as 'Tockle'.

2
A clockwork city

Outsiders had romantic notions about the Most Serene Republic of Venice. The peculiar old city of liquid streets and marble palaces made people dream and write bad poetry. They made a great deal of Venice's lovely quietness, with no noisy carriages jostling, no horses to clop over the cobbles. 'More of a magical theatre than a town!' they exclaimed. 'Or a great marble galleon upon the sea!' Those in love with Venice sighed at the memory of jade-green waves lapping gently at the arched bridges, like kittens kneading the soft belly of their mother.

But that was a different kind of Venice from the one in which Amneris and Tockle had been born. The lagoon still snuggled around the city, holding it close to its green, throbbing breast, but Amneris and Tockle were growing up in the age of automata, in a city run no longer by an elected Doge but by Fogfinger, a foreigner who had won the hearts and minds of the Venetian senators by virtue of his dazzling ability to produce mechanical devices to perform almost every single task for which the Venetians had once used their own minds, muscles and fingers.

One of the first things Fogfinger had heard when he arrived in Venice, more than twenty years before, was a proverb:

I Veneziani nasse strachi e vive per riposar – The Venetians are born tired and live to sleep.

And that was what had given him his big idea. Whoever gave the Venetians all the sleep they wanted, and indulged their natural laziness – why, that person could be in charge of them even when they were awake. And so it had come to pass that the Venetian senators gladly appointed Fogfinger as their leader and settled back to enjoy the benefits of his rule.

All the world was mad for automata in those days. But no town had adopted mechanical devices with more pleasure – or childlike excitement and simple greed – than Venice. People from other cities clucked and shook their heads when they spoke of the automata of Venice and the luxurious indolence of the rich Venetians who had grown so dependent upon them. And it was true that Venetians loved to find little machines to do their work for them.

Even the gondoliers took happily to Fogfinger's clockwork engines that made their boats glide through the water without the slightest effort on their part. Working wheels were hidden beneath the waves, so all they had to do was stand at the stern and look handsome, which suited them nicely. The rich and noble Venetians had contraptions to walk them up the stairs, to pour their coffee, to clean their shoes, to slide them into their gondolas. Or pairs of jointed tin footmen carried them around town in painted sedan-chairs. There were machines that turned the pages of books at the sign of a languid nod, and there was even a special kind of automaton with a sponge and a towel for use in the water closet. Fogfinger's devices were as human-seeming as possible, with faces and hands and bellows to simulate lungs and hydraulic systems inside circulating a blood-red liquid, so that if they got broken, they seemed to bleed and tears spilled from their opening-and-closing eyes.

There were more automata than actors in Venice's seventeen famous theatres. Mechanical cupids flew about the stages during love scenes. Planets with mobile faces revolved around stars who sang. Merchants used automata to make the attention-getting sounds and movements to attract custom to their shops: angels blowing trumpets at music shops; mechanical bears banging drums at toy shops; mooing cows at butchers'; a scribe automaton busily jabbing a quill pen at a scroll above the paper merchant's. The poultry butcher had a human-sized hen who cackled as it laid tin eggs all day long. Perfumers had glass bottles with stoppers that lifted up on the hour, releasing puffs of delicious scent; the snuff merchants had wooden noses, each tall as a child, which sneezed explosively.

Every night an army of Fogfinger's 'helpers' were sent out to rewind all the mechanical devices that had kept Venice moving throughout the day. No one ever saw the so-called Winder Uppers, but there was plenty of evidence of what they had done and where they had been: the ticking and striking and buzzing of all the automata that had wound to a standstill the night before. The morning light revealed the hundreds of bloodied white gloves dropped near the mechanical wheels, their finger-tips worn away. Very narrow were the fingers of those gloves, and very small were the palms. Those Winder Uppers lived a life apart: confined to barracks on old plague islands by day, they came out in their boats after midnight and had disappeared by dawn. Some of the poor people were sorry for the Winder Uppers, who eked out their lives in the dark, whose fingers were literally worn to the bone. When they could, the poor would leave a glass of milk outside their doors, or a small piece of bread, with a note saying '*for the Winder Upper. You will not have to hurt your hands in this house – we have no automata. But please take this food, with our good wishes.*'

Almost every poor family knew that one of those shadowy figures was one of their own. For when starvation threatened a whole household, one brave uncle or unmarried older sister would quietly pack a small bag and go to the Winder Upper recruiting office at Santa Chiara. Then a family would receive a dole of polenta and rice, but they'd never see their relative again.

The Winding Up did not come free, of course.

None of the rich minded paying the 'Winding Up Tax' that Fogfinger had imposed on every citizen. For the rich, the pleasure given by the automata far outweighed the coins they paid to Fogfinger's tax collectors. Neither were the rich much bothered by the Lambing ceremony in which, during each of the last ten years, two children had disappeared up the tower of the Frari church. All Venice knew that the sacrifice was made in order to placate the Primaeval Crocodile, a monster from the deep that had, it seemed, arrived in the lagoon around the same time as Fogfinger and had immediately launched a series of bloody attacks. Eventually Fogfinger had negotiated a tribute of two small citizens a year. The children's walk up the tower was supposed to be a game of chance – the Fate in the Box would decide if the Primaeval Crocodile would be fed, or if the child would be spared. But the Fate in the Box seemed to favour the monster. Few 'Lambs' ever came back down those stairs.

The parish priests had objected to the ceremony. 'A betrayal of the Church and everything it stands for!' So they had raged from their pulpits. And shortly after they disappeared from their pulpits and their parishes.

Fogfinger put it this way in his newspaper *Il Nuovo Postiglione*: '*Poor Venetians, your priests have deserted you and gone to live in idleness in a grand monastery in the lagoon.*' The wooden saints in the church were removed, loaded into boats and sent off with the priests. And the stone ones, too difficult to lift, had their faces covered with sinister linen masks so their sad eyes and dignified faces were seen no more.

The priests had also denounced the human-shaped automata – 'Soulless devices in human form are against all that's holy!'

In response, Fogfinger made mechanical monkey priests. At the pulpits now, each Sunday, the Venetians were obliged to listen to the tinny voices of the jointed apes, dressed in sumptuous robes and offering prayers that glorified Fogfinger and cast ever more doubt on the goodness of the old priests and the old religion. The nuns who supported the priests were locked inside their convents and their sugar rations were abolished so they could no longer make the little cakes for which they were famous.

The people missed their parish priests, who knew every one of their names, had baptized all their children and performed the last rites for their dying loved ones. The wind-up primates did none of these things, and it would have been bizarre if they had. No one liked their long muzzles or their glittering glass eyes or the way they windmilled their paws inside their red silk sleeves when delivering their sermons. They were not priests and they were not even real monkeys.

'In distress, you need a human hand in yours,' said Amneris's granny.

A widow and an ardently religious woman, Margherita D'Ago had stopped going to their church when the first mechanical primate was installed there. Her faith had been a refreshment to her spirits, especially since the shipwreck of her beloved twin brother Annibale, the sea captain, many years before. Now Granny said her prayers at home alone. She had never quite given up hope on Annibale. He was always mentioned, tenderly, in her prayers. And she spoke of him in the present tense. 'No body has been found,' she insisted. 'He was a miraculous boy, and he's a strong man. He'll be back one day. Don't look at me like that. I don't need your pity.'

Amneris knew that if a woman of such strong faith as her grandmother could withdraw from Fogfinger's new kind of worship, then the churches of Venice must be places where God was not.

Margherita D'Ago had to pretend that arthritis kept her at home, for Fogfinger ordered all able-bodied Venetians to attend on Sundays. The Sabbath sermon was the means by which he issued his decrees – a hundred times, simultaneously, via the artificial voice-boxes of the primates. And then of course, for the Lambing, even the old and sick were wheeled or carried into the Frari, whether they wanted it or not. It was the only time that the rich of each parish mingled with the poor. Amneris always looked out for the fabled daughter of Alvise Malipiero there. The girl, whose very name was a secret, was invariably swaddled in black veils, for her father, one of Fogfinger's intimates, never allowed anyone to see her face.

Rich families like the Malipiero clan found no fault with the Lambing ceremony, as their children were somehow never chosen for it. On his or her eleventh birthday, every child in Venice was weighed on a vast pair of scales that Fogfinger had installed where the public lottery used to be held – under a striped canopy at the foot of the San Marco bell-tower. The results of the weighing were always exactly as Fogfinger had secretly guaranteed his noble supporters: children who were rich – and therefore had some meat on their bones – were pronounced 'too heavy' and quietly excluded from the lots for the draw. And in this way it happened that only poor, thin children were eligible for the terrible game that Fogfinger played with their lives. If the poor guessed that it was anything but bad luck that condemned their children, they resolved not to share their fears with their sons and daughters.

So the poor Venetians minded terribly about the Lambing. But they kept quiet for the sake of their children. They had also learned to be terrified of Fogfinger's elite Fog Squad, a troop of murderers and thieves recruited from Venice's prisons, and given the freedom and power to bully to their dark hearts' content in exchange for absolute loyalty to Fogfinger.

Far too often, the poor were also too weak from starvation for vigorous protest. And this was because Fogfinger's clever mechanical devices had stolen the jobs of many maids, house-boys and gardeners. Only a few professions had survived: there were as yet no mechanical devices for carrying water around the streets, for selling fruit or silk, or for blowing glass. Those who could find such jobs worked themselves to the bone, desperately trying to keep their children well-fed enough to escape Lambing.

There was another reason why the Venetians were too afraid to complain about the Lambing.

The walls had ears: literally tiny carved ears. Inside the whorl of each ear a tube led back behind the wall to an enormous tortoiseshell horn that magnified the sound of all conversations. An 'Anagrammaticular' was attached to every tortoiseshell horn. This was a kind of writing machine that took down the words siphoned in through the spying ear-holes. It mixed and jumbled the words together until they produced a statement that could definitely be read as treason. Then miniature padlocks locked those words in place. If you said something unwise in the street – or something the Anagrammaticular could reconfigure that way – later that day, brutish men in the ostentatious grey uniform of the Fog Squad would arrive at your house and you'd be bundled into a sedan-chair with black blinds. People learned to chatter in high, bright artificial voices in the street, using words like 'wonderful' and 'what a blessing Fogfinger has brought!' and 'I'm so happy!'

Even more feared than the Anagrammaticular were Fogfinger's 'Poxers'. These were hidden in walls outside the schoolyards and were designed to preserve decorous, quiet behaviour at all times. High-spirited boys who ran out of the schoolyard whooping and hollering were likely to activate a Poxer. A pale papier mâché head with swollen glands jumped up in front of them as they opened their mouths to yell. It sneezed in their faces and gave them a horrible heavy head cold, a fever, spots and a cough. Their condition soon worsened. Such boys never yelled again outside the schoolyard.

One of Tockle's best friends, Ugo Paolin, had fallen victim to a Poxer. Whenever he had time, Tockle went to visit Ugo in his bedroom, where he sat in a wheelchair, wrapped in a blanket, gazing down at the water: his little house was on the Fondamenta Morosini where three canals converged – the Rio dei Bareteri, the Rio dei Scoacamini and the Rio dei Ferali. Ugo's lungs were failing and his voice was weak. Still, he always urged Tockle, 'It is not right, none of this! Venice is turning into a crime. Someone must do something.'

Unspoken was the terrible truth: that someone could not be Ugo, for he did not have long to live. Ugo had been the cleverest boy in the school, and the painful thing was that his mind was still working apace inside his withered body.

'Tockle, Tockle,' he whispered. 'You should join the—'

'No!' cried Tockle. 'Do not say that name. You never know who is listening.'

'I have nothing to lose,' said Ugo, simply.

Tockle squeezed his friend's hand and shook his head.

'But I do have something to lose, Ugo. And I've already lost more than I can bear.'

Fogfinger did not go entirely unopposed. There were *I Piccoli Pochi*, The Tiny Few, who bravely protested against the Lambing. The *Pochi* declared that the Primaeval Crocodile was unfairly blamed – and that those few Venetians who disappeared had simply drowned: such deaths were natural in a city surrounded by water. So there was no need for children to be offered as tribute, the *Pochi* insisted. They had also dared to point out the unfairness of the system that inevitably seemed to choose the poorest children for the ceremony at the Frari. At first, the *Pochi* had marched with banners to the Doge's Palace. The marchers did not return. A lawyer from the *Piccoli Pochi* had then tried to mount a court case. The courtroom doors closed, and no one who attended was ever seen again. The remnants of the *Pochi* went into hiding, in fear for their lives.

While Fogfinger had appropriated the Lamb as his symbol, the *Piccoli Pochi* had chosen the seahorse, a wild, delicate and fascinating creature found in certain parts of the lagoon. Members of the *Piccoli Pochi* carried small blue glass seahorses as the secret symbols of their beliefs, and for good luck. If you trusted someone, you'd show them your seahorse, and they would show you theirs. Then you'd know that you might discuss your feelings in safety – provided you were in a boat out in the lagoon or in one of the few places in Venice where Fogfinger had not yet installed one of his spying devices.

The *Piccoli Pochi* had never been many and were getting fewer all the time as they were ruthlessly hunted down. Those who were caught were wrapped in straw and bundled into boats weighed down under boxes of fruit and taken to the fortress of Cattaro, where the very air was said to be fatal and all prisoners were dead within the year. Some were sent to languish in Bohemian prisons or Serbian strongholds or were strangled in towers far from Venice. Fogfinger chose not to execute them in public, fearing that the public would sympathize with them. Instead, he delayed their trials, claiming that all the evidence had been eaten by rats, and that it was too dangerous to keep 'the traitors' in the city in the meanwhile.

An evil fate befell the man who had nailed a letter to the door of the Doge's Palace. He'd written, '*Lambing! It's not Lambing. Why give it a sweet, fluffy name? To hide the fact that it's Human Sacrifice, nothing less. Human Sacrifice is a Barbarous Act!*' The man was found severely beaten.

When a stonemason's child was Lambed, the stone-cutters of San Marcuola had staged a protest, confident of safety in their numbers and their importance to the city. But that very night flames ignited in an oil warehouse and raged through their quarter, leaving sixty families homeless. Fogfinger's newspaper, *Il Postiglione*, accused the *Piccoli Pochi* of starting the fire. But everyone knew that the *Piccoli Pochi* would not harm anyone who stood up against the Lambing.

A year ago, Tockle had paused, fascinated and horrified, on the edge of a ragged crowd listening to a man who stood on a fish-crate talking with a quiet passion. 'It is all wrong!' he urged. 'Why do you believe these lies about the

26

Crocodile? Has no one noticed that there was no Crocodile before Fogfinger arrived here?'

A crunch of boots interrupted his words. Twelve Fogs rushed through the crowd, sending bystanders flying. The man cried to his audience, 'See what is happening to me. I am Marco Gallo – tell my wife. Tell your friends too. Aggh!'

A Fog had struck him across the face with a club.

Through the blood and broken teeth, the man shouted to the crowd, 'You do not lift a finger to help me. No more than you try to save your poor children. You're like sheep in a field, who watch your young being carried off for slaughter while you tranquilly chew the grass! You are *actors* in this crime Fogfinger stages – not just the audience.'

It was rare for someone to make such a stand. More often, people took themselves far away, even though it broke any Venetian's heart to leave his beloved masterpiece of a city. If you fled, your home and belongings were forfeited and your personal papers – carefully doctored by expert forgers – were used to fatten the files of accusations against you.

Defending a friend in exile was what had got Tockle's own father denounced for belonging to the *Piccoli Pochi*. And the next day he did not come home from the Arsenale shipyard, where he worked whenever the kaleidoscope trade failed to provide enough to feed his family.

It had been two years now, and he had not come home at all.

3

The creaturely kaleidoscope

Amneris's family made their living embroidering silk
for parasols, quilts, dresses and shawls. The D'Ago
needlework was particularly prized for its brilliantly
coloured designs – so intricate that they seemed almost
beyond human imagination. And the secret of those designs
lay in a battered ebony tube full of jewel-coloured stars: a
kaleidoscope that once belonged to Amneris's great-uncle,
the sea captain, Annibale D'Ago. The captain and his other
worldly possessions had gone down with his ship. But the
kaleidoscope had somehow survived the shipwreck in the
South Adriatic, and had bobbed all the way back to Venice,
as if it had a desire and a sense of direction all of its own.
The kaleidoscope was found floating in a little wooden box,
among the fish-heads and artichoke peelings in the Beccarie
Canal by the Rialto Market.

A two-line inscription on the box helped it arrive safely
at the house Amneris shared with her family. The first line
was *reasonably* clear:

This creature is the property of the
D'Ago family in the Calle Berlendis.

But the next line had provoked three generations of headaches due to severe brain-racking:

If desperation strikes, turn the eye of the world
on its head, tap three times, and empty.

No amount of brain-racking had revealed the meaning of these words. And, in any case, in what way could a wooden kaleidoscope be called a creature?

But a use was quickly found for the device. It provided the family with a seemingly endless source of beautiful patterns for their needlework. Everyone in the D'Ago household sewed. (In fact, the name D'Ago means 'of the needle'.) Mamma was the lace-maker. Granny – who had married her cousin, Ivo D'Ago, a famous tailor – did the cutting with a sure hand. Amneris, with her excellent eyesight, undertook the fine embroidery. To the youngest daughter – or the only daughter, in the case of Amneris – was also reserved the privilege of turning the kaleidoscope seven times – it had to be seven times, no more, no less – before tipping it up to the light. This was done every Monday morning, at dawn. Then Amneris carefully placed the kaleidoscope on its wicker stand and copied the beautiful patterns she saw inside onto a sheet of paper, dabbing slender squirrel-fur brushes into her precious block of watercolours.

'The dear creature' was what the D'Ago family called the kaleidoscope, because its inspiration paid the rent of their small house in the fabric-dyers' quarter, and for their food and their clothes, not to mention the expensive paints and the occasional bowl of milk for Grillo the cat. Fortunately no automaton had yet been invented that could embroider delicate stitches on silk, but needlework was not (and never has been) a richly paid profession, and there were four mouths to feed on the proceeds of what Mamma, Granny and Amneris sewed. Poor Papà had lost his sight before Amneris was born.

Unlike her new friend Temistocle Molin, Amneris never went hungry, unless she forgot to eat because she was so absorbed in painting the kaleidoscope's designs. Still, she could not be spared to go to school. Instead, Mamma and Granny delivered constant lessons as they worked beside her, while the steam from the bronchitis kettle kept the air moist for Granny's lungs. As three generations of fingers plunged their needles and bobbins in and out of shimmering fabrics, Amneris took in stories of Venetian merchant fleets, famous battles, poems and geography. And her work with the dear creature taught her all the mathematics she would ever need to know.

For once she had finished recording the pattern, Amneris's next task was to calculate the amount of thread in each colour required to embroider the design. Silk thread was costly: they could not afford a finger's length more than was needed for each piece. After a long line of calculations had snaked around the edges of the pattern, Amneris would double-check her arithmetic, underline her totals, and set off to the silk merchant for the week's supplies.

Above the entrance to Melchior Dubbini's shop in the Mercerie was a grand but rather frightening signboard. The silk merchant's name was painted in extravagant flourishes beneath a busy automaton of a gigantic plaster hand brandishing a pair of black scissors as big as Amneris herself. The scissors sliced continuously into a bolt of green velvet. The sound of iron biting into fabric whispered above Amneris's head as she let herself in.

She would speak up clearly: 'Three skeins of Ransomer's

Red, eight of Gull-beak Yellow and ten of Uncut Emerald Green.' She would place her drawing on the counter top. 'But we'll have to check against the drawing for this pink – could be Nun's Blush or Dawn Sky?'

'Well, well, well, my dear. Let me see what you have there.' An oily voice poured smoothly out of the dimness at the back of the shop. A thin, elegant hand reached out over the counter for her drawing. Then that hand started laying down skeins of silk to match what she had painted. His fingers made absolutely no sound. When Amneris told her friend Biri about that, Biri promptly nicknamed the silk merchant 'Signor Silent Slime'.

'Watch him,' Biri warned. 'He don't mean you a bit of good. Every time he grins somefing fierce that's because he's stealing somefing off you. Reckon your family should cut with him and find yourselves another silk merchant.'

Every time Amneris threatened to do that, Melchior Dubbini raised the money he gave them – very slightly. It would pay for new needles or a fine pair of scissors. And her father sighed, 'Better the devil you know, I suppose.'

Many was the time that the silk merchant had offered Amneris a bundle of silk in exchange for the secret of her beautiful designs. He handled each sheet covetously, running his finger over the glistening colours, trying to memorize the lovely sequences of Midday Turquoise, Spun-Sugar Magenta and Lagoon Green. Amneris always whipped the sheet smartly out of his hand when she saw him reaching for his own piece of paper to make a sneaking copy.

At home, Amneris would unwind the skeins and set to work. Each Saturday afternoon, she delivered the finished piece to the shop. Then Melchior Dubbini would sell it to one of his rich customers, for three times, Amneris guessed, what he gave to her. Biri thought it was at least ten.

The silk merchant kept a roomful of orphan girls at

31

the back of the shop, stitching his own inferior designs. Occasionally he forgot to close the door behind the counter and Amneris glimpsed the girls' lowered heads, plain white headscarves and their busy little hands. It was rumoured that they ate poorly and slept on wooden bunks in a storeroom without a fireplace. Her heart always lurched with pity at the sight of those girls squinting over their sewing in the stinking light of whale-oil lamps.

The saddest thing about them was their silence.

Dubbini, it was clear, did not allow them to speak to one another. Amneris thought of the constant chatting, teaching, singing and laughing that went on when she and her family worked together at home.

She could not imagine a worse fate than being condemned to be one of Melchior Dubbini's silent little slaves.

At least, she could not imagine it then.

4
What was worrying Amneris

Dawn, Monday April 21st, 1783

It was a Monday morning when Amneris misapprehended the innocent thief Temistocle Molin. She'd already been to the silk merchant. Her shawl was knobbly with spools and skeins of silk. That was the usual state of affairs. But something had been different. This time, both she and the merchant had been baffled by her shopping list. For when Amneris had tiptoed into the workroom at dawn that morning, the kaleidoscope's seventh turn offered up a design that was, impossibly, entirely white.

'Oh my!' breathed Amneris.

Her cat Grillo, curled in a ball at the edge of the work table, opened one sleepy eye. 'Miao ... milk?' he suggested politely.

'Not now. Where have all the jewel colours gone?' Amneris asked him. Grillo yawned, rose, turned in a circle and settled down to sleep again until such time as it would be worth his while to get up.

Amneris worried. 'What's happened?'

No one answered. Apart from Grillo, she was alone in the little workroom on the first floor. Amneris loved this floating castle of a room: beneath it was nothing – just the humble Calle Berlendis dead-ending into the canal. Light washed in from two generous windows: one looked over the street and garden; the other drew in reflections from the jade-green water of the Rio dei Mendicanti. The D'Agos' house was surrounded by the homes and workshops of Venice's cloth-dyers, whose sheets of crimson, emerald and saffron-coloured fabric hung like glorious mediaeval pennants from the rooftops and windows. Although the sun had barely risen, it was warm in the workroom. The pungent smells from the dyers' vats were stealing through the air, along with the sleepy voices of the girl orphans warbling their morning hymns at the grand almshouse of the Mendicanti.

Amneris stared at the white pattern in the eye of the kaleidoscope. Nothing like this had ever happened before. Was she dreaming it? She pinched her left wrist hard. She glanced inside the glass eye again. The pattern remained obstinately white, with just a tracery of grey shadow.

For a moment, she was tempted to give the kaleidoscope a little push, to release some ruby or sapphire colours that were surely tucked up behind this strange wall of white. It was not that the white design was ugly – far from it – but how could a piece of perfectly white embroidery find a buyer? Venetians loved colour. Nothing was white in Venice! Terracotta, rose, azure, green, dove-grey – but not white! No one would pay for white stitches on white fabric, would they? You'd have to strain your eyes to see it. Anyway, the D'Ago family was famous for the rich colouring of its work.

Her fingers crept towards the kaleidoscope.

But her mother always warned that the kaleidoscope

was a sensitive kind of creature. Mamma had once been the youngest daughter herself: she had looked after the kaleidoscope and drawn its patterns. So she was especially protective of it.

'Treat it tenderly,' she always urged Amneris. 'It is because of our devotion that Uncle Annibale's kaleidoscope rewards us with a livelihood.'

Amneris picked up a pencil. She began to shade in delicate grey the outlines of the pure white pattern, gradually losing herself in her work.

Amneris was suddenly aware of her mother leaning over her. As usual, she had tiny lace bobbins looped over her ears.

'What are you up to, sweetheart?' Mamma asked. 'When are you going to fill in the colour? Hurry now. You can't be late for Signor Dubbini.'

Amneris had to arrive at the silk merchant before the shop opened to the public. Melchior Dubbini forbade her to enter when customers were there. He did not want any of his rich clients seeing the source of the matchless embroidery, or setting up to buy from Amneris privately.

It was only when her mother pointed to the sun rising in the sky that Amneris realized that she had been painting for two hours. The work lay in front of her, a tracery of grey on white, like the shadows of frost on a winter window.

'It's staying like this,' Amneris said. 'The kaleidoscope made it that way. Look!'

Her mother bent to stare at the mouth of the barrel, perched at its usual angle on the stand. The blood drained from her face. 'Did you shake it? Did you drop the dear creature?' Mamma's hands clenched Amneris's shoulders. Her eyes were wild.

'No, I just turned it seven times – carefully, as usual,' protested Amneris, guiltily recollecting the moment when she'd been tempted to give it a little shove. 'Then I placed it very gently on the stand. Don't be angry with me.'

Mamma picked up the protesting Grillo by his scruff and interrogated him. 'Did *you* bat the dear creature with your paw? It's not a toy, you know.'

Grillo used his back legs to give her a good kick in the ribs, and boxed her nose for good measure, though he kept his claws in and did not draw blood.

'It wasn't him, Mamma,' said Amneris. The cat had a transparently guilty expression for times when he stole or misbehaved. Today he was not wearing it. Mamma released him on the floor. Grillo nudged Amneris's ankle approvingly.

Her mother appealed to her in a quieter voice. 'Did you leave it in the cold last night, by accident?'

'No, it was on the mantelpiece above the embers, the proper place. Why, Mamma? Why are you so upset?'

'I fear our luck has run out,' said her mother. 'I always dreaded that this would happen. What if the jewel colours have disappeared for ever? What if the dear creature never makes anything but white any more? No! Don't touch! You know we must not stir it more than once a week. It is very sensitive. If it has done this to us, then there must be a reason. You are to tell no one, Amneris.'

'Shouldn't I take this pattern to Signor Dubbini?'

Her mother hesitated for a long time.

'Well, yes, perhaps. I would like to hear about how he takes it. But you must act as if the all-white design offers a great advantage. Then ask for the most expensive threads. In this drawing, by your shading, I see at least ten kinds of white.'

'Twenty-two, actually,' said Amneris, pointing to the calculations along the side. 'And some of them don't even have names. I had to make them up. Look, Egret Wing White, White-of-the-Eyes White, Raw Meringue White, Crest-of-the-Wave White. Signor Dubbini only has the usual named whites – Lead White, Ash White, Cream White, Ice White, Lace White and one he calls 'Frightened Face'. His little joke. I think he means the faces of those wretched girls at the back of his shop.'

'It is a shame about those girls,' agreed her mother. 'Now go and wash, poppet. Breakfast will be on the table in three minutes. Which is not to say that you should spend only three minutes washing, mind!'

Amneris did not count the minutes she spent soaping her face, arms and body. Nor did she remember the slender slice of toasted bread she ate. Or whether the narrow slick of jam was cherry or apricot. Or whether she sipped hot chocolate or barley water from her cup. Her mind was taken up with the glittering pattern of white inside the kaleidoscope. It was as if she had been drawn into it, as if her thoughts hung in the white cobweb, helpless as a fly wrapped in sticky silk.

Her mother noticed Amneris's glazed eyes and slow movements. 'You're lost in the pattern, sweetheart. It used to happen to me occasionally, if the pattern was particularly complicated. But it never did *this* to me,' she pointed accusingly at the white drawing now spread out on the breakfast table.

'Don't frown so.' She smoothed Amneris's brow. 'I'm sure the kaleidoscope means us nothing but good. I just wish I knew what it is up to now. We must not let our confidence be shaken so easily.'

'It wasn't *my* confidence that was shaken.'

'Amneris, please do not use that tone of voice. There is no

good to be had in reproaching one another. I say this not to criticize you but because it's better that you grow up as an understanding person, rather than one who must always be right.'

At his shop in the Mercerie, the silk merchant Melchior Dubbini was fascinated with the white design, though of course he pretended to be aghast.

'White on white? In the most expensive thread? How ridiculous. I'll never sell it. Or I'll have to sell it for next to nothing, just to get rid of it. A waste of silk!'

Amneris peered behind the merchant. The pale girls were stitching lurid fabrics into ragged garments that looked like pirate costumes. Who in Venice would want pirate costumes? There was no let-up in Fogfinger's decree forbidding Carnevale.

'*Until this city knows how to behave,*' he had announced, '*and gives up her traitors instead of hiding them – there shall be no masking and frolicking among the poor.*'

The girls sewed and snipped as if they had been wound up and set into motion. Their eyes shone moistly with tiredness. Amneris wondered if they had even been allowed to go to bed. Not one of the girls dared to look up. Out of the corner of her eye, she caught Signor Dubbini grinning greedily at her design, and remembered Biri's advice: 'When he smiles, it's because he's stealing somefing from your family.'

Amneris snatched the drawing from Dubbini's hands. 'What nonsense! This is the most beautiful design I've ever brought you! What can be more precious than pure white? I can't *wait* to start embroidering this masterpiece. If you don't want to sell it, then there are other silk merchants who would love the D'Ago business. Why, one dropped his calling card at our house just yesterday.'

She had not meant to lie or threaten, merely to show confidence. The effect of her bluff was gratifying, however.

'Don't take on like that, girlie mine!' Dubbini rubbed his smooth hands together. 'Just my little joke.'

'So you agree that this white embroidery will raise a good price?'

'Mmmm, perhaps it won't actually *lose* money.'

'Highest price *ever*?' she held the sheet further away from him.

He took one corner, pulling it back. A crafty look passed across his face. Amneris knew he was picturing the perfect wealthy customer for this unusual piece of embroidery. Dubbini must already know someone who really loved white. Amneris speculated briefly who it might be – a duchess? A councillor? A member of Fogfinger's inner circle, even? There were rumours that Melchior Dubbini had connections in high places. Biri swore he was a *confidente* – a spy for Fogfinger.

Now he snapped, 'It'll be extra work for *me* to convince any of my esteemed customers to accept this travesty. Which means I'll pay less for this white nonsense. And mind you don't bring me any more.'

All the way home, Amneris pulled at the fringe of her shawl and worried, 'What if the dear creature gives me white again? We cannot afford to earn any less than we do. There's Granny's medicine and …'

She tried to tell herself that the silk merchant was only pretending. But what if he was *truly* angry about the white design? Still fretting, Amneris turned into the Calle Berlendis just in time to see a boy's head disappear among the branches of their apricot tree with his dirty shoes planted on a barrel.

And the thought of stolen apricots – and cold winter nights without Granny's apricot tart – finally broke her mind free of the kaleidoscope's filmy white cobweb. It also loosened her tongue.

5

In the coils of the
Primaeval Crocodile

Monday April 21st, 1783

After Amneris D'Ago had shown him how to finish that last sum, Temistocle Molin ran off to school, the apricot in his pocket slapping against his leg all the way. By the time he removed it, the much-pecked slice of bread and jam had wrapped itself around the apricot. The clock of San Lazzaro dei Mendicanti tolled eight times. Tockle had to be at his desk by three minutes past. Three minutes was long enough to decide that green apricot wrapped in jammy bread was in fact nothing other than raw apricot pie – and also long enough to consume it in three small bites.

Feeling a little better with food inside him, Tockle slid into the chair behind his desk. The schoolmaster was pleased with the perfect sum. The rest of the morning's lessons were easy – spelling and mechanical assembly, a new subject. Fogfinger had changed the curriculum for the charity schools so that every poor child in Venice now acquired deft fingers to coil tiny wires, tap fine pins into almost invisible slots, oil

41

stiff pistons and cast ball bearings. Tockle was good at all these things, and could let his mind drift. Now all he had to worry about was his sinking boat, his overworked mother, his sister Stella's broken kaleidoscopes and the terrible look that Baffi had given him when he threw the remains of the dead rat, unfortunately in several pieces, into the canal. The cat would soon be back with another one, Tockle knew, just to show him.

Somehow he got through the day. As the final bell rang, he went gladly out into a street that was as noisy as a small war. In quick succession, he passed the violin-maker, above whose door a bow sawed at an instrument, and a tavern, whose quartet of wooden youths stamped their bare feet in a tub of grapes. And Tockle had to hold his hands over his ears each time he passed a statue.

Since Fogfinger had come to Venice, the statues on the fronts of the palaces had also developed a life of their own. At first he'd claimed the credit for it, but lately he'd not mentioned it much. The figures – saints, phoenixes, lions and classical heroes – had grown disorderly and they could not be silenced like the ones inside the churches. They were always screaming petulantly at one another. News and gossip travelled down the Grand Canal by this means. Some messages became a little distorted in transmission. So a cry of 'Fine juicy catch of clams coming in to Rialto!' might start that way at Santa Maria della Salute, but by the time it got to San Geremia at the other end of town, the news was 'Nine blue hats, a tenor and an alto!'

Most people had learned not to take much notice of the chattering statues. Certainly, the statues took no notice of the Venetians, and conducted their conversations, arguments and games of Chinese whispers – and loudly admired their own reflections in the water – as if there was no one of importance listening. Human beings counted for little in their saintly, beastly and heroic stone eyes.

As Tockle walked quickly past two angels quarrelling bitterly over the wording of a hymn, he remembered the girl he had met that morning, the girl with the heart-shaped face, who had saved his skin with that perfect sum. He wondered if he might bump into her at the Natural History Museum. Tockle smiled: it was more than likely, under the circumstances.

Now that they had so little to do, thanks to the automata, the Venetians were in need of entertainment. One of their favourite activities was to visit Fogfinger's immense Natural History Museum in a grand oriental-looking palace that once belonged to the Turkish community in Venice. Inside, Fogfinger had installed a fearsome collection of stuffed animals that seemed to have emptied the whole world of its wild things. There were two items on display that particularly fascinated the Venetians. One was a tiny mermaid, a horrid-looking thing with a shrivelled black head, ridged black ribs, glaring red eyes and an ugly gash of a mouth brimming with yellow teeth. Instead of hands, she had cruel talons. Up close, she stank of rotting fish.

'Enough to stop you ever setting a toe in the water!' people would say, staring hard. They hated the repulsive little mermaid, yet still they came to look at her.

But the exhibit that drew the largest and most faithful crowds was the skeleton of Fogfinger's 'Primaeval Crocodile'. You might even say the Venetians loved the Primaeval Crocodile. It was a love made up of conflicting emotions – fear and irresistible fascination.

When they stared at the dead Crocodile's bones, the Venetians, who were imaginative folk, always saw the living beast, clad in rippling scales and with a full complement of teeth. They saw it thrashing its monstrous tail. They saw it lunging, gnashing, killing, ripping, devouring. The museum curators had helpfully placed the stuffed body of a little white lamb beside the skeleton. It might as well have been a figure of a child. Everyone knew what it meant.

Fogfinger encouraged Venetians to visit the Primaeval Crocodile. Even poxed children like Ugo Paolin were pushed there in wheeled chairs to behold the beast.

'*The Crocodile Pilgrimage,*' hectored Fogfinger in the *Postiglione,* '*should be made by each Venetian citizen every week. Thanks should be given that our Lambing keeps such monsters at bay in a civilized and democratic way.*'

'*Civilized and democratic?*' replied the *Piccoli Pochi* in handbills scattered around the town. '*Civilized and democratic as the Emperor Nero having Christians torn to pieces by lions in the Coliseum.*'

Fogfinger claimed that he had personally hunted down and killed the Primaeval Crocodile ten years before. He had commissioned a series of frescoes for the Town Hall, showing himself in pursuit of the great scaly beast in the remotest stretches of the lagoon. The second-to-last fresco depicted Fogfinger (a slim, romantic figure in glinting white chainmail) stabbing the monster through the breast with a long iron lance. The last one showed him returning to San Marco, dragging the dead beast behind him, to the acclaim of the Venetian public, who kneeled to thank their saviour.

At the back of the last fresco, the lagoon nestled blue and green. But Fogfinger had ordered a vast grey-green tail painted into the water. For, he explained, there still was one more Primaeval Crocodile out there in the lagoon. And it was that remaining Crocodile that provided justification for the Lambing of young Venetians.

Beside the painting was Fogfinger's well-known account

of his triumph, the words etched in a stone plaque:

> **That Judas of a Crocodile, the one still lurking in the lagoon, is even more savage than the one I slew. The beast is not just evil, but wily: it betrayed its mate by luring it into a cove where I could despatch it and undertook not to snatch any more Venetians so long as Venice would agree to the Lambing ceremony in its honour every year. Two small children a year – in exchange for the safety of thousands.**
> **How could I refuse?**

The Venetians believed in the living Judas Crocodile because they could hear it every night. Recently, it had dared to swim deep into the city. It would arrive at the mouth of the Grand Canal, by the great white church of Santa Maria della Salute. Then it swam down the canal to the museum where the fellow creature it had betrayed was now kept, its bones having been stripped of flesh and bleached in a bath of acid.

And every night, the Judas Crocodile raised its body in the water, lifted its huge snout up to the sky, and uttered great roars and groans.

Of course, few Venetians actually saw it. Fogfinger had imposed a strict curfew 'for everybody's good'. Breaking it was punishable by death.

But the people who lived in the houses opposite the museum had risked peeping out of the windows. They whispered what they'd seen. Soon everyone was talking about it.

'I guess that monster's sorry for what it did,' the Venetians said. 'To betray your mate is a terrible thing.'

'Perhaps it's hungry,' said others. 'After all, it only has two children a year to eat.'

'Fogfinger should give it a basket of Bittercakes. It would soon pipe down then!'

Bittercakes were another invention of Fogfinger's, a very effective form of punishment. The pastry-chefs of Venice, known as the *scalateri*, were ordered to stop making lovely, greasy *fritole* (a kind of doughnut that had been one of the joys of the six months of Carnevale) and the delicious *galani*, the ribbons of crunchy biscuit dusted with sugar. Instead, the bakers had to cook little blackened cakes with penitential messages written in white icing.

'*I stole,*' said one Bittercake.

'*I sold bad goods,*' said another.

'*I betrayed my city,*' said the biggest and bitterest cake of all, reserved for those suspected of sympathizing with the *Piccoli Pochi*.

Those who behaved badly were forced to eat their crimes, and, considering the iron filings, rotten eggs and worms that were in the Bittercakes, they definitely suffered for their sins.

Even Tockle, who much preferred living animals to dead ones, could not but give in to the lure of the Primaeval Crocodile. The museum was on his way home from school, very close to the Corte Giovanelli where he lived. If he had not been worried about his *sandolo* sinking, he might have allowed himself ten minutes to go and visit the beast. But the little green boat was on his mind. He was torn between hoping that Stella had just been vindictive that morning when she'd said the *sandolo* was listing – and fearing that she was right. Either way, he had to get to the island of

Murano before dark. He resolutely turned his back on the museum.

And that was a shame.

Because if Tockle had visited the Primaeval Crocodile that day, he might have noticed that something very strange had just started to happen.

6
The Scarlet Loory of Manmadin

Saturday April 26th, 1783

The skeleton of the betrayed Primaeval Crocodile was displayed on an iron gibbet that hung from the ceiling, so everyone could walk around it and marvel at its size – and the power of its great jaws. Its position was changed frequently, which gave it the illusion of life. Sometimes it crouched as if ready to spring. Other times it seemed to have wrapped its great body around the gibbet pole. The Venetians saw the beast so often that they had almost forgotten how to really look at it. So not a single Venetian noticed, on the day that started so badly for Amneris and Tockle, that one of the Crocodile's skeletal claws had actually regrown a little patch of reptilian skin.

And each day after that, a tiny bit more green scaly skin began to clothe the Primaeval Crocodile's baleful bones.

Amneris's friend Biri was as loyal in her attendance at the museum as any Venetian. Despite the fact that her working days were long and hard, she could never resist a visit to her favourite exhibits, the shiny cockroaches and the velvety moths in the Wunderkammer, a room stuffed with natural wonders like a miniature universe, with every kind of thing or creature represented in its oddest possible form. It hurt Biri's feelings to see the dead butterflies and beetles pinned in patterns among the displays of whelks, conches, oysters with two pearls, corals, crystals and petrified walnuts. She hoped that the poor insects had been unconscious when they died.

For Biri, the Primaeval Crocodile was just something that she passed on the way to see the cockroaches. But it was Biri, a sharply observant girl, who was exactly the right height to pass the Crocodile's claw at eye level. So it was she who was the first – and at that point the *only* – person in Venice to notice the patch of new green skin.

Biri thought, 'Belly up! That's clever! Fogfinger's scientists are gonna turn it into a mechanical crocodile? That'll send 'em screaming!'

She shook back her frizzly wedge of hair and screwed up her blue eyes for a closer look.

Biri knew that the skeleton was the most popular exhibit in the museum. 'So them scientists *can't* take it away to their laboratory to re-skin it all at once … they'd have to do it bit by bit. At night, most prob'ly. Anyway,' Biri thought bitterly, 'it must be all under control. Like everything else in Venice. More's the pity.'

What Biri could not know was that the museum's scientists never went into the public exhibition. The things out there were already discovered. The scientists kept to their laboratory, straining their eyes at microscopes in the hunt for brand-new species, to which they might be allowed to give their own names, and thereby become famous. So not one of them had seen what was happening to the Crocodile. Meanwhile, both the old guards who looked after the museum suffered from poor eyesight. They mostly dozed peacefully in their corner of the room.

Biri hesitated to wake them now: in spite of her appearance, she was a kind girl. And she'd had her fifteen minutes of leisure and now it was time to get back outside and start earning money. The birthday of her friend Amneris was fast approaching. She'd seen a velvet pincushion in the shape of a crimson boot that Amneris would love.

Poor Amneris, in slavery to that vile silk merchant Dubbini! Biri muttered a reasonably bad adjective as she knelt and reached into a secret niche under the Megio Bridge, extracting the cage she had hidden there.

'Biri' was short for 'Birichina', which means 'the cheeky girl'. It was so long since anyone had called her by her real name that even Biri had forgotten it. (It was the very unlikely 'Ermintrudina.)' Biri looked as poor as she was. Her clothes were held together with pins and clothes pegs. People nodded their heads sadly when she hurtled past them in the street, for Biri rarely walked anywhere in a sedate fashion. Spinning in her wake, they'd sigh, '*Quella povera ragazzina!*' That poor girl!

'Poor' was certainly true. Biri didn't have much. Both her parents were members of the *Piccoli Pochi*, and had been exiled to Serbia two years before: 'too dangerous to stay in Venice awaiting trial', according to Fogfinger. They had fought to take Biri with them, but the answer from the *Magistrato alle Figlie*, the Daughters' Magistrate, had been an implacable 'No'.

'She's been weighed and found suitable. No young girl can wriggle out of the Lambing selection like that. Especially when her parents are traitors.'

Now Biri lived in a dark storeroom in the burnt-out stonemasons' yard just behind the ancient church of San Marcuola. The head stonemason, who had employed Biri's father Thadeo Fava, kindly let her stay there without rent. He risked his life giving her shelter, for the children of the *Piccoli Pochi* were also outcasts. Biri suspected that the stonemason was a sympathizer, if not a member of the *Pochi*, but she knew better than to ask. You never knew where a new Anagrammaticular might be concealed inside the wall.

Biri lived among hunks of Istrian marble, ate her poor meals off them, and occasionally stood on them to keep dry, because the ground-floor warehouse was subject to flooding at high tide. She slept on a wooden shelf up near the ceiling. She had two dresses, each as ragged as the other, and one shawl, partially unravelled, and a pair of boy's boots, well holed. She had a bowl for food and one knife. There was a white porcelain sink. A pipe with a serpent's-head tap snaked down the wall to supply a stern gush from a rainwater cistern. A squat iron stove lurked in a corner like a fat black beetle. The pile of logs beside it was carefully rationed. It took a lot of energy to steal wood from building yards and untended carts. For Biri, each winter presented a choice between freezing and starving to death. She was too proud to accept the secret help of the *Piccoli Pochi*, telling them gruffly to 'give it to someone who can't look after theirselves, why doan you?'

And now, in the springtime, she was certainly not above going through the boxes of elderly vegetables and bruised fruit that the *fruttivendolo* threw out at the end of the day because no one would buy them. 'Free is a heap cheaper than buying,' she told herself, scraping the mould off a potato. Since her parents had been sent away, she'd got used to crunching them raw, as she was usually too hungry to wait for them to boil, even if she had enough wood for her stove. She was invited to eat at the home of her friend Amneris any time she wanted, but she knew that she was watched, and that frequent visits there might bring down trouble on the

D'Ago family. For this reason too she had turned down the family's invitation to come to live with them.

From time to time, she got hold of a candle. But mostly Biri went to sleep when it got dark, exhausted by long days on her feet. Biri had two things, however, that other people rather admired: she was totally without fear and she owned a very handsome parrot. Her pet was a Scarlet Loory of Manmadin, the last gift from her father. Apart from his fine plumage, the bird had an excellent memory. It would take Biri just a few minutes to teach him to say 'Olivetti Residence' or any of the names on the brass plates on the street doors of grand palaces. The bird knew he must always utter his latest words on the sound of a doorbell.

This was Biri's trade. She would seek out houses with all the signs of prosperity, like a well-scrubbed threshold and shining brass doorknobs. Then she would teach the parrot the name of the house. When she was sure the Scarlet Loory had mastered the words, she would tap on the door and show her parrot to the fascinated housekeeper or householder.

Today the name 'Flangini' had caught Biri's eye. In a few moments, she had coached the Scarlet Loory to say 'Flangini Residence' faultlessly.

'Better than a doorbell!' Biri enthused to Signor Flangini's housekeeper. 'Your personal doorbell, and very beautiful. Just keep him in a cage near the door and when people pull the chain, he will announce the name of your residence. Reckon they will think it is magic!'

She rang the doorbell again, and the Scarlet Loory announced importantly, 'Flangini Residence!'

The housekeeper said dubiously, 'How do you wind it up, this parrot?'

'Oh no,' Biri answered. 'He will cost you no Winding Up Tax! Just a few broken biscuits or leftover cake and a little beaker of water. And then he'll sing somefing fierce! And only a ducat to you, because I can see how much he likes you. Look at that grin on his beak!'

If her customer grumbled about cleaning the cage, Biri smiled. It looked like sympathy but really it was because she knew that they would never need to do that chore. The cage had a lock the Scarlet Loory was extremely experienced at picking. Once the sale was agreed, the bird would be in that cage less than an hour.

Biri bade Signor Flangini's housekeeper a cheery farewell. Then she walked around the corner and settled down in the dust to wait. Eventually the housekeeper would need to open the door to go out for an errand. And by that time the Scarlet Loory would have picked his lock, and would fly out to find his mistress. He had an unerring instinct for where she was. He always fluttered gently down to her shoulder and gave her nose an affectionate soft peck. Biri would get up and walk home with the parrot bobbing on her shoulder. And there she would sit cross-legged on the floor and build another simple cage with a faulty door.

Her clients were embarrassed to have been fooled by the dusty little girl. So they kept her secret and Biri was careful to choose a new square or parish every time.

It was hard work, and Biri was sometimes apprehended by the constables, who knew her game all too well. Some were sympathetic but others – particularly those who were part of Fogfinger's elite, the Fog Squad – sometimes forced her to eat a Bittercake, iced with the words *I am a trickster*. They visibly enjoyed watching her cough and splutter as she forced it down. Even harder for Biri was the fact that she had been marched to a baker and made to pay for the Bittercake herself, out of whatever money she had.

The officers would pocket the rest of the money they found on her 'as a fine'. Sometimes she was locked up overnight in one of the *cofanetti*, the windowless one-roomed houses of detention to be found in every quarter of the city. And sometimes a Fog would push her a little too hard when they finally let her leave the station.

Biri had grown up fast and tough. Instead of acting like a sweet innocent victim to charm kind-hearted people, Biri had chosen the harder path of fighting her way through life.

So she put up quite a fight when two masked men approached her, dropped a black cloth over her head and another over the Scarlet Loory, and bundled them both into a boat.

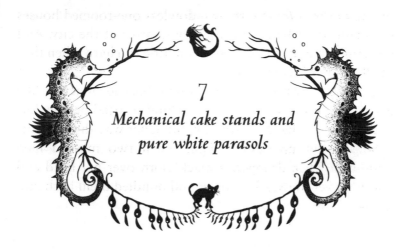

7

Mechanical cake stands and pure white parasols

Saturday April 26th, 1783

Among many pointless and expensive pastimes, Latenia Malipiero – the girl whose face was never seen – collected ridiculous cake stands. Like all rich girls, she'd been encouraged to be fond of cakes, so as to maintain a weight that would exempt her from selection to Fogfinger's Lambing. Cakes were served five times a day in the Malipiero palace: for breakfast, as a mid-morning snack, with afternoon tea at three p.m., with high tea at six and again after supper. (At luncheon, Latenia made do with three scoops of chocolate ice.) To accompany both cakes and ice, she also had cream, obtained by squeezing the linen udders of a little mechanical cow, made of papier mâché with a glass barrel inside. A kitchen maid kept the hollow rear end of the cow topped up with fresh cream at all times.

Every time Latenia ate an extra bowl of pigeon soup with Parmesan, or a second helping of wild duck with capers, her father would say, 'Good for you,' in his quiet cold voice.

Afterwards, her maids would plead, 'Just one more cake, little madam?'

Her mother did not say anything, because her mother was not there.

She had disappeared years before, when Latenia was still a baby. And now it was forbidden to mention her name in the palace. Latenia was not a very inquisitive sort of girl. Nor was she a very affectionate one. So she did not miss her mother. After all, her father gave her everything she wanted, and scarcely bothered her at all. Even though she was never allowed out of the house – except for the Lambing ceremonies at the Frari – and met only with servants, her father liked Latenia to look nice, insisting that her hair was dressed in ringlets à la Brutus, and that she wore brocaded dresses with gauzy sleeves floating from her elbows. Latenia had no objections to her fine clothes so long as someone else performed the fiddly task of getting her plump little body in and out of them. Nor did she mind the heavy veil she had to wear when she went to the Lambings.

'After all,' she told herself, 'it is much better that the common people can't look at me.'

Almost as much as eating cakes, Latenia liked playing with them. And for that purpose she had a collection of mechanical cake stands. One was a pyramid of five plates that revolved at different speeds. The fastest made the cakes spin off and splatter on the walls. Another of Latenia's cake stands was constructed of carved wooden waves. Winding its handle made the cakes bob up and down as if they were floating down the Grand Canal. It was pretty, but not as exciting as the spinning pyramid.

Latenia's room was decorated with exquisite stucco-work of fat pastel cupids trailing garlands in delicate pinks, greens and buttermilk yellow. Her bed alcove was draped with emerald and gold brocade. Her dressing table sparkled with jewelled combs, cranberry glass perfume bottles, onyx candlesticks and enamelled tweezers. She also kept a box of blue glass seahorses there. Every few weeks – until recently – one had mysteriously appeared on her pillow while she slept. She found them pretty, but, not being an inquisitive girl, she did not wonder much at their arrival or why they had suddenly stopped appearing. Living in isolation as she did, Latenia had no idea that the blue glass seahorses were the symbol of the *Piccoli Pochi*, or indeed who the *Piccoli Pochi* were. And nor would she have been very interested if she had known.

Latenia was always dressed in purest white. The maids were kept busy washing and starching her elaborate outfits, which were frequently bedecked with strawberry jam or icing or the pulp from pear-and-plum loaves or the sticky residue of elderflower fritters. They strained their eyes sewing the tassels back onto the white shawls she damaged when she kicked them across the room. Her bodices, sleeves and overskirts were white, at least until they were stained with pomegranate syrup. Her bonnets and feather fascinators were white – that is, until she dropped them on the floor and walked over them. The braided garters that held up her silk stockings were white, as were her chamois slippers with ruched ribbons at the front and the linen hoop-petticoats that kept her skirts as wide as the palace doorways. Even Latenia's parasols were pure white. She had a collection of them in silk, damask and satin. Her favourite – so far, for a rich collector is never truly satisfied – was an ivory-handled parasol in figured white velvet.

The pyramid cake stand was revolving at its highest speed when Latenia's father brought a very rare thing – a visitor – into her room. A strawberry custard pie flew straight into the porcelain buttons of Signor Malipiero's gold brocade waistcoat, exploding on impact. And the visitor – the silk merchant Melchior Dubbini – received a miniature chocolate tart to the side of his head.

Wiping the chocolate icing from his ear, he simpered, 'So sweet, so sweet, the little madam must have her fun! I do love to see the young ones enjoying themselves. And what an honour to meet the best-kept secret in Venice, Signor Malipiero – your lovely daughter. I can see why you keep such a precious treasure hidden away!'

More curious still was the reaction of Latenia's father to the cake assault. His pale blue eyes did not flash. His cynical mouth, almost invisible in the nest of his soft, gingery beard, did not frown. He did not reproach his daughter for staining his beautiful waistcoat. He didn't even really look at her. Dusting the crumbs from his braided sleeve, he said, 'Daughter, I want you to see this piece of silk embroidery that Dubbini has brought. Do you think it could be worked into a parasol for your collection?'

'I'm busy,' said Latenia rudely. 'Leave it over there and I'll look at it later.'

'Of course, of course,' Dubbini placed the silk carefully on a chair.

But even he flinched when a black-grape mousse landed on the beautiful white silk, leaving a stain that would never come out.

Latenia lifted her eyes from her spinning cake stand. They fell on the ruined silk.

'What?' she cried. '*What*?'

And then she threw herself on the ground and delivered a violent tantrum, including screams and a few tears.

'That was *exactly* what I wanted,' she sobbed. 'Papà, you must fix it.'

'I fear it is beyond repair,' her father said. 'Grape does not wash out, the servants tell me – not from kid boots, not from white gloves and not from silk.'

Latenia erupted in a new tempest of tears.

'Grape is my *favourite*. Why did the stupid piece of silk get in the way? Well, get me some more, but *better*!' she shouted, kicking over the pyramid cake stand. 'And I *definitely* want a new parasol covered in it!'

'Certainly, but of course,' said Dubbini. 'The dear little lady shall have just exactly what she desires. Such good taste! Pure breeding will out, I always say.'

'What did you want for that?' Alvise Malipiero gestured carelessly at the bruised-looking white silk.

Dubbini named a large sum. It was handed to him without comment.

'Am I to honour the young lady's request for a *better* piece next time? I am afraid that *better* will also entail a certain amount of extra expense ...'

Latenia turned on Dubbini and gave him a sharp kick on the shin with her beaded white boot.

'"Better", I said. It had *better* be better. Do you get it, mister? Or I'll make sure my father never buys another thing from you. Soon,' she added. 'Or else. And white, white, white! But send it – do not come back here. I don't want to see your slimy face ever again, do you hear?'

8
Splintered glass

Saturday April 26th, 1783

Tockle had saved his boat. After an hour of scooping and some attention with wooden bungs, it now floated again like an emerald-green leaf on the water of the Rio di San Zan Degola.

The next few days Tockle spent more time on water than on land. He did not have time for school or the Natural History Museum. Instead, he was busy visiting all the glassworks on the island of Murano. Stella had received a handsome order for twenty new kaleidoscopes. So Tockle had to row to Murano to beg for the splinters the master glass-blowers shaved and snipped off their molten vases, bowls and goblets as they turned them on their metal stakes. She used these fragments of glass to make the kaleidoscopes.

Sometimes Tockle was told to clean workshop floors in exchange for the leavings of glass. Other times, he ran errands for glass-blowers, rushing to the cookshop to fetch pies or soup. He dusted and oiled their leather gloves or aprons. They rarely spoke to him, or thanked him, merely pointing to the heap of glass splinters when they felt he'd done enough to earn them. The glass-blowers were rather full of themselves, as well they might be: their skills were legendary.

That Saturday morning, Tockle was fetching and carrying for Signor Castrauro. This master glass-blower was less uppity than most. On days like today, when he saw that Tockle was anxious, he often let him take the glass shards without requiring him to slave for them.

'Courage, boy!' he smiled. 'Off you go!'

Tockle was anxious because Baffi sat brooding in the prow of the boat. Tockle had decided that it would be safer to take him on this expedition. Stella would not have the cat in the house after the last incident with the dead fish tucked under her mattress. And it was not safe for Baffi to roam the streets.

Fogfinger did not like cats. He said there were too many in Venice. He set up a special Cat Corps, a branch of the feared Fogs. At first he tried to order a cull of Venetian felines, claiming that many were sick and must be put down for their own good. But the Venetians knew this was a lie, and they hid their beloved cats away from the Fogs, hollowing out niches in their walls and building false doors in their larder cupboards. Then Fogfinger pretended that cats were spreading diseases to human babies. No one believed him, knowing that cats are the cleanest of creatures.

Finally, Fogfinger instituted a system like the Lambing. He called it the Kittening. And for the cats, it was more of a Beak in the Box. If the cats were lucky, a dear little mouse popped up its head and they were safe (even if the mouse wasn't). If not, a cruel bird beak sprang from the box. Then the bird swelled to ten times its size, took the cat in its mechanical talons and flew away. The Kittening was held in public, between the two columns of the Piazzetta. Free cake and hot chocolate was offered to those who attended. Anyone who brought a cat was paid in gold.

Now Fogfinger succeeded where previously he had failed. There were fewer and fewer felines to be seen on the streets of Venice. Baffi had escaped so far only because humans, as well as rats, were afraid of his staring eyes and vicious paws, and because Tockle took him out in the *sandolo* whenever he rowed over to Murano.

'Hello, bad boy!' Tockle greeted his cat. Baffi looked pointedly over his shoulder.

'Suit yourself,' shrugged Tockle, carefully placing his bag of glass in the boat and untying the ropes. He lifted his oar and set off back for Venice.

Baffi did not much like the loping movement of the green *sandolo*, but he amused himself watching for fish under the water.

They were a hundred metres from the shore when a shadow fell over the cat, swallowing the prow of the boat in darkness.

'What!' cried Tockle. Then he was silenced as three lithe figures leapt from an old boat, bound and gagged him. Baffi was crammed into a wicker crab basket, where he stood spitting with his back arched. Boy and cat were placed on a wooden bench. The attackers tied Tockle's *sandolo* to the back of their own boat and sped off into the lagoon.

Tockle's eyes fell on the little sack of glass shards. At least it was safe. And so was the Molin family's livelihood for a little while longer.

If Tockle stayed alive, that is.

Tockle's first fevered thought was that he had been taken into custody by the Fogs for some new crime invented by

Fogfinger but not yet announced to the public. He had just a few copper *bezzi* in his shoe – not nearly enough to bribe a Fog to leave him alone. *They* dealt in silver *scudi* and *ducati*. But then he realized that this leaky old *San Pierota* looked nothing like the sleek grey boats in which the Fogs nosed through the canals when making their arrests. And his captors were dressed in shabby fishermen's clothes, not the black-frogged grey uniform of Fogfinger's forces. They carried no bludgeons or muskets.

Pirates? Tockle speculated. A few pirates still preyed on the smaller islands of the lagoon. Or so Fogfinger declared at the public hangings of wretched-looking men, who spoke Venetian and did not look much like pirates, except for the colourful rags they wore – that did not fit and clearly were not their own.

He could not cross himself, because his hands were tied, but Tockle said a brief prayer to San Nicolò, patron saint of sailors. 'Let these be good pirates, if they are pirates, San Nicolò. Or let them not be pirates at all. I don't want to be press-ganged into service on the high seas. Or hanged. Please, San Nicolò. I am basically a good boy, and my family needs me.'

One of his captors overheard the muttered prayer.

The man laughed heartily, and gave Tockle a gap-toothed but charming smile. 'Don't worry, lad,' he chuckled.

As the boat approached the shallow channel that bisected the island of Poveglia, Tockle became even surer of the fact that his kidnapping was nothing to do with Fogfinger. For a start, these men had been kind to him, apologizing for the shock of his capture, and politely asking him to be quiet and still 'until we are well away from frequented waters'.

At Poveglia, he was gently helped ashore. A door to what looked like a chapel was held open and the men ushered him into a long, candle-lit hall, one carrying the crab basket with Baffi inside.

In a room at the end of the hall, seats around a large table were occupied by six serious men with white beards, two Franciscan friars in their habits, a striking woman in velvet breeches and a small, scruffy girl with one arm around a crude cage that contained a magnificent parrot. With her other hand, the girl was applying a spoon to a large bowl of steaming porridge.

'Welcome, Temistocle. Welcome, Ermintrudina,' said the man with the whitest and longest beard. Two men cut Tockle's bonds. 'Please forgive the abrupt way in which we have made your acquaintance. But secrecy is essential in our line of work.'

The man asked, 'May I remove your gag, Temistocle? And offer you some porridge? However, if you intend to scream, we will need to keep you gagged. Can we trust you?'

Tockle nodded and pointed to the porridge. His stomach growled helpfully, to underline his 'yes'.

'Good. Do join us at the table. Please meet Ermintrudina—'

'Biri!' mumbled the girl, with a mouth still full of porridge.

'Very well, Biri. Meet Temistocle Molin.'

'Belly up!' exclaimed the girl. 'That's a mouthful. Nice cat, but.'

'My friends call me Tockle,' he mumbled, wiping his mouth and burying a spoon in the bowl of porridge that had been placed in front of him. He offered a spoonful to Baffi through the slats of the crab basket, but the cat was more interested in the parrot.

The lady in breeches smiled at them. She was a tall woman with rich chestnut hair that flowed loose and large eyes of lustrous brown. Tockle guessed that she was about the same age as his mother – but this woman was nothing like her. His mother and her friends were always modestly clad in a delicate shawl that they wrapped around their heads and bodies in a figure of eight. And none ever met his eyes with such a frank stare. There was strength in this lady's firm jaw and in her pronounced eyebrows. He read pride and unabashed determination in her face. In fact, if she had not been dressed in breeches, Tockle might have supposed her a noblewoman.

She caught his gaze. He blushed and looked down.

One of the friars spoke next. 'You two have something very important in common. I wonder if you can guess what it is?'

Tockle stared hard at the girl. Her clothes were held together with pins and clothes pegs. Her shawl looked like a child's half-finished knitting project. Her hair was a coarse frizz of brown in a blunt, awkward shape that spoke of a knife and no mirror. Her eyes, however, were fine – blue and wide awake. He did not think he knew her. She certainly did not attend his school. She was not from Murano where he begged for glass: all the children there were sleek and well cared for. Perhaps he'd seen her in the Natural History Museum?

The girl returned his stare gravely. She shook her head.

The man with the long white beard said, 'Both of you are without fathers at this moment. And the reason for their absence is the same. Even if you two do not know one another – your Papàs do. Rizardo Molin and Thadeo Fava are friends, and friends of ours. For they are both members of our group.'

The truth struck Tockle and Biri at the same time, so that they cried in unison, 'The *Piccoli Pochi*!' Then they clapped their hands over their mouths.

'Don't worry, no Anagrammaticulars here. Yes, Rizardo and Thadeo are loyal members. Unfortunately exiled, or escaped for their own safety, as are nearly all of our number.

As you know, Biri, your parents are both in Serbia. And Tockle, we have discovered that your father is at the great al-Mansuri hospital in Cairo. He was … injured when he fled.'

Tockle jumped to his feet, almost overturning the bowl of porridge. 'Injured?'

'If the *Pochi* are caught in the lagoon, the Fogs pretend we are pirates. They dress us in fake pirate clothes and hang us. Temistocle, your father has a flesh wound from a musket, but at least he got away. Our friends in Cairo tell us he will recover, but progress is slow.'

Tockle swallowed and said quietly, 'Thank you, sir, for telling me. It is the first news of my father in two years.' He bit his lip hard to stopper up the tears that were pooling at the corners of his eyes. 'Flesh wound?' he stammered.

'Rizardo was unlucky enough to take a ricochet of musket fire to the side of his throat. He was unable to talk for months and even then could not communicate with the Egyptian doctors in their language. It was only when another Venetian fell ill in Cairo and was put in the bed beside him that he was able to get a message out. We have only just found out his condition ourselves. That is partly why we have summoned you to talk to us. We *Piccoli Pochi* can no longer make forays into town. The situation is getting worse. The Fogs have activated a network of paid spies. It is proving effective. Venice is so small: everyone knows everyone. And everyone is known to at least one of Fogfinger's *confidenti*. Now that Carnevale is banned, we cannot hide behind masks. So we have to try a new way of working. And this is where you and Biri come in.'

'Wassat?' Biri was still cramming porridge into her mouth.

'Fogfinger does not think very highly of children. Otherwise he would not spill their blood every year. It's why

66

he poxes any who show a little spirit. He will not suspect you of carrying out missions against him.'

'Missions?' Tockle's stomach churned.

'The *Piccoli Pochi* have begun to recruit a new division called *I Piccolissimi Pochi*, The Tiniest Few. We already have some members. Temistocle, I believe that you know Ugo Paolin?'

'Ugo? But he ...'

'Is poxed. Yet even from a wheelchair, he makes a fine commander of the *Piccolissimi Pochi*. Fogfinger has exterminated his health, but Ugo's mind is masterful and fearless. He's trying to make contact with ... certain powerful forces ... who may be able to help us. As he can no longer run around, he has plenty of time to work on intricate ideas. Speaking of fearless, your own two fathers have told us that you two are the bravest, staunchest young Venetians that can be found anywhere between Cannaregio and Santa Croce.'

'Reckon,' said Biri, finally putting down her spoon. 'Somefing fierce!'

'So are you, Biri and Temistocle, ready to be sworn in as members of the *Piccolissimi Pochi*?'

'What if we don't wanna?' challenged Biri, but there was more pride than aggression in her voice.

'Then it is your right to refuse. We will deliver you safely back to Venice and never ask anything of you again, except that you keep this meeting a secret.'

'And what if we do want to join?' asked Tockle.

It was the woman in the velvet breeches who answered him. Her voice was aristocratic, low and musical. But her words were ugly: 'Then your lives are in terrible danger from this moment forward.'

'Belly up!' said Biri.

9
Getting what she deserved

His own particular branch of the noble Malipiero family tree was not as rich or as grand as Latenia's father pretended it to be. They lived in the palace's least-favoured apartments, with just two windows on the Grand Canal. Humiliatingly, Count Piero Malipiero, the head of the family, barely acknowledged his cousin Alvise in the street. Perhaps the count knew about the heavy secret mortgage and a terrifying dark hole in Alvise Malipiero's accounts where his inheritance used to be, with much of that money lost at the gambling tables in the *ridotto* where all fashionable nobles were obliged to be seen at play.

Sitting at his desk that evening, Signor Malipiero stroked his ginger beard, thinking about how he had overspent on a little item that Fogfinger liked to sell to the rich: bottles of the precious white fat found in the throbbing chamber around a dragon's heart. Only Fogfinger was able to secure this item, which he kindly sold on to the Venetians. The fat was supposed to bring success in legal matters at the *Quarantia Criminale* – and Signor Malipiero, who, to his great displeasure, was forced to work for a living, had chosen to become a lawyer. Of course, he pretended that he did it 'so as not to be bored'. It would never do to admit that a man with blood as blue as his needed the money.

Dragon-heart fat was only one of the items that Fogfinger manufactured for sale to the superstitious Venetians: he also turned a profit on sheep hearts pierced with nails to protect against bewitchment, horseshoes wrapped in fabric for warding off nightmares, the tips of rabbit tongues against poverty, acorns for lightning strikes, elder twigs against warts, peony seeds for epilepsy, fossilized shark teeth to stop toothache, coral and shell hands carved into gestures to avert the evil eye, the dried front feet of a mole that were supposed to prevent cramp. Signor Malipiero had been obliged to invest in all these things. But none were as brutally expensive as the dragon-heart fat. The cloudy white fat was displayed in glass bottles in all lawyers' offices to make their clients feel confident of a good outcome. Fogfinger 'made available' new bottles of dragon-heart fat every few months, and any lawyer who wanted to win his cases was obliged to 'invest'.

But no matter how much dragon-heart fat Signor Malipiero bought, his poor clients still seemed to fail at their cases. The truth was that Signor Malipiero was not a good or a talented lawyer. He was interested only in the fees his clients paid, and not in helping them to justice. His hands were small but he had a wide reach when it came to the pockets of those who approached him for help. People frequently left his office poorer than they went in, with their claims unsettled.

Signor Malipiero was lacklustre in defending his clients, but the fact was that he could do no better for them anyway. He could not afford to buy as many bottles of luck as it would take to win their cases. News of his repeated failures spread around the town. The clients came in fewer numbers;

latterly mostly foreigners or country bumpkins who did not know how things were done in Venice. And certainly Signor Malipiero had no noble clients with infinite purses of golden fees: they would go straight to Fogfinger and buy the outcome they wanted anyway.

And so the coffers of the Malipiero palace were emptying at a disastrous rate. But Signor Malipiero had a scintillating plan for refilling them. This plan would also enable him to give up work, which simply didn't suit him at all: he was much better suited, in his opinion, to barking orders from behind his fine desk, with its rather appropriate legs carved in the shapes of kneeling slaves.

His plan involved his daughter.

Although it was an excellent plan, it was a slow one. So in the meantime, at night, he went to the jewel box where Latenia kept all the emeralds and rubies that had been part of her mother's dowry. Every time there was a new offering of dragon-heart fat, Signor Malipiero would help himself to another necklace. Then he'd have himself rowed out to a certain glass-blower at Murano. By dawn, a tired glass-blower would be taking himself to bed, and something that looked extraordinarily like her necklace would be back in Latenia's jewel box. And the real necklace would be in the hands of the pawnbroker, who kept his discreet office at Rialto open all night for just this kind of opportunity.

Signor Malipiero was so confident of his fake jewels' lustre, and of his daughter's stupidity, that he never considered that anyone would recognize his cunning ploy. All the same, if any rich acquaintances were coming to dinner – Signor Malipiero did not have actual friends – he allowed Latenia to wear only her pearls. Her face, of course, was kept strictly veiled in black, so the pearls looked all the more luminous, and interest in the mysterious face of the Malipiero daughter grew ever more feverish.

The pearls could not be copied by the glass-blower, and so were safe from the pawnbroker.

For the moment.

However, in the privacy of her majestic bedroom, Latenia was allowed to wear her glass diamonds, rubies and emeralds to her cold little heart's content.

When he saw his daughter decked out in the false jewels, Signor Malipiero felt slightly uncomfortable. Only slightly, because his daughter was such a shallow creature that it cost his conscience nothing to deceive her. She'd never even protested when he changed her name from 'Natalia' to 'Latenia'. And the sale of the real jewels paid for her endless demands for clothes, automata and cakes, not to mention her maids and the hairdresser who came daily because you never knew when the plan might suddenly move ahead into action. Malipiero's plan meant that he must fulfil all his daughter's demands for just a short while longer. Then he'd be repaid a thousandfold. Meanwhile, if he said 'no', just once, the spoilt minx would start moaning to the servants, and gossip would get out that the lawyer Alvise Malipiero was too poor to pay for his daughter's pleasures and luxuries.

'She'll be getting what she deserves,' he thought, jingling the silver *zecchini* in his pocket. 'She is her mother's daughter, after all.'

And his face grew still and hard with hate.

10

The first task of the
Piccolissimi Pochi

'In danger of your lives,' was a phrase that easily stayed in the memory. In fact, it lingered like a Bittercake in Tockle's mouth.

'I am not ready for this,' he was thinking. 'I'm not worthy of it. How can the *Piccoli Pochi* think I am?' Even Baffi's eyes seemed to glitter with disbelief.

It was just as hard to digest the other crucial piece of information he'd received: that his father was alive. Tockle's heart kept lurching into a gallop at the thought of Rizardo Molin lying mute and hurt in a hospital bed far away in Cairo.

He was distracted from that painful thought by the startling words being spoken around the table.

'As you know, the *Piccoli Pochi* don't believe that the Lambing is anything to do with the Crocodile,' declared a Franciscan friar. 'The ceremony is a cruel trick Fogfinger's foisted on Venice to keep the city frightened and subdued—'

The other friar continued, 'He has made a game of smoke

72

and mirrors, using elements of the Christian faith like the Lamb, but twisting them. We poor fathers of the Frari were horrified when he first started to use our sacred ground for his diabolic ceremony. The preaching monkeys were the last straw. When we tried to protest we were rounded up like sheep and put in chains in the prisons of the Doge's Palace. A few days later, those who'd survived the beatings there were hustled onto boats under cover of night and taken to a labour camp on the island of San Giorgio in Alga. My brother here and I escaped.'

'So you priests didn't go off because you wanted to?' Biri asked. 'To live in the lap of luxury, eating grapes all day, like the Finger says, then?'

'I know Fogfinger put it about that we chose to abandon our parishes. But those priests at the camp on San Giorgio in Alga – they are there only because their chains are stout and there are no boats.'

'What is it you want us to do, sir?' asked Tockle.

'We need to find out more about the Lambing. We need to show the Venetians – conclusively – that the ceremony is a travesty. But we can only do that if we know what really happens up there at the top of the Frari bell-tower. Ugo Paolin has an idea about it, but of course he's in no state to undertake physical investigations.'

The woman in breeches added in her deep musical voice, 'We need to know exactly what happens after the Lambs are sacrificed.'

11
Double triple quadruple bluff

Monday April 28th, 1783

Amneris held out the new white-on-white design, trying to look proud. Under the counter, she pulled at the fringe of her shawl for comfort.

Melchior Dubbini raised an eyebrow. 'Another white piece! When I told you it was the last thing I wanted to see. The D'Ago household must be fasting at the moment. I don't see how you would eat on what I am going to pay you for this.'

Amneris flinched. But she refused to explain that she had no choice in the matter: the dear creature had delivered another white design that morning.

Then she noticed how Dubbini was rubbing his hands together. And she remembered what Biri always warned her: 'That man speaks out of both sides of his mouth at once. Whatever he swears is the truth is a lie.'

By that reckoning, Amneris realized, Dubbini must have got a very good price indeed for the first white piece. She decided to test him with a double bluff.

'Very well, Signor Dubbini. I'll have to take it elsewhere. Perhaps there is another silk merchant somewhere in Venice who has a *special customer* who likes white.'

She half turned as if to leave. And she was gratified to see him turn pale and to hear him stutter, 'Er ... er, wait a moment, girlie mine. Not so hasty.'

Although her heart was fluttering with joy, Amneris forced herself not to smile. She waited for him to speak, tapping her foot on the floor in a mime of impatience.

'I'll take it, I suppose,' he grumbled, 'but only because I am a charitable man.'

Amneris thought, 'Such a shame I never meet the customers. They would love to buy without Melchior Dubbini's fat profit in the middle. Even rich people like a bargain, Biri says. Where is Biri anyway? I haven't seen her for days. I hope the Fogs haven't caught her again!'

Worrying about Biri, Amneris almost did not hear the silk merchant saying, 'In fact, my dear, just this once, I think you *should* meet my customer, a certain young lady at the Malipiero palace. I'm sure she'll be charmed to meet a girl like you.'

Amneris was surprised. The mysterious Malipiero girl! The girl famous for never being seen, always kept at home, except for the Lambings, when she appeared swaddled in veils. A girl who lived in a palace on the Grand Canal must be very rich. Why would she want to meet a poor seamstress?

'Here's what to do,' Dubbini spoke quickly. 'Take this piece away and fashion it into a parasol – you know, one of the oriental-looking ones your family makes – the kind that looks like the roof of a pavilion at the Topkapi Palace in Constantinople.'

Amneris nodded. That style was much requested.

The silk merchant opened a drawer in his haberdashery

cabinet and counted out twelve tear-drop pearls. 'Fix these to the border. Then wrap the parasol in something decent and take it to the Malipiero palace. I shall tell them to expect you on Wednesday morning at ten. Don't mention money. The Malipiero are a noble family, so that would be offensive. I shall deal with payment afterwards.'

Delivering the parasol in less than two days' time would mean her father working all night. Although blind, he was expert at stretching the silk over the folding metal cages the D'Ago family bought in from a Turkish merchant. Then, just by touch, he would bind the delicate fabric to the struts with tiny stitches.

'Night and day are the same to me,' he always said. He was always happy for a parasol commission to make him feel useful. And, Amneris thought, being allowed inside a real Venetian palace would be exciting. At least there'd be something to pay for the next week's silk.

'Very well,' she said, 'I suppose just this once would be acceptable,' maintaining a pretence of reluctance to the last. It was better that way, because Melchior Dubbini was only ever happy if he felt someone else was miserable.

As Amneris left, she caught sight of one of his pale girls, who had dared to look up for a moment. She smiled weakly at Amneris, raising one thin hand. Amneris started to smile back.

But then she noticed what the girl was sewing.

It was a devil costume: a red suit, with a forked tail. All the girls were sewing devil suits or forcing stuffing into black satin horns. The back room was a hell of red and black. Amneris caught her breath.

The silk merchant slammed the door to the back room and the girls disappeared from Amneris's sight. He opened the door to the street and jerked his chin in the direction of 'out'.

One street away from the shop, Amneris did a little pirouette. She had got away with it! Then her face darkened. She had got away with it *once*. Rich Venetians were notoriously fickle. The Malipiero girl might want white silk today but tomorrow she'd probably want Topaz Yellow or Parrot Wing Red.

Passing the apricot tree on the way into the house, she recalled the blond boy with the half-mast stockings.

'I hope he was saved a beating for that sum, at least,' she smiled.

For a moment she paused outside the door, as if just thinking about him might make Temistocle Molin appear. The street stayed empty. She sighed and went indoors to prepare her family for a long night's work.

'I'll look for Biri on Wednesday,' she promised herself, 'as soon as I've delivered the parasol to that Malipiero girl.'

12
Boring is best

Saturday April 26th – Monday April 28th, 1783

'Farewell! Take care!' 'Be discreet!' 'Be *boring*!' urged their new friends. 'Don't attract attention to yourselves. Go to Ugo Paolin. He will give you your tasks – starting with simple ones, of course. Then you, who are able-bodied, are to come back here to us and report.'

The chestnut-haired woman in breeches strode over to Tockle and shook his hand until it was numb.

Catching sight of his watering eyes, she asked, 'Temistocle, are you all right?'

'Oh yes, except that I need a new hand.'

'I forget my strength!' she laughed. 'I am sorry. It is such a relief to be able to shake hands instead of having mine kissed all the time by the soft useless lips of noblemen—'

She stopped, looking embarrassed.

Tockle had offered to row Biri back to Venice in his green *sandolo* and she had accepted, though without pleasure.

'Not much of a girl for the water,' she groaned. Five minutes later she was leaning over the edge. ''Scuse please.'

78

She did not look up until every last oat of the porridge had gone overboard. Baffi, freed from the crab cage, eyed her with distaste.

'Now, we got to get us some new names.' Biri wiped her mouth in a businesslike manner. 'Our *Piccolissimi Pochi* names. Me, I'm going to call myself "Aulularia Cistellaria".'

'Very pretty,' said Tockle politely, though privately he considered the name did not really fit with Biri's somewhat unromantic appearance. 'But we're supposed to be discreet – boring, even. Do we need secret names?'

Biri stuck out her lip.

He said hastily, 'But if we do, something simple might be better.'

'Very well. I will be "Zuan Pollo",' she replied, using the Venetian dialect.

That was extremely simple, but a little bizarre, thought Tockle.

Aloud, he said, '"John Chicken"? A boy's name?'

'To help hide our real identities. I'll cut my hair. Your hair is blond and too long.' She looked at him critically. 'You'd make a nice girl in a bonnet. So what's your girl name?'

'I didn't agree to be a girl. Or change my name.'

'You'd better agree fast,' said 'John Chicken', pointing to a boat full of Fogs rowing towards them. Clumsily, she seized an oar.

'No, we mustn't run away from them! Or they'll think we're suspicious characters and chase us.' Tockle was prepared for this kind of situation. It would not be the first time he'd been stopped by Fogs. He kept a couple of fishing nets in the *sandolo*. He threw one to Biri, and cast his own in the water. So when the Fogs arrived, all they saw was a pair of children trying to catch something for their supper. That was not yet illegal. The soldiers rowed straight past without giving Tockle and Biri a second glance.

'Belly up!' said Biri. 'So? Who are you now?'

'My name? I'm sticking to "Temistocle".' It was Tockle's turn to jut out his lower lip.

'Boring, but,' said Biri.

'As you've just seen, boring is best at the moment.'

Ugo's mother pleaded, 'He's not having a good day. Please don't stay long. He's feverish. Keeps staring out of the window at the water. I don't know what's happening to him.'

Biri told Signora Paolin, 'Doan worry, Missis. We will be like a tonic to 'im. Better than a fried fish from the *furatole* in San Barnaba!' She smacked her lips in memory of a rare treat at one of those little shops.

Ugo's appearance worried Tockle. Those thin shoulders were like blades now, and his useless legs seemed to have wasted under the blanket.

The boy's eyes were very bright. Two spots of red on his cheeks made him look like a thin puppet. But Ugo's smile was wide in the lamp-like pallor of his face.

'I can see from your excitement that you have joined the *Piccolissimi Pochi*. You must learn to hide it. We don't want any Fogs giving you a second glance, do we?'

And he told them of missions already carried out – a child with extremely hot skin had been chosen to carry messages written on wax, 'So she can melt them with her wrists if she is caught. And she *did* get caught by the Fogs. And it worked a treat. But now she is no longer fit for active service as they have their eyes on her.

'And I had two cookshop boys carrying pots to cook in hot ashes. There should have been stew inside but actually they carried bars of melted-down jewellery and messages

80

... the boys were trained to step lightly and swing the pots as if they weighed no more than a couple of sausages and a turnip. I used to have a boy who delivered supplies and money to the *Pochi* at Poveglia, but he was caught,' Ugo sighed, 'and his boat was sunk, which was why I thought of you and your *sandolo*, Tockle. We as yet do nothing dramatic. It is more that we are discovering things. And those things are adding up to a bigger picture. I have made a kind of contact with—'

'Do all the *Piccolissimi* have mysterious secret names?' asked Biri eagerly. 'I have mine all worked out—'

Ugo smiled. 'The missions of the *Piccolissimi Pochi* are usually brief. Now we rarely use anyone more than once, for safety's sake. Everyone knows everyone in Venice. As soon as you started using a different name, people would say, "What's she up to?" So no, I am afraid not much use for secret names.'

Biri frowned. Tockle could see her bidding a reluctant farewell to her dream of being Aulularia Cistellaria or even John Chicken.

Ugo looked at them earnestly. 'What we need now – very seriously – is a girl who can sew beautifully, to stitch invisible messages into silk handkerchiefs ... I was wondering if either of you might know such a girl?'

At the same moment, and with warm voices, Biri and Tockle exclaimed, 'Amneris D'Ago!'

'What?' cried Biri. 'You know Amneris, blond boy?'

Tockle blushed. 'Not very well, but—'

'You'd like to know her better; that's what those red cheeks say!' laughed Ugo. The laugh, however, racked his thin frame too vigorously. He began to cough, and to retch. A moment later his handkerchief was shockingly spattered with red. He stuffed it into his pocket.

Biri bristled. 'Why do you want Amneris? You don't

wanna put her in danger too, do you, cos if—'

'No! No!' said Ugo. 'One of the *Pochi* leaders has a private mission for a seamstress, that's all. No danger – or very little – involved for your friend.'

'What 'bout the Lambing? On the island they said we's 'sposed to—'

'Before the Lambing, we must deal with what Fogfinger's up to with the fresh water. In fact, I believe the water problem – or should I say water *plot*? – and the Lambing are connected.'

Tockle shivered. Fresh water was his mother's trade.

He'd known there was a problem, particularly in the last few days, but he hadn't realized there was a plot.

Or that it was Fogfinger's.

13
Cake attacks and 'can't-be-bothereds'

Wednesday April 30th, 1783

The first thing Amneris saw when she walked into the noble girl's room was her last week's piece of white-on-white silk, now horribly stained with ten different kinds of cake-icing. It was being used to mop up a pool of raspberry cordial from a beaker that had just been flung at the door, narrowly missing Amneris herself. A maid was scrubbing away at the skirting board, her eyes cast down and one of her ears looking very red, as if it had been pulled.

Amneris hardly had time to be indignant. For the next thing she saw was a miniature strawberry sponge cake. She saw it as a blur because it was flying straight at her nose, which it hit with such force that she screamed as the little cake exploded into a hundred sugary crumbs. A few of them fell into Amneris's open mouth, which she quickly shut. She had never tasted anything so delicious. Her next thought was for the precious parasol in her arms. Fortunately it was sturdily wrapped in brown paper. And the Shrimp Girl rag doll, which Amneris had made as a gift for her noble customer, was safely tucked inside the parasol.

But who was the attacker?

A face was the next thing that swam into focus – a face that announced 'spoilt' from its jutting chin and long nose to its pouting mouth and perfect ringlets. Even the ears stuck out at arrogant angles. Emerald earrings sparkled on those ears. A ludicrously opulent emerald necklace glittered under that chin.

'Who are *you*?' asked the face. 'Make it good. I am easily bored.'

'So you are actually poor?' demanded the ringletted girl, half an hour later. She and Amneris were sitting cross-legged on the floor, deep in conversation. 'I never met anyone who was poor before. How does it work?'

'Well, I suppose it means that I cannot go to school, and we live quite ... simply.'

'No strawberry cake? Do have another one, by the way, Poor Girl,' said Latenia generously. 'You look as if you haven't eaten for a week. Perhaps you haven't? Perhaps it was just a bit of stale old bread? Have you been weighed for Lambing? I bet you're thin enough!'

Amneris nodded, and bit into her third cake, silently marvelling at this noble girl's fascination with her diet. The girl had not shown any interest in the rag doll on which Amneris had worked late into the night. The doll had been glanced at and dropped on the floor.

'What about your bedroom? Nothing like this, I suppose?'

'Nothing like.' Amneris pictured the bare walls, wooden floor and iron beds. 'But I share it with my granny, which is so much fun. She tells stories until we go to sleep, mostly about her twin brother Great-Uncle Annibale, the sea captain—'

'Yes, yes. But how many automata do you have, Poor Girl?' persisted Latenia.

'None. We could never afford an automaton.'

'Not one? I have twenty-six just for me. Seventeen dolls, six cake stands, a cream cow and two mechanical servant-babies. Goodness knows how many are in the palace. We have stair-walkers, page-turners, nose-wipers and mechanical gondolas, and, well, you know, ones for the little room. So what do you play with, Poor Girl?'

'I don't have time to play, really.'

The noble girl was fascinated. 'So your life is grey, miserable and without pleasure, just as they say it is for poor people? My father says the poor actually *like* to have their children selected for Lambing because death is better than the wretched lives they lead.'

Amneris said with a certain amount of heat, 'You could not be more wrong. No one wants their child killed, no matter how poor they are! We are perfectly happy. I love working with my granny and my mamma. They tell me stories all day long. I love making something beautiful every day. I love the dear— I love the tools of our trade. I even love dealing with Signor Dubbini, at least I do if I win, and I take home more money or silk than he wanted to give me.'

'Dubbini the silk merchant? I kicked him last week. Right on his skinny shin. Ha-ha! They say he is a *confidente* for Fogfinger! Who knows? He looks like a spy. And he definitely looks as if he needs a good kick.'

'Goodness! Didn't anyone tell you off?'

'No one tells me off. Ever.' The girl's tone was maddeningly smug.

'Doesn't that mean,' Amneris said slowly, 'in fact, when

you look at it in detail … that no one cares to control your temper and make you a better person?'

The girl glared at her, as if to say, 'What could be better than me?'

When Amneris just stared back, she snapped, 'No, it means that my father and our servants find me perfect just as I am. They always say, "Good for you!" when I make a scene or eat a cake, or do anything, really.'

'Don't you want to be nicer? Just for yourself?' There, Amneris had said it. Now she'd be ordered from the palace in disgrace and her family would never again receive an order from Melchior Dubbini.

The reaction was not what she expected. 'Nicer? No. Can't be bothered,' said the girl nonchalantly.

'And what about lessons? Do you learn—'

'Dancing and deportment, when I feel like it. My father says there's no point in bothering my pretty head with silly sums or jabbering in foreign tongues.'

Amneris said nothing, but her eyes roamed around the room. The priceless tapestries on the wall were stained with cake. A window was broken – a headless doll beside it showed distinct signs of violent impact.

This girl, Amneris estimated, was about her own age – at least in years. But she had never really grown out of being a baby. Actually, Amneris was beginning to feel slightly sorry for her.

Then her eyes fell on a frame of padded velvet. It was pinned with a collection of expensive tortoiseshell combs. Some were worked with diamante; others were carved into intricate crowns, roses, ladders and butterflies. Some sported mechanical devices – they could be wound up so that butterflies and bees hovered around the wearer's head, as Latenia demonstrated now, cramming one into her ringlets.

'The poor turtles!' escaped from Amneris's mouth. 'How many died for nothing, just to make these combs?'

The girl was not the least discomfited. 'They didn't die for nothing. It wasn't just to make the combs, Poor Girl. We had lots of delicious turtle soup too. Mmmm! My favourite! After raspberry chocolate cake.'

'And your goldfish!' Amneris had just noticed two cut-glass bowls on a painted dresser. The bowls were much too small for the large goldfish, who bumped awkwardly against the sides if they tried to turn around.

'Couldn't you give them bigger bowls?' Amneris asked. 'You could afford anything you wanted, I think.'

'But the shape is so pretty. Why are you bothered? Fish are just like automata. They have no brains and no feelings.'

'I don't think that's true,' said Amneris. 'My friend Biri says that even moths and cockroaches have feelings.'

'So poor people have friends?' asked the girl. 'Other poor people, presumably? How quaint. But what kind of presents can you give each other? Pebbles? Leaves? Dirt? Moths and cockroaches? I don't have friends. My father says that there is no one noble enough to be my friend so I never go out.'

'Except to the Lambings.'

'Oh yes, that's the only time, and it's quite jolly, but of course I wear a veil. What a face you are making! What do you think, Poor Girl?'

There was so much wrong with what the girl was saying that Amneris did not know where to begin in answering. Instead, she said, 'Actually, I have a name, even though I am poor. I am called Amneris.'

'Latenia.'

Amneris covered her mouth with embarrassment. If you broke 'Latenia' into 'la' and 'tenia', it would mean 'the tapeworm'. What a name to give someone! What kind of parent would do that?

Then she remembered what her mother always said: *Manners Make Ladies, not Ermine Tippets.* Amneris rose, curtseyed and lied, 'Enchanted to meet you, Latenia.' She ran the three syllables of the girl's name together as quickly as she could.

A door opened and a voice came from behind her back.

'That common accent hurts my ears, Tenni-ten-ten! What have you got there?'

A youth strolled into the room. He had a posture of rebellious boredom, shoulders slumped, chin up, fists balled. His brown eyes were a little bulbous, as if they had swelled up with too much glaring at inferior beings. His hair was a helmet of tight blond curls tied in a tail at the back with a velvet ribbon. He had a well-shaped mouth with pale lips. Amneris did not doubt that many unpleasant things came out of that mouth, and she had a feeling that she was about to sample them.

The boy did not deign to greet her, but addressed Latenia. 'Have you gone mad, picking friends from the gutter? And feeding them cake? It is probably too rich for this beggar. She will get stomach cramps and die. No point in being kind to them. You know what Papà says.'

His words were so horrible and his face was so arresting that Amneris did not at first notice that he was dressed in a most ridiculous outfit. Now she took in his purple beret, yellow gloves, and the red-trimmed green velvet doublet over a black jacket and a pair of mismatched stockings. His left leg was encased in tight stripes of black and white; his right leg was scarlet with a palm tree embroidered on the thigh. With a slippered foot, he now kicked the Shrimp Girl doll under the bed.

One of the *Compagnie della Calza!* Amneris realized. The Societies of the Fancy Stockings were an old Venetian institution, dating back to the fifteenth century, or even earlier, some said. In those days, young noblemen had dressed in spectacular clothes to stage entertainments, sports tournaments and picturesque regattas. The custom had died away as Venice grew more successful, and more serious. Young men, even noblemen, were active in the service of the state, sailing merchant ships to faraway lands, trading spices and fabrics. At home, they ran grand estates, undertook public service.

But now Fogfinger had revived the old custom of having all rich young men belong to one or other of the Fancy Stocking tribes, which had names like the *Trionfanti*, the *Sbragazadi* and the *Potenti*. He encouraged the Stockings to spend all their time amusing themselves with extravagant games that involved dressing up and sometimes hurting animals. He had added to the fun by providing special automata to make their wild games crueller and their risky sports even more dangerous. The Fancy Stockings of centuries past had played a ball game called *racchetta*. But these days the rich young Venetians even delegated their sports. There were fencing automata with blood-dripping rapiers and ball-throwing automata. The Fancy Stockings were feared for their nasty practical jokes, usually against the poor. They used their automated rackets to send little mechanical stink bombs through the windows of ordinary people's houses in the narrow alleys of Castello and Cannaregio. They painted rude words on the walls. They held belching competitions in the courtyard of the hospital. They set fire to small boats and upturned the butchers' carts.

Latenia looked at the floor and clenched her fists.

Amneris thought, 'Even *she*'s afraid of him! He *does* look like a bully.'

She had already guessed that the unwelcome visitor was Latenia's brother. He was longer and lankier than his sister, but had the same air of privilege and petulance. But unlike her, Amneris thought, he was clearly allowed out of the house. She guessed he was around sixteen years old, so well past Lambing age.

'*Well*, Tenni-ten-ten?' demanded the boy. 'A beggar in your bedroom? Standing here spreading fleas, no doubt. What are you thinking of?'

Latenia stammered, 'Actually, this one is quite amusing, and it is remarkably clean. At least it does not smell, Maffeo.'

Maffeo was taunting his sister: 'Don't you have enough dollies to play with?'

'I am not a dolly,' said Amneris with dignity, though a trembling hand was reaching to pluck at the fringe of her shawl.

'It talks without being wound up!' jeered the boy.

He slouched towards them and took a casual walk around Amneris. Her cheeks burned as he looked her up and down.

'Well, at least it looks fairly healthy,' he admitted.

'It is not a disease *not* to be rich.' Amneris could not stop herself. 'Perhaps there are people even more aristocratic and richer than you, who would pity you and think *your* lives not worth living.' She stopped abruptly, sick with fear. Would they have her punished? But it seemed she had not ruffled their composure at all.

'Richer than us? I don't think so,' laughed Latenia. 'Our father is well in with Fogfinger. He's a lawyer, and has made himself very useful. And that means that no one would dare pity us.'

'And your mother?'

'I don't have a mother and I don't need one. I have automata for everything a mother can do. I don't need anything, and I don't need to do anything. I can't even put my stockings on!' she boasted. 'That's how aristocratic I am!'

'I can't even take the top off a boiled egg,' smirked Maffeo.

'I have a special device for that. And a servant for if the egg-topper jams. And as for getting into a gondola! Only the common people climb in.'

Signor Malipiero's cold, composed face appeared at the door.

'PapàPapàPapàPapà!' cried Latenia. The whining flowed out of her without any visible thought, like the cries of a baby bird when a parent comes back to the nest. 'I want a new doll's wedding dress. With a head-dress of Honiton lace from England.'

Maffeo rolled his eyes. 'And while you're sending to the shop, do get me one of those Swiss Contortionist Dwarf Dolls. Mario Contarini has three of them, and says they are most amusing. And Ettore Flangini has a Monkey Prestidigitator in velvet smoking jacket and a monocle—'

Signor Malipiero nodded without emotion. He said, 'Daughter, you are to accompany me to a reception on Wednesday May fourteenth. You shall require a new outfit. Only the best. Practise your curtseys with Signorina Gallo.'

'I suppose so,' drawled Latenia. 'I'll need new silk slippers too. My favourite ones have jam on them.'

'Tell Miss Gallo to come to me for the money.' His eyes skittered over Amneris. 'The parasol delivery?' he asked. Amneris nodded and hastily curtseyed.

'You understand that you must tell no one that you have seen my daughter's face?' His tone was threatening.

'She doesn't know anyone,' Maffeo sneered.

Signor Malipiero disappeared.

Amneris was struck by how unashamed his children were of their terrible behaviour. It seemed to her that they treated their father as if he was an automaton.

'Does he ever say "no" to you?' she wondered aloud.

'He tried once. But now I tell Papà I'll be sad and go

off my food if he doesn't get me what I want,' simpered Latenia. 'It always works.'

Amneris thought, 'It works because he cannot bear to listen to that awful whiney voice she uses when she wants something. He says "yes" quickly to get away from her.'

She bade the brother and sister goodbye, and found her way out to the street. She fanned her hot face with her hand, gulping on fresh air.

'Now, San Marcuola,' she decided. 'Perhaps Biri's at home with a cold in the head. That's the only thing that could account for it – it's been *days* since she came for a cup of milk and a chat. I can't wait to tell her about these two parasites!'

14
Someone who could be bothered, and who made it his business to know

Nobody saw Fogfinger in public any more. No one had seen him for years; perhaps decades. No one, that is, except his intimate circle – 'the best noblemen money can buy', he called them behind their backs.

But everyone knew his most famous catchphrase.

'I make it my business to know,' Fogfinger had said, when he first arrived in Venice twenty years before – a mysterious and glamorous young man who claimed to have walked from Ireland to Italy in three months, having shot and bagged every game bird in every country along the way. He took one look at the small, rich and glamorous city and smiled.

'This will do nicely,' he said. 'Oh yes, this will suit.'

Why Fogfinger left his native Ireland, and on foot, and in such a hurry, was no one's business, apparently. When asked why, he always said that he was 'looking for information'. And certainly he questioned everyone he met, about their lives, about their livelihood, about their families. In those days, before he had power, Fogfinger had charm. People liked to linger and chat to this young man whose strong Irish accent made his fluent Venetian sound pleasantly exotic. He dressed in an extraordinarily eccentric way – his frock-coat was always at odds with his embroidered waistcoat. A single earring dangled from his left ear. Strangest of all, he wrapped a great bandeau of vivid silk around his head in a voluminous turban. He was an oddity and a novelty, and Venetians always loved a novelty – which was, of course, why and how the craze for automata had latterly taken hold of the city.

'Why did you want to know?' the Venetians would ask Fogfinger, after spilling all their secrets. He had a way about him, a knack, which made you want to tell him things you would not even confess to your best friend. After speaking with Fogfinger, people felt dazed, emptied and even a little dirty.

And to the question 'Why did you want to know?' they always received the same crooked smile and the same answer from Fogfinger: 'I make it my business to know.'

Fogfinger was being absolutely honest when it came to this statement. Knowing things *was* his business. After two years in Venice, knowing things had made him rich. After five years, knowing things had made him powerful. He had known how to provide the automata that the Venetians adored. And it was by discovering the secrets of important Venetians that he'd gradually put them under his thumb. Now he was flanked by the richest, the best-known and the most noble men in Venice. They were all bound to him because they were terrified that he would reveal the secrets that they'd entrusted to him. This meant that they would do anything for him, even the most distasteful things. As he loved to boast, 'My friends would cut off an arm or a leg for me – I just have to tell them whose.'

All the old offices of state had become emptily ceremonial – the dogeship, the Council of Ten, the Council of Forty, even the Great Council of male nobles, the Senate, the Magistrates, the Procurators, the *Avogadori*, the *Savii* (or Wise Ones) and the Inquisitors. All wore their gilded robes. But they bowed to Fogfinger.

Being powerful had made Fogfinger richer. The embroidery on his frock-coats had grown more blinding and their cut more extreme. The turbans swelled in volume. But his face remained long and thin like a pale tooth.

Over the years, Venetians had become more and more dependent on Fogfinger. He made it his business to ensure that they were. The automata – so attractive and amusing – had a darker side. For every Venetian who owned a stair-climber or a boat-slider gradually forgot how to climb stairs or get into a boat for himself or herself. They could barely open a book, so they became ignorant. And they certainly could not lift a sword or a gun with those delicate white arms of theirs, so they became helpless and defenceless.

They lived for the first day of the month, when Fogfinger sent a special decorated boat known as 'The Merchant of Delight' down the Grand Canal laden with the latest novelties from his secret workshop. The Merchant of Delight stopped at every palace, and each noble family would crowd onto the jetty, grabbing at the walking dolls, the hopping rabbits, the jugs that poured themselves, the devices for picking your teeth or plumping your pillow, for filing your nails or counting your money, crocodile toys that gnashed real ivory teeth, wooden unicorns that strutted on four jointed legs.

How could the Venetians not love and honour a man who brought them such pleasure? Between the secrets and the dragon-heart fat and the automata, Fogfinger had the devotion of every rich Venetian. His Fogs and his spies – and the Anagrammaticulars – kept everyone else nicely submissive.

'Apart,' Fogfinger recalled with irritation, 'from the *Piccoli Pochi*.'

No matter what he did, they remained a thorn in his side. They broke all the rules of being Venetian: they were tireless, brave and full of clever ideas. They evaded his *confidenti* and his Fogs.

Still, there was always the consolation of a new bride to look forward to. Fogfinger smiled: no pleasure was detectable in the drawing-up of his lips into a crooked sneer. But he was, in fact, very happy.

Alvise Malipiero was playing into his hands. It was only a matter of time before the greedy, gullible lawyer delivered that girl he kept shut up in his palace.

The face of the Malipiero daughter – and even her name – were the two secrets in Venice that Fogfinger did not yet know, even though he made it his business to know everything. The thought of the girl drove him mad. If he had to marry her to find out, then so be it.

Fogfinger had been betrothed to noble daughters a number of times before.

It was a shame what had happened to those girls, he shrugged, but it couldn't be helped. There were just so many canals in Venice where an unwary girl might drown, and so many tall windows from which she might accidentally fall.

15
Empty wells and 'Wild Water'

Friday May 2nd, 1783

It had taken a little while before the Venetians realized that their wells were in a bad state. Then it seemed to have happened so quickly that they had trouble believing it. Of course, one of the first to notice was Tockle's mother, when she had to lower her buckets further down than usual into the well at San Zan Degola. By the second day she had to buy a second length of rope to tie to the first. The water was becoming daily less clear and more brackish. All over Venice, the *bigolanti* peered into the dark wells, and worried. But they did not say anything to their customers. They were too afraid.

It was on the fourth day that Fogfinger had introduced his latest novelty. It was not an automaton this time but 'Wild Water', sold in green Murano glass bottles. Of course only the rich could afford the clear spring water in the beautiful bottles, but suddenly anyone who had a bit of money wanted to spend it on water – something that had been so cheap as to be nearly free beforehand.

The empty green bottles were soon to be found all over the city – in piles of broken glass on which children easily cut themselves or floating down the canals where careless noblemen had thrown them.

The green bottles of 'Wild Water' drew the attention of the poor to the fact that the water carried by the *bigolanti* had developed a strange, muddy taste, and that it was no longer perfectly clear. They began to crave the clear 'Wild Water' in green bottles, even though it was far beyond their purses.

Fogfinger introduced a new kind of bottle – a dark brown one, sold at half the price of the green ones. These were labelled 'Ordinary'. The water inside was not as pure as the 'Wild Water', but it was at least reasonably clear. And the poor would give up food in order to buy it. They could not afford to get sick on bad water, they told themselves.

'We are ruined,' said Tockle's mother, returning home with full copper buckets of murky well water. 'People would rather pay for the brown bottles than for *this*! Who can blame them?'

'Not even for their flowers?' asked Tockle.

Mamma shook her head.

The poor had used to enjoy the flowerboxes outside their windows, even if they could not afford a patch of garden. And everyone depended on the white runner bean plants in those boxes that provided shade and privacy as well as food. Now no one could afford to buy even the *bigolanti*'s brackish water for their plants. They had to save all their coins for the brown bottles, which had grown subtly smaller by the second week, even though the price had stayed the same.

That spring, there was no purple wisteria perfuming the old walls of Venice, except at the palaces of the rich.

The vines on the ordinary houses curled up and withered. The fig vine on Tockle's own house would be too parched to bear fruit this year. And, as spring began to warm into summer, Venice did not break out into her usual riot of pink geraniums and white petunias.

At Tockle's charity school, children were allowed two spoonfuls of water when they arrived, or their mouths would be too dry to recite their lessons.

Even the little scooped-out bowls at the bases of the wells were dry as dust. No one could spare a cupful of water for the animals. The cats and dogs of Venice had to manage as best they could, rising early to lick dew off the stones.

Worst of all, the *bigolanti* – including Tockle's mother – were talking of signing up as Winder Uppers. How else would they feed their families?

Ugo had told Tockle and Biri, 'Your first task is to break the curfew and find out what is happening to the wells. Friday night would be best. The Fogs get extra rations of rum then. Meanwhile, regarding your new role as *Piccolissimi Pochi*, you must tell no one, not your families, or your friends.'

'What about Amneris?' asked Biri.

'The sewing girl? Oh yes, she will need to know. You must explain it to her gently, and you must give her the chance to say "no". Not everyone wants to be a hero.'

At the D'Ago home, they'd been saving water as well. Plates were wiped instead of washed. Clothes were worn for two extra days before being laundered in a minimum of water. Grillo was always thirsty, mewing plaintively for a taste of the water in which they boiled the polenta, burning his tongue because he could not wait for it to cool. Amneris stroked him absent-mindedly as she bent over her work: they were busier than ever, for the rich required elegant new costumes for the Redentore.

The Feast of the Redentore, in the third week of July, celebrated the end of a pitiless plague that had cut through the city three centuries before, sending tens of thousands to their graves. On the third Saturday of July, a bridge of boats was built to the island of Giudecca so everyone could make a pilgrimage to the Redentore church, which rose like iced gingerbread above the water. As the festival week approached, all the shops were festooned with paper chains and lanterns as large as the biggest melon a man ever struggled to carry. San Marco would fill up with strolling tradesmen: you could buy candied fruits on a stick, turtles, shells, puppets, glass necklaces and have your fortune told.

All afternoon, on the Saturday of the Redentore, boats travelled down the Grand Canal to assemble in the water in front of St Mark's Square. They clustered around *il galleggiante*, a great floating ballroom lit with lanterns and beautifully decorated with garlands of flowers.

The rich arrived in grand style, with servants, private orchestras, velvet chairs and damask tablecloths. They dined on sumptuous food served on silverware. They pelted one another with sugared almonds. Then they would dance on *il galleggiante*.

The working people decked their humble boats with vervain leaves and paper lanterns. They brought their tambourines and their musical dogs, who joined in with relish when it came to singing the traditional Redentore hymns and songs. The poor shared picnic feasts laid on wooden trestles. For this one festival, even if they faced a lean month afterwards, they would sometimes run to the special Redentore dishes of spaghetti with anchovies, snails

100

in garlic, roast duck, sweet-and-sour sardines, watermelon and almond tart.

And even the poor could bask in *il galleggiante*'s light and colours. They could enjoy its music from their boats moored in a companionable circle nearby.

Then, as the moon rose high in the sky, came the magnificent fireworks display. Every scintillating bouquet of vivid light was doubled by the mirror of the water below. The glitter of the fireworks was still imprinted on the Venetions' eyes when they attended the solemn and beautiful Redentore mass next morning.

Everyone loved the Redentore best of all Venice's festivals – water, singing, music, free fireworks: what could be better?

Everyone smiled at the prospect of the Redentore, just weeks away now.

Despite the drought, everyone smiled, until the *Postiglione* printed a new announcement on May 2nd:

A Solution to the Grievous Water Problem!
The drought shall be broken by
a New and Extra Lambing.
On the day of the Redentore, at the Frari,
a Venetian Child will give Life in exchange
for Water.

Suddenly the Redentore was no longer something to celebrate.

At the D'Ago household, Amneris read the *Postiglione*'s notice aloud to her father, who put his head in his hands. Even though the whole family had saved the best of the food for her in the month before her weighing, Amneris had barely tilted the scales. She was eligible for the next Lambing selection. And now it was just eleven weeks away.

'Ugo was right 'bout the connection between the water and the Lambing,' said Biri. It was a week after their adventure on the island, the same day the grim Redentore announcement had been made. It was one hour after the curfew that neither Biri nor Tockle had ever dared to break before. She hummed a few notes and made a low mewing noise.

'Shhh!' urged Tockle. 'There could be an Anagrammaticular around here. Just because we can't see the earpiece doesn't mean there isn't one. Be quiet, Biri!'

'John Chicken,' she insisted, and resumed humming.

Tockle sighed, 'John Chicken, Jupiter Grasshopper, anything! So long as you stop making that noise.'

'I was only talking to the moths,' said Biri. 'I asked them to let me know if there's any Fogs roundabouts.'

'She talks to moths.' Tockle raised his eyebrows.

'He talks to himself!' mocked Biri.

A grey mist of moths swooped around them. Biri cocked her ear and listened intently. 'A nest of Fogs in the next square,' she reported. 'We got to go back to San Maurizio.'

'The moths told you that?'

Biri nodded. 'They are my *confidenti*, aren't they? The Finger's got his spies; I got mine.'

At San Maurizio, she bent down, shading her lantern with her hand. A tribe of cockroaches marched across the flagstones. Biri murmured to them, whereupon they stopped and began to mill around, waving their feelers.

'And the cockroaches say that the wells have been interfered with. Men come at night, climb down and block the pipes with stones.'

'How exactly do cockroaches talk?' Tockle spoke with

exaggerated patience. He had considered Biri eccentric; he was beginning to think she was mad.

'Of course they don't talk! But they mimes fings. See that group over there – 'sformed a circle, like a well-head, over that hole in the paving. Two of the others 'ave climbed over the circle – the well-head – and they's dragging a pebble. And now they's pushing it somefing fierce into that hole underneaf.'

Tockle could see the circle and the pebble, but his mind refused to grapple with the idea that the cockroaches were trying to show them something.

More moths arrived. Biri lifted her head and mewed at them. Then she listened again. She turned to Tockle. 'If we wanna see a bunch of drunken Fogs doing the same fing, we're to go to Sant'Angelo.'

Amneris was excited because Biri had come to tell her about some blond boy, an island and the *Piccolissimi Pochi*. Biri, yawning after 'a busy night', had also let fall the stunning news that the boy was a Molin – from the famous family of kaleidoscope-makers. Amneris was so distracted by the joy of hoping that he might be able to fix the dear creature – still turning out white designs – that she barely noticed when Biri started talking about 'peril of our lives' and 'total secrecy on pain of death. Painful death, see.'

She did notice, however, when Biri said, 'Boy says he knows you already. Goes by the name of Tockle.'

'Oh!'

'And we're all to meet on Monday at Ugo Paolin's house on the Fondamenta Morosini, you know, where the three canals meet, at four o'clock. It's to do with the wells and the next Lambing. The Redentore Lambing.'

'Ugo Paolin?' Amneris asked. 'Why his house? Is it safe?'

'Boy was poxed a few months ago. He's too weak to leave his house.'

'Poor thing! Is he getting worse?'

'The undertakers is leaving their calling cards,' said Biri in a sombre voice. 'But Ugo says he has something to finish before he can … leave with them dark-dressed gentlemen.'

'Oh, how sad!' exclaimed Amneris. 'What thing does he have to finish?'

'That's where you comes in, see,' said Biri. 'That's where you and me and Tockle Molin comes in. Are you with us?'

'Yes!' Amneris smiled nervously. To fix the dear creature, yes, she would do anything, even lay her life on the line. There was no need, she reflected, to bother her parents with this little matter. Hopefully, they'd never need to know about it at all.

16
A question of trust

Biri, Tockle and Amneris arrived in Ugo Paolin's house on the Fondamenta Morosini from different directions, all of them ten minutes early.

Tockle blushed when he saw Amneris again, and she reddened too, just as she'd feared she would. But any discomfort dispelled as she immediately plied him with questions about 'afflictions' of kaleidoscopes. She made sure of being somewhat mysterious about what kind of affliction the D'Ago device might have, but was most forthcoming when he asked her to explain how it had reached them.

Amneris recounted the tale of her great-uncle Annibale's shipwreck and the kaleidoscope that floated all the way back to the Venetian lagoon in a black box with a mysterious label.

'So that was how long ago?' Tockle asked.

'Before I was born. About eighteen or nineteen years ago.'

'Then your kaleidoscope must have been made by my

grandfather!' Tockle smiled. 'Grandpa Enrico Molin was best friends with a sea captain called Annibale! They used to disappear off to an old warehouse together – that's the story I always heard. And Captain Annibale said that he was "a humble apprentice". But my grandpa said Annibale was "a mechanical genius".'

'So *my* great-uncle might even have helped *your* grandfather to make the dear creature—'

Amneris clapped her hand over her mouth. She didn't want this rather nice boy to think she was soft in the head. 'To make our *kaleidoscope*,' she finished, somewhat lamely.

But Tockle did not look at all shocked. 'Some of the really special Molin kaleidoscopes have names and … well, characters. We have one on the mantelpiece that my mother calls "Sweet Nizzi". We are allowed to look into it only on our birthdays, and it is like … your eyes eating a sherbet. Fireworks! Like the Redentore, even. My sister still makes them, in fact. But now everyone is mad for automata, there's less call for kaleidoscopes. So my mother had to become a *bigolante*.'

'Oh dear,' said Amneris, licking her lips. 'Things must be very difficult for you now.'

Tockle did not mention his father but looked sad and closed his lips at the moment when it would have been logical to say, 'And Papà is …'

He asked shyly if he might 'visit the dear creature', words he uttered without the slightest trace of irony, for which Amneris liked him very much indeed.

'But should I *trust* him?' agonized Amneris to herself. 'What if he tells his mother? Those *bigolanti* are such gossips! What if some rumour reaches Melchior Dubbini – about the secret way we get our designs, or that we have a problem?'

But ten minutes later, Amneris discovered that she was about to trust Tockle with something much more dangerous.

Amneris tried not to show it, but she was shocked at the sight of Ugo.

'How can a boy be so thin and so pale and not be dead?' she wondered.

Biri nudged her ribs. 'See.'

But Ugo's voice was full of warmth and vigour.

'Amneris D'Ago,' he said. 'Welcome. I believe that Biri has explained our mission.'

Guiltily, Amneris tried to remember exactly what Biri had been chattering about when she arranged this meeting. She listened wide-eyed while Biri and Tockle talked about how the Fogs were stoppering up the wells, creating a demand for 'Wild Water' and 'Ordinary' – and the excuse for a new Lambing at Redentore.

Ugo listened to the story of the informative cockroaches and moths and said, 'Aha! I *knew* Fogfinger had engineered this drought! I just couldn't work out how.'

He turned to Amneris. 'Can you sew words in thread dyed in invisible ink?'

'I never have, and I don't have the ink … but I could try.'

'Ink is supplied.' He handed her a slender purple bottle sealed with wax. 'And I understand from Biri that you have access to the home of a Fogfinger *confidente* … a Signor Malipiero.'

'He's a Fogfinger *confidente*? Oh! Yes, it's true. I deliver needlework. Not every day, but from time to time. I'm expected again on Saturday.'

'So you could take a secret message to Latenia, daughter of the house?'

'Yes, it's Latenia I visit.'

'Isn't she supposed to be a big secret? No one sees her face. Her father keeps her locked up there like a prisoner. So what's she like?'

Amneris sighed, and began.

'They sound well 'orrible, them Malipiero brats,' growled Biri.

'Maffeo undoubtedly is. Latenia has moments when I almost ... in a way, like her.'

Tockle said, 'I don't think anyone could really like creatures like that. Not even their mother.'

Amneris said, 'I don't know where the mother is. She's never mentioned and I don't see her. But the strange thing is the way their father treats them. I think you're right, Tockle. He smiles, he goes through the motions but I feel as if there is nothing inside his heart for them. He gives them what they want, but ...'

She told Biri and Tockle about how there were no spontaneous hugs, no face lighting up when Alvise Malipiero encountered his offspring.

'He just piles on the presents, the jewels, the treats. The nastier Latenia is, the more her father gives her. But he never looks at her. He doesn't want to spend time with her. He's always standing on the threshold with his hand on the doorknob when he speaks to her.'

Biri said, 'Well, who wouldn't be?'

'I wish I could put my finger on it. When he gives them things, it is like feeding the animals at the zoo. If you ask me, there is a kind of contempt in it.'

'Well,' said Biri dismissively, 'why are we even worrying

about them mean rich children? What gets everyfing they wants.'

Amneris could barely explain it to herself. She just knew that for quite some time she had wanted to talk about the odd feelings she'd experienced when she'd visited the Malipiero family, and this was the first chance she'd had.

'I feel as if they are in danger. I cannot get away from the image of a farmer fattening piglets for slaughter. I think that Signor Malipiero indulges them while it suits him. But if it stopped suiting him ...'

Ugo said, 'Nothing we can do about that, I fear. But it could be useful, Amneris, if you'd take Tockle and Biri with you when you next make a delivery to the Malipiero household. If the three of you can cultivate a friendship with this Latenia, then it could provide us with ... opportunities.'

'I'll ask her if I may bring them,' said Amneris.

Biri said, 'Tell her it's a chance to meet even poorer children than you! But why, Ugo? Why do you want us to go there?'

He smiled mysteriously. 'No, I can't explain yet, because it's best you know the minimum. That way, if you're caught, you can't do so much damage by what you'd be forced to reveal – and hopefully you can't be hurt by what they might do to you to extract information.'

'I doan think you're just talking about Bittercakes, are you?' Biri frowned.

'Bittercakes would be a sweet alternative,' confirmed Ugo. 'Now, stones in the wells, is it? Agile swimmers with strong arms – that's what we need. Tockle, could you ask these three to come to me tomorrow?'

He whispered three names, all boys at Tockle's school.

'So many of us are involved!' marvelled Tockle.

'So many are at risk,' answered Ugo. 'Now could you

wheel me closer to the window, and open it before you leave, please?'

They left him by the window, craning his ear towards the water below, an expectant smile on his lips.

17
An awkward visit

Monday May 12th, 1783

'So your family makes kaleidoscopes?' Latenia was asking Tockle a week later. She'd been happy to invite Biri and Tockle when Amneris had nervously suggested it.

'Yes, really beautiful ones,' enthused Amneris loyally. 'The best in Venice.'

Tockle didn't answer. He was fully occupied staring at Latenia's earrings and necklaces. Today, perhaps as a treat for her humble guests, she had dressed in white satin trimmed with ermine, draping all her diamonds and emeralds around her neck at the same time.

Biri was examining the contents of Latenia's dressing table. 'Here, this box is locked!' she complained. 'What you got to hide?'

Provoked, Latenia swept across the room and produced a key from her pocket.

'Blue seahorses!' squawked Biri. 'Last place I'd expect to find 'em!'

111

Tockle and Amneris exchanged looks.

Amneris asked quietly, 'Latenia, do you know what these are for?'

'Of course I know,' blustered Latenia. 'They are for … for … putting in goldfish bowls to keep the fish company.'

'Actually,' said Amneris quickly, 'they are good-luck charms. Many Venetians keep them hidden somewhere in their clothes.'

'You mean the common people do?'

'They are a symbol of the—'

Maffeo strolled into the room, got up in his ludicrous finery. Latenia slammed the box shut.

'Who the belly is that?' spluttered Biri. 'What a poncified poodle!'

'Oh no,' thought Amneris. 'This is not going to go well.'

'More street children, Tenni-ten-ten?' Maffeo looked down his long nose. 'Have you got a new craze?'

Biri muttered, 'How is it he's worn that face for what, sixteen years, and yet no one's slapped it?'

Maffeo fanned out his cloak and sat down on a velvet stool. At the sight of his fancy stockings, Biri fell about laughing. 'Be-e-e-elllllllly up!' she shrieked, tears of mirth running down her cheeks.

Amneris whispered, 'Shhh. He's from one of the *Compagnie della Calza*. Don't annoy him.'

'The urchin has had a seizure,' said Maffeo coldly. 'When they starve, they start going mad, I believe.'

Latenia said, 'The boy's family has a trade, actually. Kaleidoscopes.'

'Kaleidoscopes?' drawled Maffeo. 'Don't you have to lift them up with your own hands to see the patterns?'

'They're not very heavy,' said Tockle.

'I know, but *the idea*!'

'Don't *you* ever do anything for yerself? Or for anyone

else?' Biri demanded. Amneris gave her a warning pinch.

'Why? How could I be sure that they would do something even better for me? I can't be bothered,' Maffeo shrugged.

Biri exploded, 'It is LOVELY to do fings for somebody else. You two is like little old ladies and little old men already. Everyfing's done for you as if you was feeble and useless—'

'No, I am just cleverer and richer than other people,' replied Maffeo, unperturbed. 'People like you.'

'Doesn't anyfing bother you?' shouted Biri. 'What about the Fate in the Box?'

'Oh,' said Latenia airily, 'our father has an arrangement with Fogfinger. And why do you think I have all the cakes?'

'Haven't you poor stupid creatures ever noticed,' said Maffeo, 'that none of the rich, titled children ever get Lambed? Our fathers all have little arrangements with Fogfinger.'

For the first time Biri, Amneris and Tockle realized something that all Venetian children should have been aware of, a fact from which their parents struggled to protect them. Now that the words had been uttered, it was impossible to un-know this terrible fact. Rich boys and girls like Maffeo and Latenia would never be Lambed, which meant that children like Biri, Tockle and Amneris were all the more likely to be.

Silence fell in the room until Latenia summoned one of her new automata to perform for them. A little rabbit pirouetted, bowing and putting its head on one side. Eventually, it ran out of winding and collapsed on the floor. Maffeo kicked it into a corner.

The silence between the five of them deepened. To break the

tension, Amneris gabbled, 'Latenia, why not show Tockle and Biri your … um … marvellous cake stand?'

'Anyway,' she thought, 'it will be a good chance to get this thing into Latenia's pocket.' She had embroidered a silk handkerchief with the words that Ugo had given her. She had dipped the thread in invisible ink first. The words were simple but still mysterious:

I cannot come to you any longer, but I am not far away, and I love you.

When she'd asked Ugo what this meant, he said, 'It is safer for you not to know.'

Tockle and Biri stood in silence as Latenia ratcheted up the speed and cakes began to hit the walls. Amneris edged closer to Latenia, and scanned her ermine-trimmed panniered dress for a place where she might slip the handkerchief. The satin skirt stretched over its petticoats without a pocket. Of course, Latenia had a maid to carry things for her.

Biri whispered, 'What 'appens to them bashed-up cakes now?'

'The maid cleans up the dirt,' said Latenia.

'Dirt? You think those lovely cakes are dirt?' It was just too long since Tockle had tasted a cake. He could not help himself. He reached down and picked up a more-or-less intact cake that the mechanical maid had missed. Half of it was in his mouth before he even heard Maffeo shrieking.

'You filthy little dog! Eating the rubbish!'

Tockle stopped chewing. The feeling inside him was somewhere between shame and rage. His blood seemed to be turning to lava at Maffeo's insult.

But that was nothing to what Biri was feeling. She stood with her hands on her hips, scorning the cakes.

She shouted, 'Reckon you're not just forgetting how to use your hands or legs, but your *hearts* as well! How can you stand here playing with food, when there's children out on the streets of your own town *starving* to death?'

Maffeo and Latenia stared at Biri. Amneris, increasingly desperate to find a place for the handkerchief, caught sight of the rack of white parasols.

Silently, she urged Biri, *Keep shouting! It's a good distraction!* as she edged over to the parasols and dropped the handkerchief into the folds of the one onto which she herself had sewn the twelve pearls.

Biri did not need any encouragement. She ranted. 'Do you know what? I am *sorry* for you! Tockle and Amneris and meself – we are richer than you, because we have somefing to live for, and to fight for, and even to die for.'

'Biri!' implored Tockle. 'Don't tell them!'

'Don't tell us what?' asked Maffeo, suddenly alert. 'And why are you plucking at the fringe of your shawl like that, sewing girl? Nervous, are you? Something to hide, eh?'

'Biri!' whispered Amneris. 'Their father works for Fogfinger.'

Biri clapped a hand over her cake-stained mouth.

Maffeo strode over to her, and removed the hand roughly. 'Tell me what you mean, you dirty starveling. Do you think you could keep your shabby little secrets from me?'

Latenia put her hand on her brother's embroidered sleeve. She said scornfully, 'They don't have secrets. They just don't have any manners.'

'Doubtless,' yawned Maffeo, giving Biri a little shove. 'They're not worth my time. Dismissed, beggars! Off with you.'

Biri, Tockle and Amneris slunk down to the street.

'Our first mission is a failure,' lamented Amneris. 'We've done more harm than good. We were not supposed to make an enemy of Maffeo. We were supposed to make *friends* with Latenia so we can find more things out, and keep delivering the handkerchiefs.'

If the three of them had looked up just then, they would have seen Latenia's miserable face pressed to the window, watching them longingly.

18
Glass diamonds and devil suits

Monday May 12th–Saturday May 17th, 1783

Amneris had managed to stuff the handkerchief inside the parasol, but Maffeo's threats had meant that she did not have time to explain to Latenia that it was there, and how she must hold a candle against it in order to make the embroidered words legible. And how she must burn it immediately after reading the secret message. All that work, wasted! Amneris was sure that the handkerchief would be screwed up and trampled on, like everything else Latenia was given.

She was still mourning the hours she had spent on the handkerchief when she realized that Tockle had changed the subject.

'They're fake, I tell you!' he was saying. 'Those are not real emeralds or rubies Latenia's wearing. They're just glass chips cleverly cut and set. Even the gold settings are false.'

'How would you know?' asked Biri.

'Well, I go to Murano all the time to pick up the glass chips to make our kaleidoscopes,' Tockle explained. 'The best glass-blower has a profitable business on the side, making false jewels. Signor Castrauro let me come to help him late one night. He showed me the difference between a real stone and a glass one. He kept testing me, until I knew all the different glimmers and angles of the cuts.'

'Why would Latenia be wearing fake jewels?'

'The only reason can be that the real ones have been pawned,' said Biri, who had given up most of her own possessions in that way.

'So Signor Malipiero is actually poor?'

'But he keeps givin' those 'orrible children 'spensive gifts,' said Biri. 'Why?'

'And what will he sell when he runs out of jewels?' asked Amneris. A cold feeling was stealing over her.

'We'll have to go and tell Ugo what's happened,' said Tockle.

At the thought of telling Ugo how badly they had managed, all three of them sank into silent gloom.

Amneris always had the feeling that her cat Grillo loved her, but that he did not entirely approve of her. Venetian cats were renowned for the smug pleasure they took in their own elegance. Where, Amneris sometimes reflected, was the cat in Venice who did not think he deserved a better owner?

So she was never entirely surprised when Grillo disappeared for a few days. She suspected him of interviewing households where fresh milk was more often available, and where grated cheese and butter were stirred into the polenta, or where the family had more money to spend on wood for the fire. Grillo did sometimes stage these short disappearances so, while she missed him, she did not worry unduly.

At least, she had not worried until the fifth morning, the Saturday after she had so disastrously taken Tockle and Biri to meet Latenia. This was longer than he had ever been absent. And, the evening after what had happened at the Malipiero palace, Amneris needed a cat cuddle more than ever. She was accustomed to whisper all her secrets into Grillo's feathery ear – giving her the relief of confession without upsetting anyone in the family. And how upset her parents and her granny would be if they knew how she had put their business at risk!

She looked at the nest of cat hairs on the cushion that Grillo regarded as his private office. The indent of his body was still there, but there was no sign of Grillo. There had been no Kittening lately – but had someone stolen her cat to sell for the next grisly ceremony?

'Oh Grillo!' she moaned. 'Please come home! I need you!'

All the way to Dubbini's she looked for him, and called for him. Arriving at the door, she hesitated, trembling. She had half expected a letter of dismissal all week. But, knowing the silk merchant, he would prefer to deliver the bad news in person and watch her suffer.

The door was open as it was a mild afternoon. As Amneris entered, a sudden breeze blew open the door to the back room, where the pale girls sat in a field of red and black cloth. One was forcing a wire into a curved sock so that it stood up like a horn. Poor girls, forced to make devil suits! Who could be the customer for those? The girls sewed at a desperate pace, their faces feverish and their white hands flickering over the red fabric.

To her astonishment, Signor Dubbini told her, 'A white shawl is required. You can take the finished silk straight to the Malipiero palace on Saturday. The girl has called for you particularly this time.'

At first, Amneris was delighted. She had been forgiven for

Biri's outburst. Her family would still be in work. Then her face darkened. What if Maffeo had engineered this so that he could interrogate her away from her friends? She was not as fierce as Biri.

'But at least I can tell Latenia where the silk handkerchief letter is!' Amneris consoled herself. 'So I will not have failed entirely.'

Back out in the street, Amneris called Grillo again. Several other cats came running, hopefully, but none belonged to her.

19
Not quite like Venice

Wednesday May 14th, 1783

Latenia followed her father out of the gondola and under the grand portico of the Natural History Museum. It was only as they passed into the courtyard that her father had told her the reason for this visit and her especially sumptuous clothes, and the sober black senatorial robe that covered his own new frock-coat.

Latenia was about to be presented to Fogfinger himself.

It did not occur to her to ask why. Latenia was a girl who thought quite highly of herself, and considered that most people would be interested and enchanted to meet her, especially in this exquisite dress with its seven floppy silk bows all down the bodice, a brocade underskirt and more bows on the gauzy sleeves. She was bothered by nothing more than a little fluttering in the stomach.

Her father asked, 'You're wearing the pearls? Not any of the other jewels?'

'Of course, Papà.' She lifted her veil and pointed to her ruffled necklace of woven lace and freshwater pearls. At the

121

last moment, she had gone to the box on her dressing table and tucked a blue glass seahorse into her sleeve too.

'But Papà,' she said, 'it doesn't seem quite like Venice in here, does it?'

Fogfinger had banished all Venetian flowers and plants from the courtyard garden. In their place he had created a jungle. Latenia did not love to study natural history, so she did not know that they were gum-trees, gourds, cacao, mangoes, bananas, palms, baobabs, cacti, Barbary figs – but she knew that they were strange and foreign, and that she did not like them. You might almost expect a hyena to lope out of the undergrowth or a parrot to roost in one of those palms.

'Fogfinger *lives* in a museum?' Latenia asked. 'Is that not odd? And somewhat dreary?'

Signor Malipiero replied, 'Is it so strange that he would choose this magnificent palace? His private chambers on the second floor are the most splendid in Venice, I assure you.'

'But the public comes in here every day! How disagreeable for him!'

'But he is kept safe by their constant presence. His enemies would never attack him here – too many innocents would be killed. More importantly, those scoundrels do not think of finding him here, as everyone believes that he lives in the Doge's Palace – everyone but a select few of his favourites.' He coughed discreetly.

'So you are one of those, Papà?' cooed Latenia.

'Indeed. Fogfinger likes to be protected by the discretion of his favourites and the ignorance of his inferiors.' He muttered under his breath, 'As you and your brother have been protected by your ignorance, come to that.'

'Why would he want to live with all these dead animals around him?'

'Ah, dead animals are something of a passion for Fogfinger,

Daughter. He was a great hunter when he was younger. You must learn these things about him.'

'Why?'

'Well, that will be explained. Put on your silk slippers now.'

'By myself? We should have brought a maid! I suppose I can manage,' she grumbled.

Latenia kicked off her high-heeled street shoes.

Signor Malipiero fussed, 'And the cloak. Give it to me. Good, let me look at you.'

Having lifted and dropped her veil, Signor Malipiero grunted with satisfaction and pointed to a large gilded cage resting on the floor.

'Step in.' His voice was tense.

As soon as she was inside, there was a shrieking of chains and the little cage began to rise through the well of the courtyard. Below her, two gilded automata tugged at the chains and above her another pair hauled on ropes.

Latenia did not panic. They had a similar device at home so the family did not have to face the tedium of walking up the marble stairs. But theirs was like a box, padded all round with velvet. The open struts of the gilded cage here at Fogfinger's palace meant she could see the courtyard disappearing below her, a disagreeable sensation. Her father was being winched up beside her, in a silver cage. His expression was grim. She wondered why. Surely it was a great honour and a pleasure to visit Fogfinger? Especially if you were one of his favourites.

The cages juddered to a halt in the middle of a second-floor room that twitched with automatic 'life'. Latenia barely noticed the human guards who opened the doors to release her. There were domes containing spun-glass models of fully rigged three-masted sailing vessels, with miniature clockwork sailors climbing the rigging. There were mechanical bears tearing the fur off each other with teeth that dripped a red liquid. Wind-up birds of prey swooped on live mice in a pen. Showy dolls beat on tambourines. Hairy spiders bigger than sparrows danced on their back legs. A rabbit poked its head out of a cabbage – only to be snapped at by a mechanical fox half hidden in a bush. An acrobat vaulted over a ladder and back. A leather-bound pig with a curly tail fried wooden sausages in a pan, next to two desperate gamblers leaning over a *biribissi* board, each with a dagger hidden under the table.

Latenia clapped her hands and ran from automaton to automaton. She tried to memorize everything: she knew it would enrage Maffeo to hear that she had seen these things, when he hadn't. She was enjoying herself royally, peering at the amusing, ingenious contraptions. The icing on the cake was the thought of Maffeo's fury. She laughed out loud and skipped a few steps from sheer joy.

Then, at the end of the chamber, she suddenly glimpsed the person whom she had really come to see.

Suddenly Latenia was not enjoying herself at all.

Fogfinger himself was no longer the romantic figure he depicted on his flags and official portraits or frescoes in the Town Hall that showed him hunting the Primaeval Crocodile. Over the years, his shape had grown increasingly odd. His face had remained thin and tooth-shaped, but there were little rolls of flesh under his chin and around his hips, which no satin frock-coat or extravagantly buttoned waistcoat could disguise. Nor did his silk breeches conceal his scrawny legs. His meaty ankles were awkwardly thrust into high-heeled slippers. The turban was now fastened with a glowing jewel, lending him a slightly oriental air, as did the earring that dangled from his left ear and the saucer-sized medal (inscribed '*for Valour in Vanquishing Dragons*') on his breast.

For a man who 'made it my business to know', Fogfinger had suffered an ironic setback: the early onset of deafness. A large tortoiseshell ear trumpet was fastened to the right side of his head. But the turtle who'd been killed to make the device had been badly cured, and this had led to an infection in Fogfinger's ear. The infection never seemed to quite go away, no matter what the apothecaries did.

All kinds of bad behaviour had caught up with him in the last few years: a suppurating wound in his shoulder from an old duel (though his opponent had died from the poisoned tip of Fogfinger's weapon), a badly set shin-bone broken by the kick of a horse to whom he had been cruel, and a griping ulcer in his side, not to mention gout in his left foot. He could walk perfectly well if he put his mind to it, but he preferred the magnificence of being conveyed in a wheeled bath chair or a sedan-chair carried by footmen.

Yet there was still a great aura of mystery and wonder around Fogfinger, from his velvet slippers to his foaming lace cravat up to the stridently coloured silk turban. The few people who saw him always left feeling shaken and intimidated – and very vulnerable.

One of the ways Fogfinger intimidated people was by keeping them waiting. As the appointed hour for a meeting passed, and then another hour, and another, people felt their worth melting away. They consulted their enamelled fob-watches and paced to and fro. They didn't know what to make of the ringlets of grey smoke that flowed into the room from a corner draped with an ornate cut-velvet curtain.

They did not see Fogfinger discreetly parting the curtain behind which he hid – for he loved to make sure that his victims were squirming, or, as he preferred to put it, 'tenderizing'. If he kept them waiting long enough, they would simply agree to whatever he asked.

And the smoke? Only those he trusted knew how Fogfinger had got his name. He appeared mild-mannered to the point of being humble, speaking in a quiet, high voice so that all must lean in to listen to him. But there was a clue to the angry fire that raged inside the man when you looked down at his hands. Curls of smoke emerged from his wrists and hands, spiralled around his fingers to form a ringlet shape, and were then released into the air.

For his meeting with Latenia Malipiero, however, Fogfinger had no reason to hide or spy.

'Little girls,' he smirked, 'come already tenderized.'

The turban, the cruel thin face, the smoking fingers, and a crowd of noblemen who hovered like flies around him, were all visible to Latenia now. Fogfinger's swollen left foot rested on a footstool covered in red gros point. Beside him was a miniature fireplace full of hot coals. Over the embers, an automaton was blackening pieces of bread with a ram's-horn toasting fork.

Servants took her by the elbow and escorted her to a square of rich Turkey carpet in front of Fogfinger. She found him disturbing to look at – not just because of the clash of his baby-blue silk frock-coat and the yellow damask waistcoat embroidered with coils of pearly smoke flowing from oriental vases and winding itself around disembodied hands and hearts. But she consoled herself with how she would boast to Maffeo about this meeting. *He* had not been chosen for this honour. She thought briefly of Amneris, guessing her new friend would be quite happy never to meet Fogfinger. Her father cleared his throat behind her.

Papà's nervous! she realized. But why?

Fogfinger's long face turned towards her. He beckoned to Latenia to approach.

'At last,' he said, 'the best-kept secret in Venice. Off with that veil, girl!'

'Greet him civilly,' hissed her father in a tone of voice she had never heard before. He snatched the veil from her face, leaving her blinking in the bright light.

'Oh!' she murmured.

Despite the ear trumpet, Fogfinger shouted at Latenia, 'Do be speaking up!' His Irish accent was still strong, after all these years. 'Not bad,' he told her father. 'But of course the best thing about that face is the aura of mystery you've cunningly created around it. *Complimenti* for that at least, Malipiero. And it will serve us both well.'

Alvise Malipiero bowed.

'Cover her up again!' barked Fogfinger. 'Not a word about this,' he warned his courtiers, who nodded fervently.

From behind her veil, Latenia regarded Fogfinger with disfavour. Close up, the most powerful man in Venice was not quite a god. He was apparently half-deaf and he walked with difficulty, Latenia guessed, seeing how he rested his hand on a clear glass barley sugar-twist walking cane. Then she noticed that his chair – silver-framed and decorated with flowers picked out in blue lacquer – was on wheels.

'Where is the grateful curtsey I'd be expecting from the girl who is about to be handed the greatest honour in Venice?'

Latenia wondered, 'What *is* he talking about?'

'Sulky, is it?' Fogfinger snapped two fingers and a servant pushed him closer to her. He thrust a long finger in her face. Smoke curled from the tip of it. He said, 'I fear you are too fond of being coddled. Now, tell me all about yourself.'

Latenia started immediately with an account of her

collection of cake stands, her love of white silk and the expensive presents in her bedroom. She was able to spin out these matters for some minutes but then ground to a halt. With a shock, she realized that when it came to the point, there really was little to tell.

Fogfinger was no longer listening. He had not even noticed when she stopped. He was absorbed in a ledger in his lap. She could see his smoky index finger had stopped at the words '*Alvise Malipiero: dragon-heart fat monies owed.*'

Fogfinger looked up, but not at Latenia. Over her head, he addressed her father. 'Malipiero! Your daughter has a violently exaggerated opinion of how interesting she is.'

Latenia's father, instead of defending her, murmured, 'Of course, Your Excellency, you are correct. She's such a precious creature that we've all petted her far too much. She has become spoilt.'

Even Latenia's most imperious stare did not extract an apology from her father for this disagreeable statement. He was busy signing a document that two of Fogfinger's servants had placed in front of him, on a portable desk. The document was splattered with red wax seals and tied with black ribbons.

'What's that?' Latenia asked boldly.

The courtiers drew in their breath in shock. Fogfinger waggled a smoky finger at Latenia's father. '"What's that" indeed. Have you bred a veritable vixen in petticoats, Malipiero? You will have this chit trained in humility before I meet her again. All I want to hear from that rosebud mouth is "How wonderful, Sir!" and "You are too kind!" Especially given the disgrace your wife has called down on you, Malipiero. The shameful way *she* has deserted your family.'

Latenia forgot about the nasty reproof. *Her mother* had called down a disgrace on the family? Fogfinger had spoken of her as if she was still alive. Latenia had become used to declaring she did not need a mother, but it still made her heart leap to think that she might have one.

20
Unnatural history

'Now, girl,' said Fogfinger, 'do you like artistic curiosities? Let me give you the benefit of my exquisite taste in these matters.'

The bath chair set off, and Latenia and her father hurried after it.

All kinds of new and experimental automata were spinning, clicking and ticking away in Fogfinger's private quarters, which were hung with lavish green velvet and damask drapes.

Even those devices that were not wound up were surrounded by flickering candles, making it seem as though they were twitching and could lunge at any moment. Several sets of human teeth had been mechanized to snap at odd moments, making Latenia squeal. And hourglasses containing viciously bright grains somersaulted every three minutes to start again. Their labels read: 'Native Arsenic from Bohemia', 'Yellow Lead from Carinthia' and 'Opalescent Iron from Elba'.

'Now – my private zoo,' gloated Fogfinger. 'How I am spoiling you!'

Fogfinger in his bath chair led the way down a marble corridor lined with onyx columns topped by chattering and gesticulating busts of Roman emperors, some of whom looked surprisingly like Fogfinger himself. They arrived at a room with walls as red and shiny as wet blood.

And wet blood was appropriate, because the room was a death chamber. Numerous stuffed antelopes, two giraffes, a hippo, a rhino, three zebras, pangolins, armadillos, a warthog and an elephant were all caught, their teeth bared, their eyes wild at the moment of death. A series of baboon heads grimaced with the knowledge that they had been about to be killed. Deer, lions and antelope had also been flayed: their flattened skins hung upside down on the walls; only their heads had been stuffed and furnished with glass eyes in a facsimile of life.

'The best of every species. Too good for the public exhibition downstairs, these! All killed by myself on various expeditions to Africa,' boasted Fogfinger. 'I decided to catch the whole encyclopaedia while I was out there.'

The next thing Latenia saw was a gorilla flattened, his belly like a great leathery rug, though his head was fully formed. She flinched from the angry look in his hooded eyes and the glint of his pointed teeth.

Fogfinger had partially automated some of his dead animals. Even though their bodies were motionless, their eyes swivelled or their ears flapped. But they were trapped inside their stuffed bodies and nailed to the floor or mounted on the walls. The effect was horrifying, even for Latenia. It would have been kinder if the beasts were entirely dead – not *living* their deaths like this.

'Wonderful, no?' Fogfinger purred.

131

'This is not natural history,' Latenia thought. 'This is *unnatural* history.'

Everywhere she cast her eyes, there was something dreadful to look at: stumps of the empty feet of elephants rolling around on hidden wheels, an anteater wagging pert ears, a grey baboon, with fur delicately stippled like an Abyssinian cat's. She could hardly bear to look at his long black muzzle and close-together eyes that blinked every second. His shapely black hands were the same size as her own. She walked past a nodding flamingo, two dancing toucans, a chicken walking awkwardly on four legs and a beaver cleaning luxuriant whiskers. Above her head, stuffed sharks swam in angry circles, propelled by iron rods. Meanwhile, eels threaded their sinuous bodies in the opposite direction above and between the sharks. On the cornices, up near the ceiling, loomed vultures and tufted owls, slowly opening and closing their glittering eyes. And high on the far wall, a pair of ostriches, without legs, fanned out their beautiful plumage.

Fogfinger muttered, 'I'm still working on a way of perfectly animating my hunting trophies, so that they function not as wild animals but as a disciplined army. My ... scientists ... keep whining that there's some conflict between the preservation methods and the mechanical implantations. Never mind. It shall soon be resolved.'

Even more fascinating and more horrible was Fogfinger's collection of grotesque furniture and ornaments fashioned out of parts of dead animals: elephant feet with tusks mounted on them, a leopard forced into an upright position, with a card-tray between its paws and a fox-fur stole around its stiff neck, a stool with an eagle's talons and a zebra-skin love-seat.

Latenia did not like them, particularly the mounted heads. They looked sinister without their bodies, though a part of

132

her could not help imagining the rest of them on the other side of the wall. Signor Malipiero walked around with a simpering grin, exclaiming and praising the arrangement. 'So artistic! Such a privilege to see this private collection, which does so much honour to Venice, Your Excellency.'

'Too kind,' said Fogfinger.

Latenia thought, 'Yes, far too kind. This is not art. It is butchery. And meanness.'

She came face to face with a pair of stuffed turtles. They gaped sadly at her with their empty faces. With a shudder, she recalled what Amneris had said about the tortoiseshell combs she collected, and about the cruelly small bowls in which she kept her goldfish. She would find them something bigger, she told herself.

Her father was rubbing his hands. 'If I might presume to ask a question, Sir?'

Fogfinger waved a condescending finger. Three curls of smoke flowed from the tip and floated across the room. They circled around Latenia's head before disappearing, leaving a faint smell of gunpowder.

Signor Malipiero asked, 'Why no *Venetian* animals, Your Excellency? Creatures from foreign lands – but none of our native species? Not even a rabbit?'

'Ah, I used to hunt here … I had an expensive pack of slavering hounds and an infallible whip and a whole orchestra of delightfully ghoulish whistles and terrifying horns for startling the prey out of their lairs and burrows. We had glorious costumes, plumed caps, elegant horses. These animals died the most picturesque deaths you can imagine. They should have been grateful to me. But alas, it seems that we finally killed every living wild thing on the mainland and on the islands of the lagoon. I already had examples of every kind of domesticated beast – look, even the famous cat of Doge Morosini is mummified here, with a rat between its paws! So then it was time to leave the last few foxes, hares, rabbits and blackbirds of Venice, and go to look for something more exotic. And plentiful. So I went to Africa.'

Latenia wondered if there were any animals left living in Africa. She asked, 'Did you ever think of making a zoo, and keeping them alive?'

'Perhaps you think it is perfectly acceptable that you do not call me "Sir" when we are in private, like this?' Fogfinger's voice was even but bushy smoke poured from the fingers of his right hand.

Signor Malipiero pincered the back of Latenia's neck, squeezing painfully. He said, 'Forgive my daughter, Sir. She is overawed by the magnificence of your collection and, ahem, of course the honour of being in your presence. She will say "Sir" at all times in future, Sir. Or "My Lord". As you prefer. I shall make sure of it.'

Latenia was unable to speak. Her father made her head nod with his hands.

'Still,' said Fogfinger, 'I shall answer her about the zoo. No, I did not think of such a thing. Dead animals are better than living ones and far more useful. What use is a living hippopotamus in Venice, hmm? Or a rhinoceros? But look at my billiard table. Four rhinocerine legs holding it, so a gentleman and his friends may spend a pleasant evening around it. Were those legs fixed to the rhino, and were the rhino living, his unpleasant odours and unpleasanter personality would have ruined the whole party. Alive, he would be expensive to keep. Dead, he is working for me.'

'So true, so true, Your Excellency,' simpered Signor Malipiero. 'So elegant. So useful.'

'And look at this chair. Yes, those legs have most unusual endings. Indeed, they are the legs of a giraffe – the top is covered with a bit of elephant. And this lamp-stand … is it fashioned from clay or wood? No, far better, this is a real python stuffed, backboned with a stake and threaded with a silken cord so that the little lanterns can hang from its jaws. Can you imagine that Signor Snake in life would be so obliging?'

'Absolutely not!' guffawed Signor Malipiero. 'Ha, ha, ha!'

'And this one, bless it, will also shoot that venom from its mouth on my command! Meanwhile, this mechanized baboon can be made to dance. In the jungle, he shambles and waddles and lopes. In my ballroom, he gavottes and minuets like a duchess. Surely that is better? And what is more, he can one day, perhaps, be trained to kill – though he does that imperfectly as yet. And then the *Piccoli Pochi* will find themselves hunted to the far corners of the lagoon – hunted, killed and eaten by my obedient animal servants.'

Latenia clutched the blue glass seahorse inside her pocket, nodding mutely. She instinctively knew that the stuffed mechanical baboon was an evil thing – evil in the making, evil in appearance and evil in intention.

'So,' Fogfinger's bath chair rolled right up to her, stopping just at her toes. 'I have some gifts for you. You like gifts? Of course you do; you are a Venetian girl. That's all you think of.'

Latenia reflected, 'Not all Venetian girls. Amneris and even Biri don't *always* think about presents.'

'Stop daydreaming!' Fogfinger was pointing to a round table in the centre of the room.

Latenia's face fell. 'But they are all just things. A fan. A doll. No automata!' she complained. 'I would have thought—'

'Think again,' said Fogfinger. 'Try the fan.'

Her father urged, 'The fan, Daughter!'

Alvise Malipiero and Fogfinger exchanged significant looks as Latenia picked up an enormous fan made of white ostrich feathers fixed between mother-of-pearl slats. It was surprisingly light. As she touched it, the fan floated from her hand and began to circle her, waving its fronds in a delicate motion like a dance. It was like being caressed by a spring breeze.

Latenia smiled and reached for the doll. Then she dropped it and screamed. The breeze of the ostrich fan had caused a side door to open. Inside the room now revealed were a hundred red devils with glistening black horns. The devils were dancing lightly in the air.

She did not stop screaming until her father had slapped her face four times.

The door had been closed swiftly by two servants, and a key turned in the lock. But not before she had realized that the devils were hollow – just costumes mounted on hooks suspended from the ceiling. It was the breeze from the fan that had made them seem to dance.

The fact that they were not real provided little consolation. Her father was friends with a man who kept a hundred devils in his house, and was training baboons to kill. And he wanted her to be friends with this man too. That was enough to worry Latenia nearly all the way home.

'If this is going out, then I'm better off locked up at home,' she told herself. 'But I shall make a terrible scene if Papà tries to take me there again.'

Then she remembered what Fogfinger had said about her mother – deserting her family, but not dead, as she had always believed.

'Papà,' she tugged his sleeve, 'tell me why—'

But the gondola, loaded with Fogfinger's gifts, had just arrived at the water gate of the Malipiero palace. Her father strode onto the mechanical walkway and stormed into the hall. Over his shoulder, he snarled, 'Present yourself in my study in five minutes. Things are about to change, Daughter.'

21
Signed and sold

Alvise Malipiero announced, 'Latenia, for the first time in your entirely selfish and ridiculous life, you are going to be of use to me. I have today signed a contract with Fogfinger.'

'What kind of contract?' Latenia's skin prickled as she remembered the document heavy with red seals and black ribbons.

'For your betrothal to Fogfinger. Your marriage will take place when you are of age.'

Latenia screamed, 'Never! I hate him! He is already an old man! He has a face like a dirty fingernail! He will be even more revolting when I am sixteen. How dare you do this? You didn't even ask my permission.'

She ran to the door and flung it open. 'I'm leaving!' she screamed. She waited on the threshold for her father to say it was all a joke, to tell her that of course she could do whatever she wanted, as usual. But he did none of those things. Instead, he asked, 'And where exactly are you going to go? You'd not survive five minutes without my money. You'll marry him.'

'I shall not!'

'Actually you already agreed.'

'What do you mean? This is the first I have heard of it, and I say no. No, no, no, no, no. Is that enough "no"s for you? No? Here are some more. Nononononono!' She stamped her feet one after the other.

As usual, Signor Malipiero simply waited out her tantrum. After it was finished, he said coolly, 'When you accepted his betrothal gifts, you greedy little girl, you accepted his hand. That's what is written in the contract.'

'A contract you never showed me! I wouldn't have—'

'It was signed in your presence, remember? You witnessed it. No one's fault but yours that you never asked. You only ever ask for silk and cakes and automata. Or shall I say, nag and whine and demand them. How was I supposed to know that you might want to read a contract? You never even want to read a book.'

'You tricked me!' screamed Latenia.

She recalled the glance her father exchanged with Fogfinger when she picked up the ostrich plume fan. That had been the moment she had ruined her life.

'Well, it was easy enough. Fortunately you have not inherited your mother's wits. Look where they got her.'

'And that's another thing!' cried Latenia. 'What's all this about my mother? I thought she was dead!'

'Did I ever say that to you?'

'No,' admitted Latenia. 'But you never mentioned her. So I thought she was.'

'I never mention the Emperor of China,' sneered her father, 'but he is doing very well, or so I understand.'

'So where is my mother?'

'Paris, it seems, living it up at the expense of our family's reputation – that's the latest whisper I heard. The shame! I pray that Fogfinger never learns of it. And now it is your turn to pay for her crimes. God knows I have spent the last eleven years putting up with you, so now it is my turn to get some good out of you.'

'What good?'

'With the signing of this betrothal contract, I am promised the Admiralty when the current admiral dies.'

'But you know nothing about ships or sailors or wars.'

'It's an honorary position. But it's paid in gold. And it shall put me in a position of extreme *influence*. And there'll also be lots of fat little envelopes being poked into my pockets by people wanting jobs in the Admiralty. Now run away, Daughter. Start planning your betrothal dress.'

'When?' asked Latenia desperately. '*When* is this … betrothal?' She could barely bring herself to say the word.

'At the feast of the Redentore,' said her father.

Latenia slumped against the wall.

'And in honour of your betrothal,' he gloated, 'the extra Lambing, the one against the drought, is going to be *extremely* special. I'll let you in on a secret – now that we are part of the family, so to speak. *Three* children instead of one, in honour of Fogfinger's new fiancée!'

Latenia whispered, 'More children will be killed in my honour?'

Signor Malipiero continued, 'No expense spared for the ceremony – you can dress yourself in cloth of white gold for all I care. Now that you're safely betrothed, you can go about the town shopping to your heart's content, so long as you keep the veil on. You might keep buying dresses for five years and still not spend all I'll be earning soon.'

Latenia gaped at him. Suddenly clothes had lost all their glamour.

Signor Malipiero's proud voice grew quieter, harder.

'I've been keeping your brother in fancy stockings and the two of you in all the automata you want. Did you never think there would be a cost?'

'Not this cost! You are Lambing *me* too!' shrieked Latenia. 'You should be ashamed! And grief-stricken!'

'I suppose I am,' said Signor Malipiero. 'Lambing you, that is. But no, I'm not ashamed. Or sad. Unlike the poor people, I'm giving up a child that I don't much mind losing.'

The coldness of his voice was not unfamiliar to her. It was just that usually her papà said 'yes' in the same tone as he was now saying 'no'.

'It's not fair! What about Maffeo? Why isn't he going to pay?'

'I don't think he'll particularly enjoy being sent to Dalmatia. The son of the admiral traditionally serves there. Not a lot of automata in Dubrovnik. The boy will have to learn to use his legs.'

Latenia felt the heat of satisfaction in her cheeks. Yes, Maffeo would hate going to that barbarian place. But Maffeo's misfortune did not really lighten her own.

'You should stop frowning like that. It is most unbecoming.'

Suddenly Alvise Malipiero flinched and looked uncomfortable.

'I did not see you sneak in, girl,' he said to Amneris. 'Stop cowering by the door and let me look at you. Are you spying? What have you to say for yourself?'

Amneris had let herself quietly into Signor Malipiero's study about five minutes before. Seeing the brown wrapped parcel in her hand, the maid had escorted her straight there. So Amneris had heard the words exchanged by Latenia and her father.

Somehow she made herself answer now, as Latenia, standing still with the colour drained from her face, was clearly incapable of uttering a word.

'I brought the new order, Sir. I shall sew the most lovely silk for your daughter's betrothal, Sir,' Amneris gabbled. 'It shall be an honour.'

'You'd do anything to get in with a family on the rise, I suppose?' Signor Malipiero looked at Amneris with a mixture of repugnance and speculation. 'I had heard there is this underclass in Venice, too poor for automata, full of greedy ambition. You're starting young, girl. But if you make yourself useful, there might be some *zecchini* in it for you.'

Amneris hated to be thought of in the way that Latenia's father saw her. Her cheeks burned with the unfairness of it.

It was only when Signor Malipiero pushed them both outside his study and slammed the door behind him that his daughter gave way to a storm of uncontrollable sobbing.

Finally, Latenia hiccuped, 'I shall run away and sell my jewels, and never come back to Venice.'

Painful as it was to do so, Amneris felt obliged to explain what Tockle had noticed about the jewels.

'Fakes? Papà pawned the real ones? No, I don't believe you – how can you say that we are really poor?'

'Not poor like us, obviously. But not as rich as you thought.'

'My father has sold me to Fogfinger so he will not be poor ever again,' wept Latenia.

Amneris patted her shoulder. 'Could you not find your mother? I heard what he said – that she's not dead after all.'

'Just in disgrace. But I don't know where she is, and I have no way of finding her. I was just a baby when she left. I wouldn't even recognize her in the street. And just think, she abandoned me. My own mother!'

Latenia burst into fresh and wetter sobs.

Amneris let herself out of the palace and walked home sadly, calling out for Grillo every now and then. It was only when she saw the apricot tree at the Calle Berlendis that she realized she had completely forgotten to tell Latenia about the secret silk letter in the parasol.

22
Just a few more sleeps

Latenia had hoped that her first visit to Fogfinger would be her last, but she was obliged to wait on her fiancé-to-be again the following week. She was supervised by her father. His strained face seemed to shrink and hide inside his ginger beard, showing that he enjoyed these occasions as little as she did.

Fogfinger chattered gaily about the betrothal ceremony while dipping biscuits in a porcelain cup of hot chocolate. Latenia stood silently, the tears dropping on her cheeks.

'I fear my engagement will be a disappointment to many a beautiful lady,' sighed Fogfinger. 'As my choice, you should show humbleness, and pity for all the other girls I could have chosen instead. Presumably that is what your tears are for.'

'No!' wept Latenia.

Fogfinger did not betray any anger, unless you counted the swirls of fog that started to issue from his fingertips.

'Disgusting!' wailed Latenia.

143

'Signor Malipiero,' said Fogfinger, 'I see that your daughter has inherited your wife's wilful character. In compensation, I have added five thousand *ducati* to the dowry she will bring with her. For I must employ some people to groom her manners until she's as *amiable* as I require. In fact, I have already employed them.'

He snapped his fingers.

Two figures shuffled into the room. Something about their mutual ugliness made it obvious that they were married to each other. Latenia thought, 'They must be – no one else would have them.'

The man's face was goat-like, with small yellowish eyes placed far apart and high on his muzzle. His nose was mottled with moles and freckles. Greasy hair clumped in grey wisps on his awkwardly shaped skull. His lips were thick and leathery. His wife had no visible softness to her shape, presenting merely a squat and solid square. The skin stretched tightly over her moonish face. Apart from their grim looks, the couple shared a single expression: a cynical sneer, with an undertone of cruelty.

'Signora and Signor Drossi, my personal housekeepers,' said Fogfinger. 'And shortly to be yours, my dear. I present Latenia Malipiero, the latest girl.'

Latenia curtseyed. Privately, she marvelled that Fogfinger could bear to keep such hideous creatures around himself. She tried to imagine the Drossi couple stuffed and mounted – but they were still more terrifying than anything in Fogfinger's collection.

Signor Drossi chuckled horribly. His wife barked, 'Charmed, I am sure,' in a voice that made it clear that she felt exactly the opposite. She did not curtsey back to Latenia, or even lower her large head to a bow. And when she walked away, it was with a mannish, arrogant swagger.

She heard Lardo Drossi repeat a Venetian proverb to his

144

wife: 'An old man in love is like an ass who plays the lyre.'

She snorted, 'In love? Ha!'

Latenia did not know how they dared.

They dared a lot, she noticed. When Lardo Drossi and his wife walked past them, even Fogfinger's warrior baboons and killer snakes stood to attention.

Success had taken the D'Ago family by surprise. Instead of the dismissal Amneris had feared, suddenly there was a great demand for the all-white designs that the dear creature continued to generate. Alvise Malipiero had naturally boasted to his friends and clients about his daughter's exquisite fabrics: other nobles were not slow in finding Melchior Dubbini. The silk merchant was not slow in sharing the D'Ago work with these new grand customers. And when news of Latenia's betrothal was announced in the *Postiglione*, everyone craved the 'Malipiero' white silks all the more.

As if to confirm the D'Ago family's new popularity, Grillo had come back. Amneris spent hours with her arms around him, her nose buried in his vanilla-scented fur, telling him of all the strange and terrifying things that had happened in his absence. He licked her hand sympathetically.

Ugo had sent Amneris a new message to embroider. But just when she most needed to see Latenia, Amneris had no excuse for an official call at the Malipiero palace. She was too busy stitching duplicate designs for other noble families.

Finally, Dubbini deemed a new piece of white-work perfect for 'my favourite little client', and sent Amneris around to deliver it.

The maid who showed her up warned, 'Miss is in a foul mood.'

Amneris felt in her pocket for the candle and flint she had brought from home. She did not know how long she'd have with Latenia before they were interrupted. Maffeo could walk in at any moment. She still had to find a way to show Latenia how to use the candle to reveal what was written in the hidden ink.

Latenia greeted her without enthusiasm. Eyes wide open, she was curled up on the floor.

Amneris was struck by Latenia's listless look.

'No cakes?' she said, kneeling down to take Latenia's hand. 'Are you not well?'

Latenia burst into tears. 'How would *you* feel if you were about to be betrothed to an old goat?'

'I wouldn't be in her shoes, for anything,' Amneris thought with compassion. But she needed to deliver Ugo's message. Brusquely, she said, 'I'm truly sorry. But you have to watch this. Quickly. Before someone comes in.'

She produced the handkerchief and the candle from her pinafore pocket.

'Someone is going to send you letters. Letters sewn on silk. By me. For safety, I'll sew them in invisible thread. If you receive a silk handkerchief, wave the candle like this, slowly in front of the stitching, careful not to set fire to it. The words will appear. Read the letters quickly and then burn them with the same candle. You must not keep them.'

'Who wants to send me a silk letter? Why all the mystery?' Latenia's voice quivered with suspicion.

Amneris smiled reassuringly. 'I have no idea. Apparently, it's better for me not to know. But trust me; it comes from a good place.'

'How could Amneris betray me like that?' Latenia brooded,

holding the two invisible ink letters gingerly between her fingers. She had retrieved the one from the parasol too.

'I thought all the poor people hated Fogfinger,' she frowned. 'So why should Amneris help him send me these ridiculous love letters? And why on earth does Fogfinger need to use invisible ink? It's a stupid, stupid game.'

And why had he chosen to write such babyish words?

'Just a few more weeks, tiny one, till I can kiss your little soft cheek.'

Amneris brought more messages over the next few days, on the pretext that she needed to make adjustments to the embroidery designs for Latenia's betrothal dress. The two girls were awkward and quiet with one another.

The messages said things like '*I think of you, my little one. Do not think badly of me.*' And '*Do not believe everything they say about me, my child.*'

With trembling hands, Latenia burned the silk letters as quickly as she could, but their words were etched in her memory for hours afterwards.

As bad as the letters was the realization that Lardo Drossi or his mannish wife had been sent to spy on the Malipiero palace. Twice, she'd seen the awkward shape of Signora Drossi waddling away from her front door. It must have been her. Could there be two completely square women in Venice? And once Latenia saw Lardo staring up at her with an insolent expression on his face. She avoided looking into his eyes, staring instead at the stubbly groove between his spongy nose and slack mouth.

He mouthed, 'Watch yourself, sweetheart!'

She marvelled that he dared. After all, little as the idea pleased her, she did have the status of Fogfinger's fiancée-to-be. But Lardo clearly cared for no one's opinion of himself or his manners. And this was perhaps why Fogfinger had chosen him as his henchman. Just by his contemptuous presence, Lardo put people exactly where Fogfinger wanted them: in a state of anxiety.

Anxiety was general in the Malipiero household. The servants were in a frenzy about the betrothal preparations, Signor Malipiero was in distress about the extra dowry Latenia's tantrum had cost him, Maffeo was in a state about the threat of being sent to automata-less Dalmatia – and Latenia was so choked with sorrow that nothing would pass her lips.

Latenia's father berated her. 'You will get as thin as a poor girl,' he warned.

A programme of relentless snacking was devised for her.

But Latenia refused to eat.

Latenia was burning a letter when Maffeo strolled into her room, exclaiming, 'Pooh! What's that cheap smell? A new scent, Tenni-ten-ten? Oh, what are you up to there? Something secret?'

Latenia spun around waving the burning handkerchief so that it flew about the room in splinters of glowing ash. But as she did so, her blue glass seahorse flew out of her pocket. It landed at Maffeo's feet.

'Oho, what is this then?' He pounced on the seahorse. 'Tenni-ten-ten, what are you mixed up with?' he said, advancing on her.

'Nothing!'

'What are you doing with a *Piccoli Pochi* talisman in your pocket?'

'I don't know what the *Piccoli* thingies are and what is a talisman?' Latenia sniffed. 'I never heard of such things.'

Maffeo's voice was full of speculation. 'I suppose that is possible. She does not go out, and she has no education, and

148

she does not read the *Postiglione*, and she thinks only about cake and dresses ... but those street children, they know!' He tilted Latenia's chin up and glared into her eyes. 'Did those dirty urchins give you this seahorse? Did they?'

'No! I found it on my pillow! I used to find them quite often. I have a whole box of them. Look!' She broke free from Maffeo and ran across the room to her dressing table, flinging open the box.

'Well, well, well. Ah. I see,' said Maffeo.

'What do you mean?'

'I can see that I have a few things to explain to you,' drawled Maffeo, taking the box and emptying its contents out of the window into the Grand Canal. As he did so, he muttered, 'And I have a few things to work out quietly on my own, that might be profitable for me later.'

He turned back to Latenia. 'Sit down. You are about to hear how things are in Venice, and after I tell you, you will not be associating any more with those street urchins. Ever again. You'll be sorry that you ever met them and you'll wash your hands every time you think of them.'

23
An Ark at Arsenale

Wednesday May 28th, 1783

The Feast of the Redentore and the extra Lambing loomed in just a few weeks, but Venice was distracted by stories of an Ark being built in the Arsenale shipyard.

Fogfinger had changed his tactics about the *Piccoli Pochi*. He had now decided, as he put it, that '*Venice should have the populace she deserves.*'

A new poster on the walls announced:

> Anyone who does not like
> this new Crocodile-safe and orderly Venice
> will NOT be hunted down or even punished.
> Why should this Kind State be so barbarous?
> No, instead, from motives of generosity and a desire for peace,
> we shall allow all who find fault with this lovely city
> to leave her. They are free to depart. Godspeed!
> We have even assured a sunny paradise for them to go to –
> the beautiful island of Hvar on the Dalmatian coast,

a miniature Venice with a proper Venetian theatre,
an azure lagoon
and abundance of grape and grain.
Sign up at the Town Hall.

'It's a trick,' Tockle said, when Stella brought home one of the handbills that duplicated the poster in miniature.

'An island with a theatre and lots of food?' said Stella. 'We should be off to the Town Hall immediately. Even in paradise, people will still want kaleidoscopes.'

'But where would we get the glass?' worried Mamma. 'And perhaps there are already *bigolanti* there to carry the water? What would I do? Things are not so bad now. At least the wells are working again.'

This was true. Ugo's diving boys kept unblocking the wells as fast as the Fogs plugged them up. Biri's moths reported each new blockage and it was now usually repaired the same night. 'Ordinary' water in brown bottles stood unsold in the shops and Tockle's mother was as busy as ever.

They talked about the Ark deep into the night. The temptation was strong: a new start in a place without Lambing or Kittening, and the prospect of never being hungry again. Redentore was drawing closer, and with it the chance of Tockle being Lambed.

'What if Papà should come back?' argued Tockle. 'He'd find the house empty. He'd think we had given up waiting for him.'

'He'd never think that,' declared Mamma. 'But it is something to consider.'

'To consider for five minutes, and then go to the Town Hall and sign up,' chivvied Stella. 'And what's wrong with leaving a letter on the mantelpiece for him?'

In all the poor homes of Venice, the talk was of nothing but the Ark and the possibility of escaping to the paradise

151

island of Hvar. People who had children of Lambing age or cats were particularly tempted.

'We owe it to our children to go,' they told themselves, even though their hearts were breaking at the thought of leaving their beloved Venice.

At first, the signatures came in at a trickle. But after each family signed up, cousins and friends followed. The lists grew longer: they were posted on the wall outside the Town Hall. Suddenly it seemed that no one wanted to stay in Venice.

New posters urged:

Reserve your space now for the Paradise Island of Hvar.
A dear little house for everyone, and a garden too.
Departure date: June 25th, 1783

Tockle's family's names were on the list now.

Tockle had told his mother that his father was in Cairo in the hospital. When she asked him how he knew, he said that he'd overheard two Fogs talking about it. It hurt him to lie, but it meant that his mother at least knew that there was hope – something he could not bear to deny her. It also meant that she could not ask Tockle any more questions.

Now, for Tockle's mother, the Ark represented a way of getting out of Venice and the first step in the journey to Rizardo Molin's side.

'Surely there are ferries from Hvar going further south?' she asked. 'Even to Egypt?'

Tockle's name was on the list, but he had decided to stay. He continued to insist there must be someone in the little house in the Corte Giovanelli in case Rizardo Molin made his way back.

'And Sweet Nizzi shall stay on the mantelpiece,' he insisted. 'To show this is still our home.'

Only to himself did Tockle admit why he did not want his family to go to Hvar. There was something about the Ark that he mistrusted. Every time it was mentioned, he felt an emptiness in the pit of his stomach.

Why would Fogfinger make it so easy for people to leave?

The lists continued to fill, as May ripened into June.

It was not that the poor Venetians trusted Fogfinger. Tockle was not the only one who suspected that the promises of the Ark were too good to be true.

But the prospect of the extra Lambing at Redentore drove them to sign up. Who could risk losing a child? The only certainty was that more families would do so, if they did not sail with the Ark.

24
Thin enough to be Lambed

Wednesday June 25th, 1783

The mechanical pigeon tapped on the D'Ago front door.

When no one answered immediately, it flew in an open window and pecked importantly on the kitchen table where the family sat eating a sombre luncheon. It was June 25th, the day the Ark was due to leave, taking many of their friends with it.

Its mechanical voicebox whirred into life. 'Amneris D'Ago, Amneris D'Ago,' it said. 'Message for you.'

It dropped a curled-up cake-wrapper from its beak.

'Who do we know who can afford a bird automaton?' asked Granny.

Amneris was reading the cake-wrapper with a frown on her face. 'This is odd,' she mused. 'It doesn't sound like Latenia. She said "please". Three times.'

Her mother looked over her shoulder at the note. 'It's been at least a month since you were called there, has it not? Is that not in itself strange? You must go to her, my pet. She

154

may be very rich and very unpleasant, but she is clearly in trouble. Take that nice boy Tockle with you. He'll be lonely today – his family will have boarded the Ark this morning. And he might be able to help.'

The first thing that Amneris noticed was that Latenia's plump figure had shrunk greatly in the weeks since she had seen her last. Her brocade bodice was bunchy around the shoulders and drooped over the places where her hips and stomach used to provide comfortable cushions of flesh. She paced the room energetically – a far cry from her old languid pose.

It struck Amneris that if Latenia were to be weighed at this moment, she would be thin enough to be Lambed.

'What has happened to you?' Tockle asked kindly. 'You do not look … yourself. You sent the pigeon to Amneris – is there something we can do for you?'

Latenia jerked her thumb at Amneris. 'Yes! *You* are a double agent, aren't you? I've worked it out. You're in Fogfinger's pay to deliver those horrid letters. And you're all in the *Piccolissimi Pochi*, aren't you, you and Tockle and the girl Biri?' whispered Latenia. 'That's what Maffeo meant when he was interrogating you. That's what you were about to tell me about the seahorses.'

'No, no, no, no!' Amneris was shocked. 'Fogfinger? I do not work for him!'

Tockle protested, 'Of course she doesn't! Except in that all of us work to pay his Winding Up Tax. How do you know about the *Piccoli Pochi*?'

Latenia scowled. 'The *Pochi*? I bet you've both got a blue glass seahorse sewn into your clothes somewhere, like they all do. Don't you? Like you tricked me into doing.'

She told them what had happened with Maffeo.

Amneris tried again. 'I just sew. Tockle goes to school. Whatever gave you these wild ideas?'

Latenia tapped the side of her nose. 'I'm like Maffeo. I'm not stupid. I see things. I understand things.'

'But,' asked Tockle, 'how did you get those blue seahorses?'

'You tell me: perhaps you had something to do with it?'

'Stop being mysterious,' exclaimed Tockle. 'This isn't a game. Tell us what you mean.'

'I know it's not a game,' said Latenia. 'That's why I am hiring you two as my private killers.'

25
Pointed and pointless

Wednesday June 25th, 1783

Amneris stood very still. Had she really heard correctly? 'You two have to kill Fogfinger,' Latenia repeated. 'Not just for me. I know you wouldn't do it just for me. You don't care a button for me, for all your pretending to be nice. However, I have information to sell you. In exchange for your help. And it's this: I happen to know that Fogfinger is raising an army of mechanical killing animals. I've seen them myself. Gorillas, baboons, snakes with venom. And who do you think he is planning to kill with them?'

Tockle paled. Amneris was too shocked to answer. Ugo had wanted her to befriend the rich noble girl so that she might obtain just such crucial information. But the pale, thin Latenia who had jumped to her feet and was now striding up and down the room … this was not a spoilt little girl: she was a feverish, dangerous creature. Perhaps she was making it all up? Perhaps Latenia had started to lose her mind?

Amneris exchanged a look with Tockle, who said, 'Slow down and tell me where this has come from.'

157

'I'd rather be dead than betrothed to Fogfinger. It's better *he*'s dead than me. So I want you to kill him. Simple.'

'But Latenia,' said Tockle, 'look at us. We'd never kill anyone.'

'Not even Fogfinger,' said Amneris. 'Can't you just run away?'

'Where? With what? You've told me my jewels are false. *You're* too poor to look after me ... and anyway, you may not even be alive by the Redentore.'

'You mean the Lambing,' said Tockle faintly.

Latenia's eyes fell on her miserable goldfish.

'I am just like the fish, just as pointless, just as pitiful, just as trapped,' she said. She ran to the beautiful glass bowls. Before Amneris could stop her, she had heaved one of them to the window and tipped the fish out into the Grand Canal. Then she ran back to get the other.

'Latenia,' Tockle blocked the way, 'it is *salt* water down there. You've just killed your pet.'

He grabbed the second bowl just in time as Latenia collapsed on the floor, weeping, 'Save me!' Amneris was sorry for the fish, but in this moment she was just as sorry for Latenia.

Maffeo strode into the room, his cape swirling. He grabbed Amneris by the scruff of her neck and Tockle by his ear. 'I know who you are now, you spies! You are members of the *Piccolissimi Pochi*, aren't you?'

'Let go of them!' shouted Latenia.

'Eavesdropper!' muttered Tockle. 'You'd never work it out for yourself!'

Maffeo grinned. 'I know you little guttersnipes think I'm useless, but you're about to see I'm very effective indeed.'

'Please!' pleaded Amneris, her teeth rattling. 'I think you're very clever ... very effective.'

The floor shook with booted footsteps. Ten Fogs burst into the room.

'You sent for us, Sir? About a matter of treason?' The captain bowed to Maffeo.

'It has come to my attention,' Maffeo drawled, 'that there's a girl in San Marcuola, a dirty beggar who lives in a stone-cutters' old warehouse. Goes by the name of Biri Fava. Well, I have reason to believe she's a member of the *Piccolissimi Pochi*.'

'Do you, Sir?' said the captain. 'That must be the Corte del Tagliapietra, near the church? A right nest of traitors since the fire. We'll be asking that lot a few questions and post-haste. And these two?' He nodded at Amneris and Tockle.

'I'll deal with them,' Maffeo declared.

The Fogs marched out of the room. From the window, they could be seen climbing aboard the grey boat they had tied up against the San Samuele *traghetto*.

Maffeo grinned at Amneris and Tockle. 'Now you see what'll happen if you don't tell me everything you know.'

'Why didn't you give us to the Fogs?' stammered Tockle.

Latenia said in her new, hard voice, 'Don't you see he wants the glory of delivering you to Fogfinger personally? And the rewards! He wants to show everyone that he's the most intelligent person in Venice.'

'But did you think of this?' Tockle shouted, twisting his ear out of Maffeo's grasp. 'That we can run faster than you?'

Tockle grabbed Amneris's hand. She screamed as she tore her hair out of Maffeo's fingers. The two of them bolted out of the room and hurtled down the stairs, through the courtyard and into the street, where they halted for a moment to catch their breaths and listen for their pursuer.

There were no footsteps.

'Of course,' said Amneris, 'Maffeo does not run! He does not do anything that requires an effort. He's forgotten how. He has automata for that.'

She shook her head, panting. 'But what about poor Biri?'

26
Chinese whispers and flying chickens

Wednesday June 25th, 1783

'How can we warn her?' Tockle jumped from one foot to the other. 'The Fogs have a boat – they'll be at the Corte del Tagliapietra much faster than we can run.'

'I don't know!' Amneris could not bear the thought of the Fogs dragging Biri away. She knew they would not be gentle.

'Corte del Tagliapietra, you say? I was born there.'

The street was empty: the deep, crackly voice seemed to come from above their heads. Was someone spying on them?

'Who said that?' asked Tockle, craning his neck upwards.

'I did,' said the statue above the door, a smooth life-size face on a pedestal. 'It was at the Corte del Tagliapietra that the stonemason Thadeo Fava first cut me out of living marble. I suppose you could call him my papà.'

'It talked to us!' squeaked Amneris. 'To humans! And it's talking about Biri's father.'

Ordinarily, of course, Venice's talking statues spoke only to one another.

'Well, I don't make a habit of it,' said the statue. 'But when needs must, I can talk. Holler too. So, this "Biri" is in trouble? If you wish, I can send a message down the Grand Canal to her.'

'Quicker than a boat?' breathed Amneris.

'Quicker than a seagull,' said the statue. 'Quicker than a blackbird. Or an egret. Or a vulture, or a—'

Tockle interrupted, 'We need to tell our friend Biri to run away from her house – well, the stonemasons' storeroom in the Corte del Tagliapietra …'

'I know it well. As I said, I was made there,' said the statue impatiently. 'But I'd better not call out "Biri", had I, or those nasty old Fogs might guess what the game is.'

'It's not a game!' cried Amneris.

Tockle said, 'This is what you should say: "Tell John Chicken to fly!"'

He whispered to Amneris, 'John Chicken is Biri's secret name. She'll understand.'

'Whatever you say, I suppose.' The statue pursed its lips and cried out in its gravelly voice, 'Tell John Chicken to fly! Pass it on! Tell John Chicken to fly! Pass it on!'

The stone lions sunning themselves on the terrace of the Ca' Erizzo opened their sleepy eyes and listened.

'Yoohoo!' called the lions, 'Yoohoo! Tell the roast chicken to die! Pass it on!'

'Oh no!' said Tockle. 'They're making a mess of it!'

The statue sniffed, 'Typical! You do a human a favour and all you get is nitpicking. Stop worrying. These things have a way of working themselves out.'

Meanwhile, the lions' 'Yoohoo!' had caused a noisy consternation among the seven heads that adorned the front of the first of the four Mocenigo palaces.

'Never!' said a man's head. 'I'm not telling anyone what to do with their knickers!'

'Well, we don't have to agree with it. We just have to pass it on,' pointed out a woman.

The other heads chattered disapprovingly among themselves. Finally they yelled in a loud chorus, 'Hang your knickers out to dry! Pass it on!'

This was heard by two marble angels holding a shield on the top floor of the Ca' Garzoni.

'All right! All right!' called one of the angels grumpily. 'We heard you. Yes, of course, we'll pass it on. Yoohoo! Tell the fish supper to fry! Pass it on!'

At this point the message had already overtaken the Fogs who had in fact stopped for a glass of warm wine at a stall outside Ca' Rezzonico. Gossiping among themselves, they did not hear the statues' words. The statues chattered to one another all day long, and the Fogs were much more interested in the latest news about a shipment of muskets.

But the message for Biri was heard by the phoenix carved into a burnished stone panel on the first floor of the Ca' Viaro. He flapped a few feathers and squawked, 'Pass it on! Put your fist in your eye! Pass it on!'

The seahorses on the Ca' Corner Contarini dei Cavalli neighed loudly, 'There's thick mist in the sky! Pass it on!'

The angel on the Rialto Bridge passed it on to the kneeling Virgin Mary carved on the other side of the arch. She cried, 'There's a feast by and by! Pass it on!'

On the apricot wall above the balcony of the little palace next to the Ca' Michiel delle Colonne, the two figures nodded to one another, 'Greasy buns – buy! Buy! Buy! Pass it on!'

A pair of stone lions perched on a balcony at Ca' d'Oro took up the tale. One cried, 'Hip, hip, hooray!' But the other roared, more loudly, 'By the pirate's black eye! Pass it on!'

Two life-size statues at water level next door at the shining new Ca' Miani leaned out of their niches to call to the busts on the third floor. 'And don't ask us why!' they shouted, adjusting their loincloths. 'Pass it on!'

A rat carved into a fat white column at the jetty at San Felice chittered, 'It'd make a cat sigh! Pass it on!'

On the Palazzetto Barbarigo, a Madonna sheltering a cluster of stone people under her outspread cloak mourned, 'What a dreary goodbye! Pass it on!'

The toga-clad statues on the gates to the garden of Ca' Vendramin Calergi cocked their ears at the noise. They swivelled slightly and called down the canal, 'Bring me beer and cream pie! Pass it on!'

Finally a marble Virgin at the top of the Ca' Gatti Casazza bent to make sure she was hearing correctly. Then she called to the shaggy-legged eagle fixed to the side of her palace that faced the church of San Marcuola, 'It's urgent! Tell Biri to fly or she'll die!'

The eagle's head shifted in its bed of stucco, sending dust crumbling to the ground. He looked up to the Madonna as if to ask if it was truly acceptable for him to do the one thing forbidden to all bird statues in Venice – and the one thing they all longed to do: to break loose and stretch their wings. The Madonna nodded. With a caw of delight, the eagle erupted from his wall, circled three times for sheer joy, and then swooped down to the old stonemasons' courtyard to the door of the warehouse that Biri called home.

He tapped on the door with his beak before flying in the window.

'Belly up!' said Biri. 'Stone birds flying? You keep away from my insects, you! Or I'll pluck you somefing fierce!'

The eagle cast a longing eye at the moths that hovered around Biri's lantern.

Then it opened its beak and spoke. 'Message for you. "Tell Biri to fly. Or she'll die."'

'Fly?' Biri had leapt to her feet and grabbed the cage with the Scarlet Loory. 'How?'

'Get on my back,' cawed the eagle. 'I reckon I can get you to the other side of the canal, to Santa Croce. Then you're on your own, mind.'

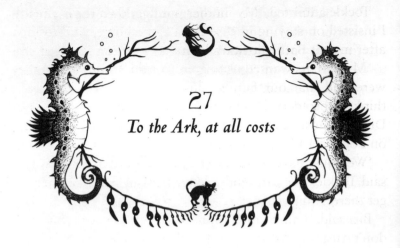

27
To the Ark, at all costs

The eagle dropped – rather literally dropped – Biri and her Scarlet Loory at the square of San Zan Degola, just as Amneris and Tockle arrived there. All three rushed together in a jumble of noses, elbows, tears and laughter.

'But,' said Biri inspecting her grazes, 'what zackly we got to laugh about?'

Tockle said grimly, 'Yes, it's only a matter of time before Maffeo denounces us too.'

'We's marked for Lambing,' said Biri. 'Ain't no doubt.'

'Three Lambs this time,' Amneris said. 'I heard Latenia's father say it.'

'That nasty Maffeo will make sure it's us,' said Biri. 'Latenia said he wanted the glory of handing us over. He'll get all the more glory if we are the Lambs.'

'We have to get on the Ark,' said Amneris. 'I didn't want to say it before, or even think it. But it's the only way. The boat's leaving this afternoon so it's too late to put our names down.'

166

Tockle admitted, 'My mother put me down for it already. I insisted on staying in case Papà came home. And to look after my cat Baffi. He hates boats.'

'My parents wanted us to go too,' said Amneris. 'But they were told that our family runs a necessary trade. I don't think embroidery is vital to the state, do you? So Signor Dubbini must have told his rich clients to use their influence on Fogfinger to trap us here.'

'We'll just have to sneak you two aboard as stowaways,' said Tockle. 'We can send a letter to your parents when we get there, Amneris.'

Biri said, 'I ain't going on no boat on no ocean voyage. I don't trust that Ark as far as I could frow it. Anyway, I would sick up my whole skeleton. And what 'bout our mission? We got to find out 'bout the Lambing. I been thinking 'bout that. Keep coming back to the same fing. The only way we can really find out about it … is to be Lambs ourselves.'

Amneris said, 'Surely the *Piccoli Pochi* don't want us Lambed? They are *against* the Lambing.'

Biri stuck out her chin. 'They told us when we joined that our lives would be in terrible danger from that moment forward.'

'But if we get Lambed ourselves, we'll probably die, so how can we tell them what happens? Ugo hasn't actually told us to get Lambed, has he?' Amneris appealed to Tockle.

Biri said, 'Isn't none of you *listening* to me?'

'We're listening and we're disagreeing,' said Tockle. 'We're disagreeing because we want to stay alive.'

The feet of at least a dozen Fogs thundered down the next *calle*. A rough voice shouted, 'Reports of three suspicious-looking children in San Zan Degola!'

'I'm already enjoying thinking about what we'll do to them when we get the little tykes.' The voice that barked these words was close – too close for comfort.

'We got to separate!' Biri hissed. 'Meet you behind the lions at Arsenale. In one hour.'

'What time does the Ark sail?' asked Amneris. 'Isn't it—'

Tockle looked at the clock on the church tower. 'In one hour and a quarter!' They scattered.

Tockle had to fetch Baffi and the special kaleidoscope, Sweet-Nizzi-on-the-Mantelpiece.

Sweet Nizzi fitted comfortably into his pocket, but Baffi refused to budge from his place in front of the embers of the fire.

When Tockle tried to pick him up, the cat clung to the rag rug.

Tockle promised, 'There'll be plenty of rats on the boat.'

Baffi yawned.

Tockle tried to appeal to Baffi's undoubted sense of adventure: 'Imagine being able to see Venice from a distance. Imagine travelling high above the waves ...'

'Actually, it's verrry nice,' said Baffi.

Tockle rubbed his eyes. 'I'm so tired and frightened I'm imagining things,' he told himself. 'And you know this, do you?' He spoke to the cat as if Baffi really had uttered human words.

In answer, Baffi rose and presented his neat left flank. In front of Tockle's eyes, a wing unfolded itself from the fur and fluttered gracefully. Then Baffi tucked it away again.

'So,' the cat said, 'I don't need to come on that leaky old Arrrk with you. Any time I want, I can fly high above the wavesss.'

'You really, really said that, didn't you?' Tockle asked. He leaned against the door, needing something sensible and solid behind his back. 'But cats don't fly and they don't talk.'

'That'sss where you're wrong. There is a generrral agreement among cats that we don't speak unless it's been prrroved that there'sss absolutely no other way of getting a human to understand what'sss what. And what's what is thisss: *I'm ssstaying.*'

'But I don't want to leave you,' pleaded Tockle. 'Especially now I know you can talk.'

'Shaveling thinksss there's something suspiciousss going on with that Arrrk.'

'Who's Shaveling? Another talking cat?'

'I don't like yourrr tone, boy.'

Tockle cried, 'Then you don't have to listen to it any more. I'm off.'

'Don't go!' miaowed Baffi to Tockle's retreating shadow.

Amneris did not want to tell her family where she was going. She was desperate not to worry them either.

She waited until she'd stopped panting before she inched up to her mother and gave her a hug. When might she be able to do that again?

'Mamma?' she began.

'Yes, my sweet? How is the Malipiero girl?'

'Latenia? Oh, well … the thing is … I'm going to stay with Biri for a few days. She has … a … bad cold. I'll take some sewing with me, so the orders won't suffer.'

'I'll come with you and see to the poor girl. She does not look after herself! *Why* won't she come and live with us? So stubborn! I'll bring her some food and a *tisana*.' Her mother put down her lace bobbin.

'No, no, Mamma! It's not serious, honestly. I'll take her some of your apricot tea myself—'

The argument went on for fifteen minutes that Amneris

didn't have. In the end, after whispering her secret in Grillo's feathery ear, she simply ran out of the house, clutching a little bundle of clothes and food.

Grillo yowled after her. His frantic miaows sounded strangely like 'Don't goooo!'

Clutching the searing stitches in their sides, Tockle and Amneris hobbled up to the lions at Arsenale as the clock struck a quarter to four. Biri was waiting for them with her parrot and a very small sack of provisions. The three of them peered through the two towers that guarded the entrance to the Arsenale's private harbour.

'That must be the Ark!' pointed Biri. 'But—'

They were shocked to see that the Ark was an old sailing ship in a perilously shabby state. She looked more like a prison hulk than a vessel to take people to paradise. Venetians crowded on deck. On many faces, fear and doubt mingled with grief. If the Ark was a trap, it was still their only hope of saving their children from the Redentore Lambing.

'Hey!' Tockle shouted. 'She's moving!'

The Ark had cast off and was already being towed towards the mouth of the harbour.

'She left early!' gasped Biri. 'I guess they wanted to stop stowaways from creeping on at the last minute.'

'Why didn't we come straight here?' lamented Amneris.

'We're dead,' said Tockle.

28
The right answer

Thursday June 26th, 1783

In his private drawing room, Fogfinger was surrounded by weapons arranged in vases like brutal flowers: daggers, swords, bayonets, carbines, rifles, blunderbusses, knuckledusters, Hottentot clubs, Mexican lassoes. One vase bore a discreet sign, '*Peruvian poison arrows. Do not dust.*'

Fogfinger told Latenia, 'Here are more presents for you.'

She mumbled, her eyes downcast, 'I don't want anything to do with you. If you gave me a musket, I would turn it on you. Why did you have me brought here?'

Fogfinger swivelled his ear trumpet towards her. 'I see you are choking on admiration for me. But do try to speak up, my dear.'

Her father forced Latenia's chin upwards, and tweaked her nose painfully. 'Answer clearly when you are spoken to. And *appropriately.*'

Fogfinger smiled. 'Now, I have some questions for you. Has anyone been trying to communicate with you? I speak particularly of recent weeks. Did you never receive any secret notes that you can show me?'

Latenia shook her head. No letters ever arrived for her at all, in fact, except Fogfinger's own silk handkerchiefs with their sentimental sweet nothings that made her shudder. She had no friends to send her letters.

Self-pity engulfed Latenia. Her only real friends were Amneris, Tockle and Biri, and they probably couldn't write. Amneris had refused to save her from the betrothal – which, she supposed, meant that the girl was more on the side of Fogfinger than the *Pochi*. But ... Amneris was poor, so ... so shouldn't she hate Fogfinger ... ? It was so confusing that it made Latenia's head hurt.

'The girl is distracted,' observed Fogfinger. 'Or is she just a bit simple?'

Latenia said clearly, 'Nothing has come,' muttering under her breath, 'nothing that you don't know about already, you old goat.'

Or had something come?

Latenia thought again about those little notes in the invisible stitching. Why would Fogfinger try to communicate with her like that? He had no need for secrecy, not with all Venice terrified of him, or in his pay and with the contract signed for her betrothal. But Fogfinger did not seem to know about the letters. If he did, now would be the moment to say something, to boast about his cleverness. It would not be like him to neglect an opportunity to do so.

If those loving notes did not come from Fogfinger then ... ?

I think of you, little one. Do not think badly of me.

Do not believe everything they say about me, my child.

My child! A *mother* might say that to her daughter. Of course, Fogfinger and her father had tried to tell her that her mother was a runaway and a disgrace. And if she was a good mother, how could she leave her children? But when Latenia recalled who had been telling her these things, their words were instantly transformed into lies.

A thought opened up in her mind like a flower. What if her mother was not in Paris? What if she had been kept away, rather than running away? Her father never mentioned her without an expression of hate on his face.

The more she thought about it, the more Latenia became convinced that her mother had been trying to make contact with her! Amneris had not betrayed her – she was trying to help. Suddenly, in the midst of all her woes, Latenia felt a sharp joy.

'Why is the girl smiling like a loon?' Fogfinger asked suspiciously.

'Your kindness is overwhelming,' she said dutifully. 'I am smiling at my great good fortune to be your bride. In four years' time, of course.'

'The right answer. And as you are proving so sweetly tractable today, I must have something from you. I believe that you have – accidentally, of course – been associating with some rather dangerous children. Your brother has informed me that you've even invited them into your house.'

'My brother?' Latenia began to tremble.

'Obviously, in your ignorance, you did not realize they were plotting to gain your confidence so they might find a way to get to me through you.'

Latenia knew a trap when she heard one. She dared not defend Amneris, Tockle and Biri. She kept her lips firmly pressed shut, and smiled as stupidly as she knew how.

Biri, Tockle and Amneris huddled under an upturned gondola on the slipway at San Trovaso. It had been their home since the Ark sailed the day before. None of them was accustomed to luxury, but they were accustomed to a real roof of sorts over their heads at night.

The shock of watching the Ark sail had given way to a kind of edgy optimism in Biri's case, and a desperate fear in Amneris's. Tockle was trying to calculate their next step. Did Maffeo know where he and Amneris lived? Was it safe to go to one of their homes? Or would they have to take up permanent residence under this boat at the gondola workshop at San Trovaso? If they did, was that really what you'd call living? Waiting in despair for the Fogs to come and take them? And what would they do for food?

'Miaow!'

'Baffi! How did you find me here?' Tockle stroked the cat's ears. 'What's that in your mouth? Oh, thank you! Clever cat! He talks, you know.'

Biri scoffed, 'Yes, he says "miaow". Very clever, him.'

'Miaow,' said Baffi.

'No, he really talks, but only when he feels like it – oh, never mind. Let's eat.'

He tore the ham roll Baffi had brought into three equal pieces. The cat refused to speak in front of the girls and quickly loped off.

'Typical!' thought Tockle.

With a little food inside them, a sense of hope returned. And an idea.

'Let's go to Ugo,' said Tockle. 'He's never had contact with Maffeo. He's already poxed – the Fogs won't bother with him now. He needs to know we've been betrayed. He'll tell us what to do.'

29
Rather dangerous children

'In spite of their mischievous ways, I'd *really* like to meet your dear friends. In fact, I have presents for them too,' purred Fogfinger.

Latenia knew all too well about the dangers of accepting gifts from Fogfinger, but she forced herself to say, 'How generous, Sir!'

'I know.' He pointed to a hanging lantern in the shape of a glass parrot, with a candle in its hollow green belly. 'For Biri.'

'I don't know any Biri.' Latenia did not know why she lied, but she had an instinct it was the right thing to do.

'Ah, but your brother tells me that you know the girl in question quite well in fact. You must have just forgotten for a moment. And here's a Mathematical Machinator for your friend Amneris. I understand she is a good little arithmetist.'

'Who?'

'And a cat automaton for your friend Temistocle. All you

175

have to do is tell me where they're hiding, and I'll have my men deliver these lovely gifts to them.'

'But I don't know where they are!' screamed Latenia. 'How would I?'

She dared not say, 'And I would not tell you if I did.'

'So you admit you know who they are? Just your little game, to pretend you didn't? Not a very good little game. The kind of game where someone might get hurt.' There was no mistaking the menace in Fogfinger's voice.

Latenia whimpered, 'They have been to our palace, to deliver things, you know. The poor send their children on errands.'

A rustle of silk and a slither of embroidered stockings announced Maffeo's arrival. He made a theatrical bow to Fogfinger, who chuckled, 'Ah, just the thing, just the thing. Welcome, my dear boy! The information about the seahorses is proving most useful.'

With a pang, Latenia understood that Maffeo had already made himself a favourite of her future fiancé by telling tales on her friends.

Maffeo got straight down to business. 'In exchange for this list of automata, *I* can tell you where the guttersnipes live, Sir. My sister doesn't have any wits, Sir. I'm like you, Sir. I make it my business to know. And speaking of business ...'

He handed over a sheet of paper covered with his rather childish handwriting. Latenia glimpsed the words '*Flying machine, monkey valet with functioning tail ...*'

Fogfinger dropped the list on the floor without looking at it. Maffeo wrinkled his nose, but continued hopefully, 'I made some enquiries.'

He picked up his list of gifts and held it out again. 'Sir, you'll find Amneris D'Ago at the Calle Berlendis in Cannaregio.'

'Well done, boy.' Fogfinger took the paper.

'And Temistocle Molin is at the Corte Giovanelli at San Zan Degola.'

'Ah yes, his father is in the *Pochi*. We know that house.'

'And the one they call Biri – as you know already, she lives at the Corte del Tagliapietra at San Marcuola. In a warehouse. She sleeps on a shelf, I believe.' Maffeo's lip curled. 'But the big news is they've got another friend. He's called something or other. And he's the leader of their gang, really.'

'I am sure you will remember his name.' There was a slight edge to Fogfinger's voice.

Latenia shivered as Maffeo answered, 'Presently. I must do more research. If I find this leader, I require an undertaking that I'll not be sent to Dalmatia as the son of the admiral usually is.'

'I understand,' said Fogfinger. 'You have the makings of a first-rate spy. And I love the way you are prepared to betray even young children.'

'Drossi!' he shouted. Lardo Drossi appeared instantly from a side door. 'Send men to these addresses. Capture all children who dwell there. You don't need to be too careful about breaking arms or noses if they put up a fight.'

Fogfinger grinned, 'Now Maffeo, I'm about to give you your first taste of honour and power. How would you like to be the Master of Ceremonies at the Grand Ball to mark my betrothal to your sister?'

'With a mechanical butler to announce me?' asked Maffeo. 'And the seat of honour at the high table?'

'Whatever you like by the way of grandeur shall be yours, boy.'

'Hmmm?' Maffeo, Latenia realized, was lost in dreams of his night of triumph.

Fogfinger turned to Lardo Drossi. 'Take the girl home

to her father. She's not turning out to be much use at all. Her skin's all blotchy – she needs that cunning cosmetic treatment you've told me about – raw strips of veal soaked in milk on her face every night. See to it, Drossi.'

Drossi gurgled with mirth. Fogfinger ordered, 'Tell her father that if the fiancée proves defective, the dowry is still forfeit.'

After Lardo Drossi left, the walls of Alvise Malipiero's study seemed dark with the imprint of his ugly words. Malipiero paced the floor. Suddenly, he turned to face Latenia. 'You might as well get used to it. And you may not enjoy living here much longer. I'm looking for a new wife, one with a fine fat dowry to replenish the cost of selling you to Fogfinger.'

'But my mother is still alive! You cannot marry again while she lives.'

'I'll have her declared dead. I have a Gradenigo or a Memmo in mind. A Golden Book family, anyway. Fit for an admiral like me. My next children will be true princes.'

'Next children?' asked Latenia faintly.

'Well, of course my new wife must breed.'

Other children in the palace? Other children who would be treated more nicely than Latenia and Maffeo?

She said, 'What if the *Piccoli Pochi* win, and Fogfinger is brought down?'

'Since when are you interested in politics, Latenia? The *Piccoli Pochi* are on their last legs. It is only a matter of time before they take a wrong step. By trying to recruit the bride of Fogfinger, of course, they have opened their web of young spies for our inspection. They will be brought down, like your mother—'

178

'You want her dead, don't you?' Latenia whispered. 'Did you never love her?'

'Love? What's that worth? I valued her, and then she lost her value by running away. Now I hate her because she stands in the way of my bettering myself. Simple as that.'

Latenia could not avoid the thought that was only a logical extension: 'If I do not do what he wants, I shall lose my value and stand in the way of him bettering himself. Simple as that.'

30
Baffi's friend

Thursday June 26th, 1783

Unbeknown to Tockle, his cat Baffi had friends in high places. Notably, he was friends with a certain cat who was kept by Fogfinger to protect his kitchens against the rats. Fogfinger had never yet perfected a cat automaton. He'd made mechanical cats that looked soft and luxurious as a proper animal, but he had never been able to make a cat who could capture and despatch a wily Venetian rodent.

So if he needed a rat dealt with, Fogfinger sent his real cat Shaveling, so named because some cruel Fogs had taken a razor to his tail. Now it was bald like a rat's except for a ridiculous pompom at the end.

Not being very presentable, and therefore liable to be kicked and shouted at if he presented himself, Shaveling had made a secret nest for himself among the spare cushions kept in a wicker basket at the back of Fogfinger's bath chair. From that vantage point, he often eavesdropped on his master's business.

Now Shaveling was a fine ratter but he did not consent

to be kept inside the palace at all times. He was a roamer and extremely sociable too. He loved to talk of the great things afoot at the Natural History Museum, keeping half the cats of Venice much better informed than the humans. Shaveling's late-night expeditions had brought him into contact with Tockle's cat Baffi and Amneris's Grillo. And his ears had pricked up when he heard Baffi's and Grillo's humans named by Maffeo.

He slipped from behind the cushions, made his way through a tunnel of velvet curtains, padded down the marble stairs and was out of the pantry window and across the garden before Lardo Drossi had even left the building.

'It's all right, Shaveling, the young ones are already safely in hiding,' said Baffi.

'Thank goodness they did not get on the Arrrk,' added Grillo.

'Some of my family did,' mourned Baffi.

'We have to do sssomething about that boy, Maffeo,' said Grillo. 'My second master – you know, the apothecary – says that some of those stupid Fancy Stockings wrecked his shop the other day. Maffeo Malipiero was one of them. Now he's causing trrrouble for my mistress. Loaded up with ssspite to the muzzle, and dangerous with it.'

'Curse him, I say,' growled Baffi.

'I sssuppose you know a friendly witch who'll do that?' sighed Grillo.

'Why do we need a witch? I can do a Cat Curse myssself,' said Baffi.

'Wish his milk will go sour? Wish his herrings will be rrrotten?' Shaveling sniffed.

'You're not taking me ssseriously,' warned Baffi.

181

'That'sss not ever a good idea with a cat,' said Grillo.

'So what kind of cursesss can you do?' asked Shaveling.

'Lots,' said Baffi airily. 'I can do a Featherrrs-in-the-Mouth where the human never stops being thirsssty and keeps licking his paw, I mean hand. Orrr I've got a great one for making your ear rrreally infected, as if you have ear mitesss. It is terribly uncomfortable and can lead to madness in the end. Or the one about the fleas of a thousand dogsss infesting your arrrmpits.'

'I don't think those are going to get Maffeo out of the way.'

'Aw,' said Grillo. 'Why not give it our best ssshot?'

'The Toothache Curse?' purred Baffi. 'It's almost not worth bothering for a boy who eatsss so much cake. He's going to end up at the apothecary'sss for a pulling some day sssoon, without my help.'

'But what if all three of us curse his teeth at the sssame time,' said Grillo. 'Ssso every single one, top and bottom, is on fire with pain?'

'We-ell,' said Baffi, 'I suppose so. If we do this for about four daysss.'

Grillo added, 'With sleep and food brrreaks every fifteen minutesss.'

'Of course.'

The three cats hunkered down, closed their eyes, and began to yowl.

31
The bells of San Salvador

A mneris, Tockle and Biri found Ugo by the window, staring into the three canals below, his eyes shining.

'Perfect timing. You must take me down to the water,' Ugo urged. 'I have succeeded in contacting the … I must join them now.'

'Ugo, didn't you hear what we said?' Tockle pleaded. 'We have been betrayed. And you might be too. Who are "they"? Who must you join now?'

'In due course you shall understand, but for now it would be dangerous for you to know,' said Ugo. 'Now if the worst happens – please remember me saying this: "*It will all be all right.*" They … have explained to me what happens. But it must still be kept a secret, even from you. I'm sorry. So,' his voice rose, 'please take me to the canal.'

'How?'

'Lift the wheelchair down the stairs to the front door. And then you can carry me out to the canal. Tockle, I'm half the weight I was. You can do it. And you *must* do it now, while my mother is at church.'

It was true: Ugo was a slight weight. The three of them easily carried the chair down the stairs. When Tockle picked Ugo up, his bones felt as brittle as icicles. As he carried the boy in his arms, he was close enough to hear Ugo's painful wheezing.

'What do you want me to do with you?' he asked. A dark suspicion was forming in his mind. Was Ugo in so much pain? Could he really want to—

'Is it eleven o'clock yet?' Ugo's voice trembled lightly. 'It must be eleven. They wait for me every day at eleven. They watch for my signal – I flash a mirror from the window upstairs.'

The bells of San Salvador began to toll.

Ugo ordered, 'Throw three stones in the canal right now!'

Tockle worried that Ugo's keen brain had finally been affected by the poxing.

But he raked the crumbling wall for pieces of stone and threw them in.

'Thank you,' said Ugo. 'That is the signal they're waiting for, you see.'

Tockle didn't see at all.

Ugo smiled, 'Now, on the eleventh stroke, you are to throw *me* in the canal.'

'No!' cried Biri and Amneris in one voice.

Amneris was crying. She took one of Ugo's hands into hers and begged him, 'Please don't give up hope.'

Ugo replied calmly, 'Hope is the last thing I will give up. Throw me, please, Tockle. It is time.'

'Ugo, you are too weak to swim. The water is awfully cold,' protested Tockle.

'Stop arguing with me. Just throw me. I'll die if you *don't* do it.'

Nothing in Tockle wanted to cast his frail burden into the dark water of the canal. But there was something compelling in Ugo's sureness. And in his heart, Tockle knew it was true: Ugo was dying. He might have one last choice: *how* he died. Was drowning better than choking on your last drawn-out breath as your lungs collapsed? Tockle felt oddly distant from it all: he fancied he heard sweet singing in his ears and all the colours of painted stone and water seemed somehow more intense and yet intermingled. As in a dream, the strangest things seemed to make sense.

Still, it was the hardest thing he had ever done, to take the few steps to the edge of the canal and release Ugo's body into the water as the bells tolled for the eleventh time.

The dark green waves swallowed the boy in a moment.

Tockle's dream dissolved abruptly. The girls were staring at him, open-mouthed with horror.

Suddenly Ugo rose to the surface, smiling. His eyes met Tockle's, and he mouthed the words, 'These things have a way of working out.'

'How could he be *smiling*?' agonized Tockle. 'He's about to drown. Because of what I did.'

An azure tail thrashed the water near Ugo. And a pair of pearly arms rose and fastened themselves around Ugo's waist, lifting him up and settling him on top of a muscular scaled back. Then, as if seated on a living throne, Ugo sped through the water, disappearing from sight as the Bareteri Canal turned sharply into the Rio della Fava.

'Is that ... was that ... the Judas Crocodile?' Biri's voice came from high in her throat. 'Did we just Lamb that poor boy?'

'It can't be!' Tockle refused to believe he had just dropped his friend into the jaws of a monster. 'The Crocodile agreed to eat children only if they were Lambed.'

'Not very honest, that Crocodile, though,' Biri pointed

out. 'It betrayed its own friend to Fogfinger. If that's true, of course. Perhaps it ain't, as it were Fogfinger who said it.'

Amneris broke in. 'But that … thing … wasn't big enough. Or dark enough to be a crocodile. Was it?'

'And it had pinky-white arms,' said Tockle.

Signora Paolin appeared from the direction of San Salvador.

'Hello, my dears,' she said. 'I thought you'd be upstairs visiting Ugo. He seemed a little over-excited this morning. Such a hug he gave me! He said he'd had a message. Was it from you?'

32
A better place?

It was impossible to explain to Ugo's mother that her son had been hugging her goodbye.

Tockle bolted around the corner, feeling as cowardly as a hyena. The girls followed him. So, five minutes later, did the cries of Signora Paolin, who had discovered the empty chair and the emptier bedroom upstairs.

'Lady's got her faith, ain't she?' panted Biri. 'We could go back and tell her that her boy's gone to a better place.'

Amneris looked as stricken as Tockle felt.

'Why did we do what he said?' she lamented. 'We must have been mad! What must poor Signora Paolin be feeling now?'

'Can you imagine what a wonderful son Ugo was?' said Tockle. 'He was kind and clever and gentle. Signora Paolin is a widow. Ugo's her only family. She may allow that his soul goes to heaven – but she will never forgive us for taking him away from her.'

'Even though Ugo had decided that it was his time?' asked Biri.

'Signora Paolin will call the Fogs and denounce us for murdering him,' said Amneris. 'All three of us. She saw the guilty looks on our faces.'

'We's on the run already,' said Biri. 'And if they catch us now, you know what will happen?'

'We have to disappear,' whispered Amneris. 'Our homes will be the first place they look.'

'Where can we go?'

At that moment Tockle almost wished that the silvery blue tail and the pearly arms would rise out of the canal and take all three of them wherever it had carried Ugo.

He could not rid his mind of the thought that Ugo had seemed to know what would happen in the water. He'd said he had an *appointment*: 'They are waiting for me.' And he was visibly happy to go.

But no, Tockle would have to think of his own kind of escape. He looked at the two girls – Biri so sturdy and defiant, Amneris so delicate and distressed. He'd get them into his *sandolo* and row out to Poveglia, to the *Pochi*.

The most important thing now was speed. Fortunately, the *sandolo* was not far away.

'To the boat,' he told the girls.

'*That* boat?' asked Biri, pointing. 'That green one? Belly up!'

And indeed that was what the *sandolo* was doing – floating half-submerged in the canal.

33
Wanted for torture and murder

'That looks a bit like Amneris!'

Latenia ordered the gondola to stop so she could lift her veil and take a closer look at a poster hanging from a bridge. Three familiar faces were pictured above the words.

**WANTED FOR THE CRUEL TORTURE
and MURDER**
of the helpless cripple, Ugo Paolin
Do you know these wicked children?
Temistocle Molin,
Ermintrudina 'Biri' Fava
& Amneris D'Ago?
Substantial reward for their capture

'Well, I never!' exclaimed Latenia. 'Murderers all the time. And torturers. Who'd have thought it? And I let them come into my bedroom and eat my cakes!'

189

Doubt, an unusual thing for Latenia, entered her head. She mused, 'But it was Amneris who showed me how to read those letters from my mother.'

Amneris's sweet old-fashioned face swam up in Latenia's memory. It was not the face of a liar. Or a murderer. Or a torturer. Tockle's tense, sincere features joined Amneris's in Latenia's mind. 'They did not *seem* like murderers. I don't suppose that there has been some mistake? Anyway, I don't like seeing them like this.'

Being a girl who until recently never put up with anything she didn't like, Latenia ripped the poster off the bridge and crumpled it up. Then she told the gondolier, 'Proceed!'

A minute later they passed another poster, and another. Even with the floor of the gondola heaped with posters, there were still more on every corner of every alley and every canal. Latenia did not give up until her hands were sore and bleeding.

But eventually she had to go home, little as she wanted to – for home, these days, meant the daily torture of deportment lessons with the Lardo Drossi and his wife, and the nightly outrage of milky strips of veal on her face.

Back at the Malipiero palace, Melchior Dubbini was waiting for Latenia with two new bolts of embroidered white fabric.

'I told you I never wanted to see your slimy face again!' she told him.

'Obviously,' he simpered, 'we shall not soil your home any longer with the work of that young murderess. So I've made haste to bring you some new material from some girls I've hand-trained almost from birth to do the most exquisite sewing.'

'So *you* think Amneris hurt that crippled boy?' Latenia

asked, fingering the silk. Her eyes were irresistibly drawn to it. They found fault. The workmanship, while lovely, was nothing like as brilliant as the D'Ago family's stitching. Of course Latenia had no idea that Signor Dubbini's pale girls were starved of light as he was too mean to allow them lamps until the darkness was profound.

The fact was that Latenia needed a new dress. Indeed, the matter was urgent. She was worried about what her father had said, about three children being Lambed at Redentore. Was that a coincidence? She was thinking that she'd go to Fogfinger and explain the mistake about Amneris, Tockle and Biri. She'd have to argue against Maffeo. But as Fogfinger's fiancée-to-be, her word would surely have some value? If she did such a thing, she'd need to look like a princess.

But now she was also aware of the need to save money.

'How much is this one?' She pointed to the bolt on the left.

'Ten *ducati* is a bargain ...'

'And the other?'

'Ah, what exquisite taste you have, my lady. Of course you would pick that one. It is, of course, fifteen *ducati*.'

'What is the difference then?'

'Why, five *ducati*, my dear, but you've no need to worry your pretty head about sums.'

Latenia thought, 'That's where you're wrong, you nasty old wormtongue.'

'I shall keep them both overnight and make my decision tomorrow,' she told him firmly.

He simpered and rubbed his hands.

'Why are you still here?' asked Latenia.

'Wanted for Torture and Murder?' Biri's voice rose from its normal gruffness to shrill disbelief as she read the poster the Fogs had nailed on the gates of the *squero* overnight.

They were back hiding under the upturned gondola. It was starting to feel like home under the black-painted arch. A damp, stone-floored, comfortless home. But it felt safe, at least. Baffi had just dragged in a whole roast chicken. And the weather continued warm.

Amneris lamented, 'They say that we tortured poor Ugo? How could they lie like that? Have they even found his body?'

Tockle said, 'No, not a trace of it has been found, I'm sure. The torture charge is fabricated to make people hate us. Fogfinger wants to get the city's blood up. We will be made scapegoats for all the discontent in Venice, you realize that? And next he'll associate us with the *Piccoli Pochi* – don't you doubt it for a minute. Anything to get his hands on us.'

34

The worst toothache in the world since day one, ever

Sunday June 29th – Monday June 30th, 1783

Maffeo had never known pain like it. Every tooth seemed to be burning with a separate fire. He woke screaming, his eyes bubbling with tears.

His mechanical valet had dressed him with difficulty and the butler had bundled him into the gondola.

Now they were standing in the apothecary's shop, specially opened on the Sabbath when Maffeo threatened to smash down the door. Maffeo was still gibbering and dribbling with pain, quite oblivious to the beautiful room in which tall dark shelves were lined with majolica and glass jars, and the smell of herbs – deliciously clean and faintly medicinal – filled the air. There was still a little pile of broken jars from the raid Maffeo and his *Compagnie della Calza* friends had mounted for a prank a few weeks before. But Maffeo barely remembered that: his toothache pushed every other thought from his mind.

The apothecary, dressed in a long yellow robe and white cap, frowned over the top of his spectacles as he forced

Maffeo's clenched jaw open.

'You must brace yourself,' he said, 'for some major extractions. You know the saying – away with the tooth, away with the pain.'

Maffeo screamed again. 'Don't patronize me with stupid proverbs, old man! I'm the most intelligent person in this town. You don't have to tell me anything. I know it all. Your job is to be silent and fix this.'

The apothecary forced his little wooden stick deeper into Maffeo's mouth. He tapped the teeth one by one.

'But this is strange,' he mused, putting down his pen and making copious notes in his day book. 'Very strange.'

'You mean you can't do anything?' sobbed Maffeo. 'You useless, vile man. Don't you realize who I am? Fogfinger's particular favourite! I'll have him shut you down. I'll … ah! I think I'm dying. Aaah!'

The apothecary stood pale and dignified under the verbal assault that ended with a howl. Then he said, 'Just to be sure, young sir, is the pain as if a cat's claw is raking through your gums, shredding the soft tissue?'

'Yeesss!' howled Maffeo.

'And do you hear in your head a kind of hum or buzzing that might approximate a cat's purr?'

'I told you that I did. Are you deaf? Every throb of pain will cost you, I assure you.'

'And can you taste in your mouth a kind of fishy breath?' asked the apothecary in a composed voice.

'Can't you smell the stink from there?'

'Indeed I can. So the matter is settled. There is little I can offer against a Cat Curse,' the apothecary said. 'The best I can suggest is that if you have offended any cats, or the owners of any cats, you must apologize and make good.'

'You're joking!' screeched Maffeo. 'Cats? Cats are good for kicking only. And the same for people who are soft on them.'

The apothecary and his handsome cat gazed at Maffeo with hatred.

Unseen by his second master and his second master's client, the apothecary's cat now rose from his cushion by the fireplace and jumped up to the desk. He ran his paw down the notes in the apothecary's day book until he came to the name of this disagreeable patient. His little triangular mouth opened to mime the name 'Maffeo Malipiero'.

'Might have guesssed!' Grillo hissed quietly. He jumped off the desk and made a discreet departure through a window.

Meanwhile, inside the shop, Maffeo was still berating the apothecary.

'If you refuse to placate the cats,' replied the apothecary, 'the only treatment I know is the Celtic Skull-cure. Go to a churchyard alone by night, to the corner where bones from the old graves lie in a heap. Choose a skull and bring it home. Fill the skull with water, and drink deeply from it.'

'Stop!' Maffeo struck the man on the side of his head, knocking off his spectacles.

But the apothecary continued calmly, 'You must drink everything from the hollow of the skull, including all the dust and little pieces of something-or-other that float inside the water. In fact, they will do you the most good of all. Having done that, your toothache will go away. Maybe. I can do nothing more for you.'

35
Son and daughters of traitors

Friday July 4th, 1783

Exactly as Tockle had predicted, few days passed before new handbills were pasted on the city walls. Baffi arrived under the gondola with a damp torn one rolled up in his jaws. He dropped it in front of Tockle and batted it emphatically with his paw. Tockle read aloud to the girls:

JUST REVEALED
Child Fiends are Son and Daughters
of Known Terrorists!
Temistocle Molin & Biri Fava
- two of the Gang of Three
who tortured and drowned a crippled boy -
are the children of members of the
PICCOLI POCHI
Spawn of the devilish traitors!
Links to violent criminals in exile!
Increased reward
for information leading to their arrests.

'Someone won't be able to resist the mention of "increased reward",' said Amneris. Baffi nudged her hand in agreement.

'Absolutely not,' said a smooth male voice. 'Chaps, turn the boat over. There's gold here for us.'

'I know who that is!' cried Amneris. 'No!'

The gondola creaked loudly as strong hands pushed it off its stand, revealing Amneris, Biri and Tockle cowering on the slipway. Baffi arched his back and hissed.

Signor Dubbini stood rubbing his hands. 'Nice to see you again, girlie mine,' he said to Amneris. 'You've found a new way of making money for me. Reward money, no less.'

He ordered the six Fogs behind him, 'Seize them. And you know where to take them. There shall be universal pleasure at the capture of these devilspawn.'

'Of course *you* know all about devils!' whispered Amneris.

'Signor Slime!' said Biri. 'You're exactly what I 'sposed you would be!'

36
All kinds of uses

Friday July 4th, 1783

'Now that I have you, I have all kinds of uses for you.' Fogfinger's smile was wide. An ostrich feather fan floated around him, gracefully dispelling the hot air. Tockle, Biri and Amneris stood in front of him, shackled at the ankles and with their arms tied behind them.

'First of all, there's this one.' Fogfinger held out a piece of paper. 'It's a new announcement for the *Postiglione*.'

Murdering Child-Fiends apprehended!
Guilty verdicts certain;
Grand Triple Lambing on Redentore Sunday
to mark the Betrothal of our Leader.
The murdering thug Temistocle Molin and his friends
to be spared only
if his traitor father gives himself up in their place.

Biri, Amneris and Tockle stared in silence at the words and the smoke curling from their captor's fingers.

'My father is too poorly to come from Egypt,' thought Tockle. 'The journey alone would kill him … and then Fogfinger would.'

Tockle said quietly, 'I shall not allow you to use me as bait.'

'What alternative do you have?' asked Fogfinger.

Amneris said, 'We could *offer* to be Lambed.'

'But Amneris,' Tockle stared at her, 'your parents are both here in Venice, and they're not in the *Piccoli Pochi*. You don't have to do this. Not for my father. You don't even know him.'

'I know *you*,' said Amneris, quietly.

'It's an interesting suggestion,' said Fogfinger. 'And the girl who made it surely deserves the honour of being the first of you to be Lambed. This gets better and better.'

Fogfinger hummed gaily as he seized a quill and added some lines to the poster.

What kind of people are the *Piccoli Pochi*?
The kind who will allow their own children to be Lambed
rather than give themselves up to the law.

'That's *worse*,' groaned Tockle. 'You shame my father. Of course he'll give himself up for execution if you make it a choice between him and me.'

'But I understand your father is far away,' said Fogfinger, 'and not in the best of health.'

Tockle realized, 'He doesn't know exactly where my father is. He's fishing for information.'

He gave warning glances to Biri and Amneris, who nodded.

Fogfinger said, 'Within two weeks the *Postiglione* will be at the furthest corners of the Mediterranean Sea.'

Tockle grimaced, 'But it's only two weeks till the

Redentore. If my father comes back, we will already be dead, and he'll have given himself up for nothing.'

'Beautiful, isn't it? So, we have two girls and a boy for Lambing,' said Fogfinger, smiling, 'followed by the return of a traitor. The timing should be just about perfect: Rizardo Molin will have a *hope* of saving his son, but not enough time to actually do it.'

'The only traitor in Venice is the one sitting in your chair!' shouted Biri. 'Look at you! You're on *fire* with badness!'

'Smouldering a bit, perhaps,' laughed Fogfinger.

'This is the worst!' cried Tockle.

Amneris suddenly remembered the words Ugo had uttered with such conviction before he ordered them to throw him in the canal.

'Now if the worst happens – please remember me saying this: "*It will all be all right.*"'

'Now the worst has happened,' Amneris thought, 'and there is no possibility of it being all right.'

'Take them away. Solitary confinement in the *piombi*, times three!' Fogfinger ordered his captain. 'Cells spaced wide apart, so they can't talk.'

He turned back to the children. 'It's a kindness, really. Two weeks as my guests in lead-lined cells at the top of the Doge's Palace in this heat – alone, with short water rations – why, it will make you grateful to be Lambed, my dears. And marinating in fear is worse than actually dying.'

'How do you know that the Fate in the Box will kill us?' asked Biri. 'Maybe it'll send us home happy. Did you ever think of that?'

In answer, Fogfinger brayed with laughter and the smoke poured out of his fingertips.

37
No appetite for Lamb?

Saturday July 19th – Sunday July 20th, 1783

On the night before a Lambing, Fogfinger had trestle tables full of food laid out in the poorer streets of Venice. Despite the hunger that growled in their bellies, the Venetians, heartsick at the prospect of losing another child, would never touch the feast. It seemed wrong to fill their mouths when a child was most likely about to die. The three children to be Lambed this time had been incarcerated up in the roof of the Doge's Palace for the last two weeks, and no one had been allowed to visit them, even send a note. Some whispered that the little ones could not have survived the pitiless heat of those infamous lead-lined rooms.

Fogs soon devoured the spurned food.

This year, preparations were muted for Redentore. The shopkeepers did not bother with the Chinese lanterns or paper chains. Boys and girls did not pester their parents to start decorating their boats early. The strolling tradesmen did poor business.

By the eve of this strange, sad Redentore, Venice seemed

like a city in mourning, not one about to celebrate its favourite festival. A few boats straggled out to the *bacino*. Only the rich attended the festivities on *il galleggiante*, watching the fireworks in splendid isolation. They had brought automata to do the cheering for them.

This time, for once, even the poor Venetians were invited to *il Grande Ballo dell'Amore e della Morte* – the Grand Ball of Love and Death, to prolong the party after the fireworks, presided over by Maffeo Malipiero in the fanciest stockings that anyone had ever seen, though his expression was far from cheerful and his hand was clasped to his grimacing jaw.

Maffeo had stood at the great gates of the palace, ready to condescend to his guests. But the rich were already tired out by the fireworks. And the poor were nowhere to be found. They were all at home, praying for the Lambs and fretting about their family and friends on the Ark. Nothing had been heard from them.

So the echoing halls of the Doge's Palace, hung with streamers, stood almost empty apart from a few sullen Fancy Stockings, who dared not turn down their chief bully's invitation.

Amneris was to be the first Lamb, just as Fogfinger had promised.

In her stifling cell, she listened to the fireworks. A tiny, high window let in their colours, dulled by the sheets of lead that lined the walls.

Then she lay sleepless on her pallet, thinking about Biri and Tockle. She'd tried tapping and calling their names, but there'd been no response. So the last two weeks had limped along in a lonely, hopeless daze of searing heat. But tonight

202

– her last night, she thought – the minutes seemed to be galloping. She tried to think of what the *Pochi* said, that the Primaeval Crocodile did not eat the Lambs.

But then why, she asked herself, don't the Lambs come back? Perhaps the fall is fatal? But why do they find no bodies? There must be something down there below the Frari.

Her memory hovered over the image of the vast skeleton in the museum, now fully re-skinned. She thought of the metre-long jaws, the underwater howls in the night. Clutching her blue glass seahorse, which she'd unpicked from the hem of her skirt, she lay gasping in the soupy air.

She must have dozed, because morning came abruptly. After so many days without human contact – just trays pushed through a slot in her door – Amneris was dragged out of her cell and hustled down three flights of stairs to a mirrored room. Fogfinger's minions were both so big and so coarse that Amneris felt as vulnerable as an insect in their presence.

The woman who rough-handled Amneris into her Lambing clothes was the shape of a low, stout column. Her husband, a man with a face like a jowly, shaggy goat, called the woman 'Maschaccia' – 'Nasty Great Lump of a Man', and urged her to hurry.

'No point in trying to make the little brute look pretty.' His accent was as coarse as the whiskers on his face. 'We don't get paid any more for that.'

Maschaccia cut a hole out of the bottom of a sack and tugged it over Amneris's head. She tied the waist with a rope. Then she pinned a long red velvet cape to the corners of sack that rasped Amneris's shoulders. She crammed a wreath of white roses over Amneris's hair, none too careful about the thorns. A trickle of blood fell past Amneris's ear.

Finally, Maschaccia jammed a wax taper into a holder fixed to the wreath.

Lardo grumbled, 'Candle's crooked and she's bleeding like a piglet. You've made a mess as usual.' He lowered his voice. '*He* won't like it.'

'Will he even notice it, Lardo?'

'Don't be smart. Here, clean it up.' He handed her a rag from his pocket.

Amneris felt the blood wiped away. A powder puff was dragged over her face, and some carmined wax was dabbed on her nose. She caught sight of herself in one of the mirrors: her face was almost fluffy with white powder and her nose was pink. With the white roses above her ears, she did in fact look something like a lamb.

She was spun around and inspected from all angles.

'It'll do,' said the man. 'You've two more to dress after this. Get on with it!'

Amneris thought, 'Biri and Tockle! How cruel of them to prepare us separately. We cannot even say goodbye to each other.' She began to cry softly. 'Still, perhaps it's better this way. I don't want them to hear me die.'

A slap on her legs shocked the tears away. 'Don't you start snivelling. The Lamb doesn't snivel,' snapped the man.

'You forgot the blindfold, idiot!' The woman's voice was not even angry. Amneris suspected that it never rose to anger, because it was permanently embedded in a state of cold, reptilian contempt, not just for her husband, but for everything and everyone.

A strip of white silk was wrapped around her eyes as she was hustled into the gondola. For some minutes, she felt the waves tugging beneath her and the sun caressing her head. She knew when they had arrived at the Frari when she heard the desperate singing inside the church. Hard hands reached into the boat and hauled her up to the *fondamenta*.

'Get moving, girl. One foot in front of another.' It was the captain of the Fogs who had arrested them.

Amneris tripped on the cape, and received another slap for her mistake.

'Not on the face!' growled Lardo Drossi. 'You'll leave a mark.'

The bundled end of the cape was thrust into her arms. 'Don't you remember? You're supposed to carry that until you get to the church door.'

She did remember. Amneris had seen six Lambings. She remembered each blindfolded, wreathed child being led into the church by the Fogs. Feeling the crunch of stems underfoot and scenting perfume, she recalled how flowers were always strewn over the square in front of the Frari for the Lambing. She heard the soft snapping of flags in the breeze. She remembered craning her neck for a glimpse of the unfortunate boy or girl. Twice, it had been someone she knew: a boy called Adelino from San Polo and a girl called Sofia from her own quarter. Neither of them had come back.

The doors of the church must have opened – music billowed out into the square.

'Drop the cloak,' she was ordered. She felt hands tugging it into position behind her.

'Now, four steps,' she was told. 'Stop! Light the candle, Lardo!'

A drip of hot wax fell on Amneris's cheek. With a Fog at either elbow, she walked up the stairs and into the nave. The hot July air suddenly cooled as she entered the great brick building.

The sounds were all as they had been at the last Lambing she attended – the same urgent prayers, the same lamenting hymns, the same weeping of the women, the same pain in the men's singing. As on previous occasions, a slight rustling could be heard as the saints seemed to be struggling to mutter protests through the linen masks that grew damp as their stone eyes shed tears. Her own family, she knew, would be hidden away in the choir, so that she could not see them. The family of the Lamb were never allowed to see their child in case it led to unfortunate scenes.

'Mamma!' she whispered. 'Papà!'

She tried to make out her family's voices in the midst of the singing, but it was impossible. She knew the soldiers must be marching her towards the little door at the left of the nave. They guided her down the three steps and through the low door. Inside, a Fog ripped the white silk off her eyes and pointed to a set of stairs.

'Up,' he said briefly. 'There's a ramp. Climb. Follow the lamb.'

A life-size automaton of a lamb jittered out of the shadows and began to march upwards. Amneris turned to look at the Fog in mute appeal.

'Do you think I haven't seen that look before?' he said, roughly. 'Away with you!'

He and his colleagues marched out of the door. Three vast bolts slid shut behind them. The door was a little fortress in itself. It would be opened again only if the Box decided in her favour.

Then she heard the churning of restless waves very close by.

'Water? Inside the tower?' she thought. 'How? Why?'

And she answered herself, 'The Primaeval Crocodile lives in water.'

Amneris began to climb, following the lamb.

38
The Redentore Lambing

Fingers of dull light from the red-paned lanterns poked at the plum-coloured curtains. Ringlets of smoke curled around her head.

Amneris faced the Fate in the Box. Her heart made deadened beats. She thought, 'Biri and Tockle will be doing this too, very soon. I wish it was only me.'

The Fate in the Box teased her, opening a tiny bit and then snapping shut again. She wound and wound the handle, the sinister tune tinkling out over and over, but always stopping and starting again just before the '*Pop!*'

A penny for a spool of thread

A penny for a needle

That's the way the money goes …

Just when her shoulders had started to sag with exhaustion, the Fate in the Box surprised her.

Pop!

The noise echoed around the chamber like a bullet. At the same moment, the lid popped open and a grinning skull with string for hair nodded in front of her. Amneris heard the trapdoors creak and suddenly there was nothing but air underneath her. A scream tore out of her throat.

For a moment she was blinded by the light of the belfry. Then she plunged back into the darkness of the tower's shaft.

The cloak fell off her shoulders immediately. It rushed down ahead of her, like a fast-moving storm cloud. The sack floated up to cover her face. She held it down with one hand and flailed with the other to find some kind of hold, anything to break her fall. But the shaft was too wide and her progress too fast.

It was not completely dark inside the tower. Every few metres there was a niche in which a single candle smouldered, revealing the great arches in ghostly blurred outline as she fell.

She gave up trying to find a handhold on the sides and resigned herself to plunging downwards until she reached whatever lay at the bottom of the shaft.

Down and down she plummeted.

In the church, Biri, waiting her turn to be Lambed, heard the trapdoor drop. She heard Amneris's scream. She stumbled against Maschaccia, but was soon slapped back into an upright position and marched into the nave.

Through the weeping and the screaming of the congregation came the blast of a trumpet. This meant that Fogfinger had a new decree to issue.

Biri's scalp tightened. 'No! Get on with it!' she muttered. 'Don't torture me with waiting.'

The captain of the Fogs stood up in front of the altar and unrolled a scroll.

'People of Venice. Another child has been Lambed. What does this tell us? The Fate in the Box has chosen against her, as a warning. And our Protector has already taken steps to make Venice more secure. To deal with the increased danger from the criminal *Piccoli Pochi*, the old Poxer has been improved. If it hears people talking treason, it will no longer be a question of a bad head cold and a loss of the use of the limbs.'

The captain explained how the new poxing would afflict anyone who even mentioned the name *Piccoli Pochi*.

'Those traitors,' announced the captain, 'shall die in parts. Each day they will become a little smaller, like dolls, though in perfect proportion. Their vital functions cannot survive this miniaturization: human circulation is insufficient. They will die in one part a day for thirty days, gradually losing the use of their toes, feet, fingers, knees, and finally their hearts. And they grow perfectly white, being perfectly bloodless in the end. Grown men shrink the fastest. When they are dead, they will fit into a coffin that could easily hold a cat.'

There was a profound silence in the Frari, apart from a slap administered to Biri when she kicked Lardo Drossi and ripped off her blindfold.

'I trust this is understood.' The captain rolled up the scroll, his eyes roaming around the nave. 'All one hundred and forty thousand Venetians shall be *protected* now, on each of the one hundred and seventeen islands of this city. There will be no blind spot, no safe places for traitors to conspire.'

Two Fogs and both Drossis were now fully employed in stilling and silencing Biri. All eyes were fixed on her hopeless struggle. The captain tried to draw the congregation's attention back to himself: 'People of Venice, now let us celebrate, for we shall greet the betrothed of our great leader!'

209

The Venetians in the church bore no trace of celebratory smiles on their faces. They looked grim and gaunt. And frightened. As Fogfinger's new fiancée was paraded around the church on a litter, they barely looked at her, even though the child was weeping as if she was about to be Lambed herself. The rose in her hair had slipped awry. Her skin was the greyish colour of veal and her dress hung on her as if she were a scarecrow.

Fogfinger himself did not attend the betrothal ceremony. Lardo Drossi acted as his proxy, ramming the ring on Latenia's shrinking finger and speaking the bridegroom's part in his coarse, mocking voice. But it was hard to hear a word of the formalities through the tearing sobs of the bride.

'Does it count?' asked a young boy, 'if she didn't actually say "Yes"?'

Biri's mouth was firmly covered by Maschaccia's hand, so she could not reply. But for one long second her eyes met Latenia's across the nave.

'I tried!' Latenia wept. 'I tried to have you spared!'

Amneris had landed with a splash in dank, suspiciously warm water.

Young voices cried out. Something cold, wet and soft struck her arm. Pushing it away, Amneris realized that it was the arm of a dead child. An arm with no child attached.

The weak voices were stronger now. Amneris guessed – those who were still alive in this lightless underwater cavern could have survived only by eating those who were dead.

'I am this Lambing's fresh meat,' she thought, as the

splashing grew louder and she felt the water spiralling around her legs, and then the touch of a clammy hand on the back of her neck.

39
Severed arms and steaming hot chocolate

'Stop struggling!' shouted a girl's voice.

'And do give over all that kicking,' said a boy.

They dragged her to a rock ledge, pulled themselves lithely out of the water and then reached for Amneris.

'Don't eat me!' Amneris shrank away in the water. 'I am still alive! Please wait till I've drowned before you start—'

'We're not going to eat you, you great goosy thing!' said the girl. 'Why would we save you if all we wanted was a meal?'

'You're lying! I touched a dead arm!' Amneris protested. She was on the ledge now, shivering under the blanket that had been thrown over her shoulders. 'I know it was.'

'It works!' giggled the girl. Peering through her salt-blurred eyes, Amneris believed there was something familiar about that girl. She looked a lot like Sofia, the girl from her own quarter who had been Lambed.

'Do you mean this thing?' the boy waved a crudely carved wooden arm around, to which some pink velvet had been

212

sewed. 'We made a few of these in case the Fogs come down to investigate. So we always put them in the water when there's a Lambing. The Fogs think that the so-called Croc has taken the rest.'

'So the Lambed children really don't get eaten?' Amneris asked. She realized that she knew the boy too. 'You're—'

'Yes, it's me, Adelino!' he confirmed. 'Living proof that the Lambs don't die! And I believe you know Sofia already. Here you are.' He offered Amneris a goblet full of steaming hot chocolate he poured from a gilded flask. 'Are you going to stop kicking us now?'

Amneris looked around her. The ledge led to a passageway lit by candles mounted on golden sconces in the shape of scallop shells. Hanging from the sconces were dried wreaths of white roses: Lambing crowns like the one she had worn. She saw that Sofia had fished her own wreath out of the water and draped it over a sconce to drip.

Amneris scrambled to her knees and took the goblet, gulping down the hot liquid gratefully. It had a gamey, spicy taste and a little fiery kick to it. The only thing embittering her relief was knowing that Tockle and then Biri would also suffer the fear she had experienced, being rough-handled by Maschaccia and then making that terrible walk up the tower. Was there some way to save them from that fear? 'My friends, the next Lambs—' she began.

Adelino said, 'No, I'm sorry. I know what you're going to ask, but we have no way of reaching Lamb children before they get to the Frari. And we could not risk their revealing what happens down here, even if they didn't mean to. We don't die, but we cannot go back to our families, because they are watched. Fogfinger expects what he calls "traitorous" behaviour from grieving parents. He's waiting for a chance to arrest them if they show anger. They have to be sad, dignified—'

'How awful for them, and for you,' said Amneris. She asked, 'And the cats who have been Kittened?'

'Saved, every one, and eating their weight in fresh fish and eels every day.'

'Don't you … don't you miss daylight down here?'

Sofia laughed. 'Oh, silly, we don't *live* down here on this ledge. We only come here for the Lambings. Then we take the Lamb back to where we live. Which is what we're about to do with you too. Adelino, turn your back!'

She handed Amneris a roll containing a dry skirt, shirt, shawl and jacket.

'Are you … by any chance … *Piccolissimi Pochi*?' Amneris asked, struggling into some woollen stockings. 'Like me?'

'Yes. The Lambed who have survived have all joined.'

'So do you … did you … know poor Ugo Paolin? He was a kind of leader of the *Piccolissimi Pochi* before. I think he might have known about what happens to the Lambs. He said "if the worst happens – *it will all be all right*." Poor Ugo!'

'Why the past tense? Why the sad voice? Ugo's still our leader.'

'I thought he had been taken by a sea creature and killed. He was so weak with the Pox already—'

'What a dark imagination this girl has!' the boy said in a light, teasing tone.

Tears of relief spilled down Amneris's cheeks. She suddenly realized what a burden of guilt she had been carrying about Ugo's disappearance.

A long, deep roar came from far below them.

'What's that?' The air shivered around Amneris's body.

'The She Sea-Saur has smelled you. She's always very upset about any new Lambs. Come on!'

'Sea-Saur?' wondered Amneris, hurrying along the passageway. 'Upset?'

Within moments, she was ascending mossy steps and crawling under some sails into a boat on the Grand Canal.

'Keep down,' said Sofia. 'We'll be at the House of the Spirits in no time.'

There was a faint cry and a splash behind them. 'That'll be your friend Biri,' said the boy. 'When she's dry and warm, she'll be coming along too in a separate boat, with the other Lamb. We never travel in a big group. For obvious reasons.'

40
A tail? Fancy!

Allthe way down the Grand Canal and up the Canal di Noale, Amneris was working things out. She tried to ask a few questions, but was always shushed abruptly. They passed the Misericordia and rowed into the small harbour in front of the House of the Spirits. Then, one by one, they climbed over the gate, crept across the garden and into a little chapel. When it was her turn, Amneris found that the pretty little building had a trapdoor in the floor opening to a lighted stairwell. There was also a table with baskets of buns and more hot chocolate.

'We'll wait here for the other Lambs,' she was told.

Within half an hour, Biri and Tockle, pale and tearful, had also arrived at the House of the Spirits.

'Quicker than you,' Adelino told Amneris, 'because they didn't argue as much. Look how quiet they are. Quiet as Lambs.'

Biri and Tockle hugged Amneris with trembling arms.

Tockle was still silent, and pale as milk. Amneris realized, 'He went through the worst of it. He had to live through both me and Biri dying before he found out the truth. And he's worrying about his father too. What if he's on his way back to Fogfinger's trap?'

When he finally found his tongue, Tockle told them that the last mean thing that Maschaccia had done was rifle his pockets and steal Sweet-Nizzi-on-the-Mantelpiece. 'My last connection with my family. She just pocketed it!' His teeth chattered with shock and indignation.

Neither Biri nor Tockle could manage any food, so Adelino said, 'Well, down we go then. You won't be left to go hungry, anyway. What's that?'

With a blur of feathers and beak, the Scarlet Loory had flown into the chapel and alighted on Biri's shoulder.

'Well, *that*'ll be at home where you're going next!' said Sofia.

As they filed down the stairs, Adelino told Tockle, 'Ugo will be so pleased to see you. He told us to tell you that he was sorry to trick you into throwing him in the water, but it was the only way to get him here.'

Sofia added, 'He was furious about the posters. The ones that said you tortured a helpless cripple. As if! But—'

'Who ... what took him?' asked Amneris. 'He did not swim here on his own. I saw a tail ...'

The children laughed. 'A tail? Fancy!'

Amneris was beginning to feel well enough and safe enough to get annoyed at the mysteries these Lambs were making. She had important information of her own to give them, after all.

'Wait,' she said. 'I need to tell you ... My friend Latenia Malipiero ...'

'The one just betrothed to Fogfinger? How can you be *her* friend?'

'It's true that Latenia would not be everyone's cup of tea,' said Amneris. 'But she wants Fogfinger dead more than anyone. She doesn't want to marry him. He's an old man! She'd rather be Lambed.'

'Well, I am not too sorry for her – living in the Malipiero palace, surrounded by luxury.'

'Latenia has been to Fogfinger's palace and she told me something that could be valuable. It is about his stuffed animals. He's been doing experiments, trying to turn them into an army—'

They had come to the bottom of the flight of stairs. Amneris could hear the ripple of water and smell a sweetly salty, almost perfumed tang in the air.

'What Fogfinger needs is Magic.' A beautiful, musical voice floated out of the darkness. It seemed to pronounce the important words in capital letters for emphasis.

'And Fogfinger,' the voice continued, 'is a Deeply Unmagical Man. The only Magic He manifests are the Curls of Smoke that issue from his Fingers – when He is Frustrated in His Plans. He is a Man of Coils & Springs, of Lies & Machinations. Nor do We believe He has the Wit to create the Automata with which He has seduced Our Sad City. Some Poor Genius must be enslaved by Him to perform that Task.'

As the voice spoke, the candles on dozens of scallop-shell sconces started to flicker into life.

Ugo's voice rang out, 'Hello, Amneris! Biri! Tockle!'

They craned their necks to see him, but the cavern was still too dim. There was a shine of old, tarnished gold about the walls that reminded Amneris of the mosaics inside the basilica of San Marco. Hanging from the ceiling were gilded cages of parrots as handsome as Biri's Scarlet Loory, but decked out in a full rainbow of feathers. The parrots craned their necks towards the new arrivals, making admiring whistles at Biri's bird, who preened and strutted on her shoulder.

The beautiful voice persisted above the parrots' din, 'Fogfinger has only His Wickedness & His Particular Irish Charm & Menace that have placed so Many Humans under His Unworthy Thumb. We, however, have Magic. And That may succeed where Fogfinger has Failed.'

The words were accompanied by a splash.

'Who said that?' asked Amneris.

'I did.' The owner of the voice broke through the surface of the water just as a large ship's lantern, suspended from the ceiling, lit up. Its mullioned glass winked as it swayed.

Dazzled by its light, they heard Ugo's voice saying, 'I'm sorry. I wish I could have prepared you for this. But it was too risky to tell you. About this, about the Lambing. About everything.'

But Amneris didn't hear him. Her eyes had adjusted. She was gazing at the creature in front of her, at the coral lips, the sea-green eyes, the tousled blonde hair.

'Are you ... are you ... a *mermaid*?' she stammered.

'Yar.'

41
Flesh-knitting Canticles

Sunday July 20th, 1783

'Why do You stare so, Children?'

As the mermaid spoke, dozens of tousled blonde heads with slanted sea-green eyes poked up out of the water.

'Bless my old soul!' said one mermaid. 'It's the New Lambs arrived. Two maids and a stripling. Well met!'

It was Biri who had the courage to say, 'You don't look a whole lot like that nasty shrivelled mermaid in the Natural History Museum. For a start, you is twenty times bigger. And a thousand times prettier.'

'Yar,' said the first mermaid, who seemed more grown-up than the rest – none of whom looked more than sixteen years old. 'Ugo told Me of That Heinous Thing the Humans pretend to be a Mermaid. 'Tis Nothing more than the Top of a Dead Monkey that has been Thrust inside a Fish whose Head has been cut off. 'Tis a Vile Travesty. Fogfinger wants the Gullible Humans to believe that Mermaids are Ugly. And Small. So the Venetians shall not think of Us as their

Saviours, even though We have served as the Protectresses of Venice for Thousands of Years. I am Lussa, the Queen.'

'You don't look that old, though!' Biri exclaimed, while Amneris thought, 'I like the sound of that word "Protectresses". I wonder, should we kneel?'

'Mermaid Years are Slower & Longer than yours. Death does not love Mermaids. We have no Natural Predators, saving Vampire Eels, who have not been seen in these Waters for Centuries.'

'Vampire Eels!' keened the younger mermaids. 'Sufferin' seahorses!'

'No! No! No!'

'Sink me standin'!'

A red-haired mermaid, who seemed to be the second in command, huffed, 'Madam, prithee do not talk of those stinkin' worms. It gives me the pip like a lemon sandwich.' She screwed up her strong features.

Lussa nodded, 'Yar, 'Tis best that way, Chissa.'

Amneris asked, 'So the Primaeval Crocodiles do not eat mermaids?'

'Firstly,' sighed Lussa, 'You must understand that these Beasts are not Crocodiles, Primaeval or otherwise. They are Sea-Saurs, an Ancient & Honourable Race of Aquatic Lizard. A Pair of Them has always inhabited the Venetian Lagoon. They breed but rarely, and their Eggs take One Hundred & Eighteen Human Years to hatch.'

'But Fogfinger said that—'

'That drivelswiggin', lie-lickin', cabboblin'!'

'I'll settle his brazen hash—'

Lussa held up her hand. 'Belay, Pretty Ladies! We well know the Slander that Evil Man has spread among the Landlubbering Venetians. Sea-Saurs do not devour Mermaids, or Humanfolk. Or Lambs. They are clean Beasts of Mild Appetite. Why, They eat All the Tiny Crumbs of

Waste from the Ocean Floor, like Kindly Brooms with Mouths.'

Chissa said, '*And* they are our fine scaly friends. So it don't sit well with us, when his nobship the Finger insults them.'

'Shame on da Finger!' shouted a young mermaid. The cry went up, 'He should be cat-cursed and dunked in dog doings! Da dribbling, whey-faced slubberguts!'

'Pretty Ladies,' intervened Lussa, 'Kindly belay your Gadzookery in front of the Human Children. They may be Gently Bred.'

'Not me, anyhows,' said Biri.

'So why did Fogfinger ... ?' Tockle began.

'Kill the Male Sea-Saur? Well might ye ask. Yoiks!' said Chissa darkly.

'Purely for his own Power-Mongering Purposes,' explained Lussa. 'He created a False Fear, and then He created a False Solution for that Fear. He made the Foolish Venetians believe that He had saved Them. In fact, He had merely murdered an Innocent Beast, and murdered the Happiness of his Loving Mate who survived.'

Amneris was momentarily distracted by a large green object floating in the water near her feet. She craned her neck to see it better: it had the size, texture and colour of a watermelon, with two big holes in it.

Tockle was saying, 'So when the living Croc – I mean Saur – cries at night, it is *not* out of guilt for betraying him, as Fogfinger says.'

'She's pining for her mate?' asked Amneris, keeping an eye on the green object. She could have sworn it twitched. 'Oh, poor thing. She doesn't know her husband is just a skeleton now? With a bit of skin grown back?'

'She knows That Terrible Thing, and She suffers also from knowing the Bloodthirsty Slander that Fogfinger spread about Her ... that It was in Exchange for Little Human Lambs to eat that She betrayed her Mate. She does not eat Meat, as You now know. But, more importantly, She would never have given up her Dear Husband for any Price, any Treasure, any Thing. Sea-Saurs mate for Life. And are passionately affectionate Couples.'

'Specially these two,' agreed Chissa. 'The most romantic aquatical lizards ye ever saw. Quite affectin', it was, to see them billin' and cooin' and duckin' and divin' together in the briny.'

She wiped away a sentimental tear.

'Yar,' Lussa said. 'Imagine how It is for the Female – You pass Hundreds of Years loving a Creature, whose Body is suddenly destroyed, and whose Soul is trapped in a Skeleton inside a Prison of Stone, where other Creatures come to point & stare. And hate.'

'So he is not exactly dead? The male's soul is still alive?' asked Tockle.

'Fogfinger's Hunt may have stripped the Husband of his Skin, but not of his Life or his Spirit. However, without Flesh, his Spirit is a Helpless Thing, trapped inside the Remains of the Ruined Body. Imagine how It is for the Male – your Soul lives in a Cage of Bones and your Beloved cries for You every Night. You feel her Pain. You long for her Sweet Company. You Remember your Free Lives in the Azure Waters. And You know You can never be with Her. Because a Murderer has divided You. Ah, 'Tis a Rotten Fabric of Lies Fogfinger has woven, laced together with Cruelty.'

Tockle said, 'It is like what has happened to my parents. My father is in exile, and my mother must bear the slanders that are said of him. That he is evil. Now he—'

Lussa raised her hand. 'Fear not, Temistocle Molin. One of our Sisters was despatched to the Nile to warn your Father against returning to Venice. He knows You are Safe and that not a single Lambed Child has ever been Eaten.'

'Not a wibbling one!' said Chissa. 'Sorrily, two pore mites drowned before we realized what was happening. When we found their bodies in the lagoon, we made enquiries of the fishes and discovered the dreadful truth. Since then, the Lambed childer, as you see, end up here with us. Safe as stinkbugs.'

Lussa explained, 'We keep Them in a Comfortable Barracks by the House of the Spirits. And We teach Them – We run quite a little Schoolhouse here. When They are old enough, We send Them to Safe Places where They can start a New Life. Meanwhile, We also instruct Them in the Arts of War, as one Day soon – a Day I both hope & fear – They shall need to use those Violent Arts to defend this City. And in that Task, the Sea-Saurs shall be our Defenders too.'

'Both of them?' asked Tockle. 'But the male ...'

'Have ye not heard the female croonin' at night?' asked Chissa. 'Sad and low loik a creaky hammock.'

The children nodded.

Lussa said, 'The She Sea-Saur is singing her Husband whole once more. The Songs She sings – They are called Flesh-Knitting Canticles. They have gradually covered his Skeleton with Skin. Her next Task is to sing his Soul back into his Body.'

Biri breathed, 'I saw the skin growing back on a claw! Saw it my own self!'

'For such a loving song, it sounds so sad,' said Amneris.

'Would make a weasel weep,' agreed Chissa. 'Weasels being hard-hearted little landside beasties, 'tis said.'

'The She Sea-Saur's song is indeed solemn,' said Lussa. 'Sometimes We call it her 'Him-Hymn'. But You must wait & see what Kind of Song she shall sing when her Mate is restored to Her. It shall break your Heart with its Unearthly Beauty. Meanwhile, I believe that all You Little Human

Lambs carry Talismans in the Shape of a Seahorse, who is, of course, but a Very Small & Delicate Dragon or Saur.'

'I never thought of them like that,' said Amneris. 'But they certainly don't look like creatures of this world.'

Lussa said, 'Dragon Talismans are also helpful in Matters of Love & the Heart, or so the Chinese Mermaids have told Me.'

'Chinese mermaids?'

'Oh indeed, a very Brilliant & Ancient Race. We meet Once a Year at Atlantis, along with Representatives of all the Magical Creatures, including the Tender-Hearted Saurs.'

'Surely,' said Amneris, licking her lips nervously.

'No, let Me show You how tender They are.' Lussa laughed and sang a crystalline note.

A wave of foam surged up out of the water just where the watermelon had floated – and there was the She Sea-Saur. Biri and Tockle screamed, scrambling as far away as they could, which was not very far. Amneris was too frightened to move. Her neck prickled with the realization that the She Sea-Saur had been lying a metre below them all this time and the green object she had seen was the bulbous chamber at the end of its jaws.

Amneris's eyes flicked around the cavern. Unlike the mermaids, the Sea-Saur was amphibious. It could climb out of the water and be extremely tender to her at any moment.

Biri shouted, 'I don't want no Sea-Saur kiss, thank you!' She too was scanning the cavern for exits.

'By Neptune's Mandibles,' exclaimed Chissa. 'Be nice to the poor creature, childer! Her feelings are hurt nuff already.'

The Sea-Saur did not lunge at them. She sat upright in the water. Chissa swam into the circle of her front claws, using a large sea sponge on a stick to dab at the Saur's green eyes. The lids were thick and inflamed with weeping.

'Pore old peepers!' said Chissa. 'Here's aloes for you, and

borax juice. Settle down, my beauty. Look – the Lambs are safe, every one. There, there!'

As the Saur subsided back into the water, a mermaid in a chef's white hat swam up and announced in an important tone, 'Supper is served.'

There was a general thrashing of tails and a cacophony of exclamations like 'I could eat a lighthouse, me vitals is gnawing at me so!' and 'Prithee bring on da hot stuff!' and 'Seconds all round, sirrahs!'

Chissa said proudly, 'No empty bellies on my watch, nossir! Get your ivories into this! I've a hankering to see some fine fat human childer roundabouts.'

Food was floated in on silver salvers laid in baskets. And such food! Everything smelled of saffron and coriander and other exotic spices that Biri, Tockle and Amneris had only ever sniffed in their fragrant pyramids at the Rialto Market before being chased off by the merchants. Sauces bubbled around vegetables that they had never seen before. The chef-mermaid explained, 'Chilli and garlic Sea Cucumber, spiced granadilla dipping sauce, ginger and cumin rice-balls, pickled sesame-oiled Sumatra samphire, tamarind cassava chips, toasted coconut double-fried soufflé, buttered basmati buns, palm-sugar toffee-ed pumpkin slices, lemongrass pakora, peri-peri red beans, truffled cashew and callaloo, chickpea and sweet potato mascarpone. Leave a little space, prithee, in your belly parts. For to follow there'll be pomegranate and pistachio baklava with coddled raspberry and rose-water crème brûlée with pearl-blossom syrup.'

Amneris swayed on her feet, dizzy with hunger and the fumes of the food.

'Help yourselves!' said Chissa. 'Get in quick. All the others'll be here in a minute, fangin' for their feeds.'

'Ugo, too?' asked Tockle eagerly. 'I think this food smells good enough to undo a poxing!'

'True!' It was Ugo's voice that answered him.

Ugo floated into the cavern on a diminutive boat with wheels like his old chair. He turned the wheels with his arm, dextrously navigating to the centre of the pool. His face was fuller and his skin bloomed with a healthy colour.

'He ain't wastin' and dyin' no more!' marvelled Biri, bursting into tears.

'Don't cry,' he said. 'I have been well and getting better all the time. The mermaids have a chilli-jam antidote to the Pox. I might even be able to walk again, if I live. If we all live.'

Chissa growled, 'Belay that loose talk bout wastin' and dyin', stripling – when your moufs should be full of vittles! Time nuff for that nogging kind of chatter when our bellies are sticking out proud in front of us!'

The living Lambs knelt by the edge of the water and filled golden bowls with food.

The food, while delicious, burned their tongues with furious flavours while their ears strained to take in the approving exclamations of the mermaids as they fed. 'Baggin' brilliant, dis dippin' sauce!' 'Dat'll strip da lining offa yer tongue!'

'How much chilli is in this?' spluttered Tockle.

'Just a snattock, stripling,' insisted Chissa.

One young mermaid let out a satisfied belch, immediately imitated in chorus by the parrots and followed by a reproving finger wag from Lussa.

'We Venetian Mermaids just adore Spicy Curries,' explained Lussa. ''Tis a Gift from Human Sailors. They have a Taste for Fire in their Mouths, having dined in the Indies where the Humanfolk are handy with the Spices. Our Species tasted the Scraps floating in the Wakes of their

Ships … and We improved upon all those Recipes They had brought away with Them from Madras & Bombay. We took the Creatures out of the Mixture and improvised with Greenery instead.'

'So you are vegetarians?' asked Tockle. 'So are most Venetians these days, but only because they cannot afford meat.'

'Yar, We are Half-watery Beasts Ourselves, so It does not behove Us to consume Once-Living Flesh.'

'Anyways,' observed Chissa, 'I'd rather kiss six smelly sea goats than put a dead thing between me loverly pearly gnashers.' She showed off their brilliance in a wide grin.

At the entrance to the cabin, a great splashing of washing-up commenced, accompanied by some ditties that would make a nun's hair stand on end, with refrains of '*Tan yer buttocks blue and lumpy*!' and '*How many fleas in* your *Flea-Flea bag?*' And '*Sixteen kinds of Parrot Particular! Pooh!*'

'Your language,' said Amneris, very carefully, 'is like your food – quite, um, colourful.'

She wiped her mouth on a soft seaweed serviette and settled back on her cushion. Her mouth was a furnace; her stomach was warm with pleasure. She could not imagine needing to swallow another thing, ever. Anyway, human food would have no taste after what she had just eaten.

'Where do ye think we got our grasp of Humantongue, girl?' asked Chissa. 'Same place we got the curry – sailors and pirates – by eavesdroppin' on *them*, obviously. And *they* speak, well, most ungently.'

'Rough as guts!' said a younger mermaid approvingly. 'Did ye ever know a sailor wot couldn't curse fluent, little maid? None of your namby-pamby mealy-mouthed girly talk. Though I's been a-noticin' that *you*,' she smiled at Biri, 'has got a good salty tongue on you.'

'But Lussa?' asked Amneris carefully. 'She speaks so elegantly.'

'Well, she's da Queen, ain't she?' said the young mermaid confidentially. 'Also, she got extra electrocution lessons from a prince, a human boy-prince, wot got shipwrecked in the Lagoon a few centuries back. Isn't dat right, Your Majesty?'

Lussa swam over to them. She had a faraway look in her eyes as she sighed, ''Tis True. He was my One Great Love …'

'But Lussa had to stay here, to protect Venice. So she took his elegant language, but not his wedding ring,' Chissa explained. 'And saved herself a big headache too, if ye ask me.'

'I did not ask You,' said Lussa crisply.

'What would of happened when the prince grew up and ye disappeared in front of his eyes, pouf!' Chissa explained to the Lambs. 'No humanfolk over fourteen years can see or hear us.'

'Something sweet!' called the chef-mermaid. 'Desserts all round.'

'Reckon this'd take away the taste of any of them Bittercakes,' said Biri, wiping her mouth with her sleeve, before digging her spoon back inside the scallop shell full of rose-water crème brûlée and taking another swig of Cove-Cherry cordial.

'Bittercakes?' asked Chissa. 'What in wibble are they? Sounds nasty as numping.'

Biri explained.

'Little black cakes, eh?' asked Chissa. 'With writing on them? Believe we could make some little black cakes of our own for the *Piccolissimi Pochi* to spread around the town instead. Something palatable.'

The chef-mermaid agreed. 'Instead of iron filings and rotten eggs, we could use some of our sea-beet sugar caramelized and tinted with essence of liquorice and black mustard seed.'

'Very noice! Yoiks!' agreed some of the mermaids.

Biri enthused, 'The *Piccolissimi* could put 'em in the bakers' trays just before they put the icing on! They'd never know the difference!'

'What shall we do with the real Bittercakes?' asked Amneris.

'The childer can bring yon scurvy things back to the cavern,' said Chissa. 'We got some old muskets we liberated from some Ottoman pirates a few years back. Believe those Bittercakes would make fine musket-balls.'

'Musket-balls?' asked Amneris. 'For shooting?'

'Little maid, did ye really think we'd be changing this sorry old world without having to spill a little blood?' asked Chissa.

42
Where is the Primaeval Crocodile?

Wednesday July 23rd, 1783

In the days after the Redentore, Venetians returned to their ordinary lives, a little sadder and just a bit more frightened. A larger than usual crowd of people attended the Natural History Museum. And for the first time, people started to notice the layer of new skin growing over the Primaeval Crocodile's body.

In fact, its hide was not as scaly as you might expect. It was smooth and green, like the skin of a frog. The other thing that was surprising was the expression on the monster's face, now that it had one, instead of just a skull. Everyone had reasonably expected it to look even more ferocious. But the beast looked utterly tragic. And the fleshier it grew, the sadder it looked. Its snout seemed to yearn towards the window to the canal. Crystal tears dropped from the newly lidded eyes, making an increasingly large pool around the creature, no matter how often the old guards mopped it up.

When news of the skin was brought upstairs to him, Fogfinger had quickly issued a handbill. He claimed that it was none other than himself who had turned the skeleton into a creature that now approximated a whole animal.

'There is nothing I would not do for the Venetians,' he proclaimed. 'They love their Primaeval Crocodile, so I have given them a bit more Primaeval Crocodile for their money. Of course, now there will be a few changes …'

'For their money?' asked the Venetians.

Until now, admission to the Natural History Museum had been free. Suddenly it was not. And this meant that only the rich could go to visit the Primaeval Crocodile. Three days after the Lambing, Maffeo was there with his friends from the Fancy Stockings. Maffeo's toothache was no better. His pride was smarting too, from the dismal humiliation of the Redentore Ball, which was supposed to have been his moment of triumph. He could not forget how he'd had to stand grinning at the room, empty but for a few Fancy Stockings he'd intimidated into attending. Those same craven fellows were with him now at the museum.

He'd forced Latenia to come with them too, even though she disliked his rowdy friends and flinched at the mention of the museum. She was looking distinctly poorly and quite shamefully thin. She'd hardly stopped blubbing since her dirty little friends got Lambed. But now that she was Fogfinger's betrothed, Maffeo wanted all his friends to keep in mind that he was connected, well, practically with *royalty*. He smiled to himself, thinking that the other Stockings had absolutely no idea who lived upstairs.

Latenia had uttered a shriek at the sight of the re-skinned Crocodile. 'It looks almost alive now!' she whispered fearfully. She wept as she stroked the stuffed lamb that had been placed beside the monster. It too wore a terrified expression.

'Silly girl! You still crying for your traitor friends? Nothing left of them but bones. And there's nothing to be afraid of here! This ugly brute is long dead. But what a stink!' said Maffeo, strutting around it. 'It even smells like a live lizard. Like a barnyard. Eugh!'

Maffeo did not see the angry glint in the Sea-Saur's eye because he had just lost his footing, slipping in the puddle of water that had collected around the Crocodile.

He landed with a painful thump on the ground. His upper teeth collided with his lower jaw and a new pain roared inside his head. His Fancy Stocking friends laughed at him, clearly happy for the chance to see the bully-in-chief cast down for once. Only Latenia moved forward to offer a frail arm to help him up.

'You'll be sorry,' Maffeo thundered. He pushed his sister aside. 'Fogfinger will hear about everyone who laughed at me today. He'll hear about how you once gave a poor girl a cake, Giovanni. He'll hear about how you helped an old lady across a bridge, Piero. Nothing to say for yourselves now, eh?'

Maffeo was so busy revelling in the fear on his friends' faces that he hardly noticed the creaking behind. He didn't even feel the shadow falling over the room as the Primaeval Crocodile rose from its crouched position and loomed behind him.

'Yes,' he sneered at his friends, gratified by their terrified expressions. 'Look afraid! Look very afraid! You should see yourselves! Like mice in the jaws of a wily tomcat.'

The great Primaeval Crocodile bent and roared in Maffeo's ear. Its rank breath sent him tumbling to the ground again. Then the creature thundered by him, pausing to take Latenia gently in its teeth. It crashed through the window and disappeared into the Grand Canal with a neat splash.

From outside in the water came a crooning howl. It sounded somehow feminine, and very, very satisfied.

A few minutes later, a song of unearthly beauty and joy began to well up from under the water, filling the whole of Venice with a sensation of being wrapped in velvet and fed on rose petals.

People stopped in the streets to kiss one another, without really knowing why. 'I love you!' they cried spontaneously, to strangers.

From under the water came long howls of joy.

But from Latenia Malipiero, there was just silence.

'Not even a scream when she was taken, poor creature,' people said. 'Let's hope it was quick.'

For days after the Redentore Lambing, and the snatching of the noble girl in the Natural History Museum, people tried to think positively – of all the Venetian children who had safely got away in the Ark to the paradise island of Hvar. But nothing was heard of the Ark. There were rumours of a storm in the Adriatic, but no merchant vessel reported a sighting.

Then a bottle bobbed up at the Rialto Market with a twist of paper inside it. A fishwife pulled it out of the water. She took it to the parish clerk at San Giacometo. Although the priests had been exiled, their clerks were kept on to maintain the parish records.

'What does this say?' the fishwife demanded, thrusting the paper at the clerk.

The clerk's face darkened as he read:

FROM THE VENETIAN ARK. July 10th. It is not as they said it would be on this ship. As soon as we were out of the lagoon, some of the passengers turned out to be Fogs in disguise. Now we are in a floating prison,

surrounded by armed guards. Anyone who protests
at our treatment is beaten and put in chains – even
children. Whoever picks up this bottle and reads this
message, please tell our families what is happening. Don't
let anyone else be tricked into boarding one of these
boats. We would ask you to send help, but we know that
there is none. And we do not know where we are. If we
are truly going to the island of Hvar on the Dalmatian
coast, we are taking a strange route. The coastline is
unfamiliar. And the winds are too strong. And a dark
ship is following us.

'My cousin is on that boat, with all his little ones,' wept
the fishwife. 'Where are they taking them?'

The words in the bottle were soon whispered in every
square: also in the square of San Zan Degola where
Temistocle Molin had lived before he was Lambed.

'Poor boy!' said the neighbours. 'At least he has been
spared this awful news.'

Maffeo's mouth was still on fire with agony. The incident
with the Primaeval Crocodile had made it worse, for he had
bitten his tongue when the beast came to life so unexpectedly.

Maffeo did not for one moment believe in the apothecary's
maundering about a Cat Curse. But he had started to look
at Venetian cats in the street in a different way. They all
looked incredibly self-satisfied, not to say triumphant as
they sidled past him with their tails in the air.

He experimented with the idea of an apology in his head.
Not an apology: just the idea of one. The apothecary's Skull-
cure came into his mind daily, then hourly, then every few
minutes as the pain worsened.

Finally, Maffeo was driven to the Campo dei Morti at Santo Stefano, where the old graves had recently been dug up to make more space. It was only a few hundred metres from the Malipiero palace: Maffeo managed the walk on his own, stumbling and complaining under his breath all the way. The old bones awaited transport to the ossuary on Sant'Ariano. They lay unguarded by the north wall: no one was likely to steal dead people's remains.

Until now.

Gingerly, Maffeo approached the corner where the bones glowed faintly in the moonlight. He reached through the thicket of thighs and pelvises to a small skull – a child's, from the look of it.

Grunting with effort, he extracted it from the heap and thrust it into a pocket of his cape. He made his way home, completely unaware of the pair of Fogs who had observed the whole thing, and who had decided to follow the grave-robber to his door.

When they saw what door it was, they whistled under their breath.

43
Rehearsing for a revolution

Wednesday July 23rd, 1783

Latenia curled up on a pallet in a corner of the cavern, sobbing into a seaweed pillow.

'Why are you crying?' Amneris patted her back. 'Aren't you happy that we're all alive?'

'How would *you* like to be snatched in a monster's jaws, dragged under water, carried down the Grand Canal and then thrown into a cavern full of mermaids and dead children?'

'We aren't dead, we've told you,' sighed Tockle.

'I fink it would be an adventure,' said Biri. 'Better than being Lambed, anyway. And the Saur was that gentle! It didn't close its teeth on you at all.'

'It drooled all over me and I could feel how sharp those teeth were,' whined Latenia. 'And now I'm a prisoner here, with none of my things, and a dirty dress on.'

'You'd rather be in Venice, getting married to Fogfinger?' asked Tockle.

'I'd *rather* be in my bedroom with the revolving cake

stand and some grape mousse,' wailed Latenia. 'But no one has asked me what I wanted. Not for days and days and days. Years, actually.'

And she wept some more.

'Yoiks! This one is wetter than a spit sandwich,' said Chissa. 'I ain't impressed with her nobship one bit. Not going to be much use in a revolution, is she?'

The chef-mermaid muttered disparagingly, 'No wonder da Saur spat it out. Must of tasted like jellied water!'

Lussa exclaimed, 'And It is so Hard to imagine whose Daughter She is!'

'Whose daughter?' Latenia sat up, sniffing ostentatiously. 'I mean, apart from my horrible father's?'

'Come now. We have explained how your Mother is with the *Piccoli Pochi*, and so was forbidden Contact with You. You know She has gone to an Extraordinary Effort to reach You. Indeed your Friend Amneris has put Herself in Danger to facilitate the Communication.'

'Silk handkerchief letters! How was I supposed to guess they were from my mother? She was supposed to be living it up in Paris, with no thought for me.'

'But You've admitted that You did guess the Truth, in the End. Did It never occur to You to reply to Her?'

'Why should I?' asked Latenia stubbornly. 'She left me. So she should win back my affection. With proper gifts and not just letters.'

'Stab me vitals!' exclaimed Chissa. 'Sharper than a serpent's tooth is—'

Amneris shook her head. She had guessed what was behind this. Latenia needed a mother more than any other girl she had ever known. How many years was it since someone had given the poor girl a hug? But Latenia did not want to admit how stupid she had been, thinking that the letters came from Fogfinger. It was better, in Latenia's mind,

238

that the mermaids and other children believed that she was proud, needing no one, rather than that she was simply not very clever.

Latenia still refused to reply to her mother, who had sent another loving letter, written in bold black ink this time, along with the baskets and baskets of glass flintstone that had been made by Signor Castrauro and the men of Murano. Tockle told Amneris that he'd not been at all surprised to discover that the kindly Signor Castrauro was in fact a member of the *Piccoli Pochi*. The adult members of the *Pochi* did not come to the mermaid cavern in person, as they would not be able to see Lussa and her comrades.

Amneris sighed and picked up another glass flintstone, fitting its thicker end into the cleft of a narrow stick that had been whittled by Biri. She counted the pile of arrows beside her. She had made a hundred and fifty of them that morning.

Tockle was fashioning bow after bow – delicate but strong – from driftwood and woven seaweed. He tested each one with an arrow before laying it on the heap.

When she thought no one was watching, Latenia had left her mattress and was quietly helping him to polish the finished bows with dried seaweed.

'They are beautiful,' thought Amneris watching them at work, 'those bows and those glittering glass arrows. Beautiful as a piece of embroidery.'

But would *she* ever be able to fire an arrow at another human being, even if he was a Fog? Or Fogfinger himself?

'Surely,' she told herself, 'an arrow is nothing more than a great big needle?'

She brightened momentarily and then drooped again. She'd spent her life plunging needles into silk, but she'd never stuck one into living flesh and then watched its owner die.

'Snotties away!' Chissa urged them into the boats.

'Why snotties?' asked Biri, wiping her nose.

'Old sailor term for midshipmen,' said Chissa. 'Ye's all officers at arms now.'

The children were armed with bows and arrows and the old pirate muskets ('Fell off the back of a galleon, didn't they,' said Chissa) and a daily supply of Bittercakes for ammunition. It was midnight and they were off to practise their skills in the 'Old Bone Orchard', as Lussa called the private cemetery of the white-robed Camaldolese monks on the island of San Michele. The monks, of course, had been sent into exile, so the island was now deserted.

'Ye can't hurt anyone in the Bone Orchard,' Chissa observed. 'Them that's buried there is already well past hurtin', even by green-tailed snotties like yesselves.'

Whether tucked up in their bunks in the barracks, or feeding on the mermaids' spicy food, or shooting at targets by lamplight on San Michele, the talk among the Lambs was all about how and when the revolution would come. Lussa was quiet on the subject, saying only, 'The *Piccoli Pochi* at Poveglia are still Depleted in Numbers. It would be Murder if we despatched such a Tiny Force against the Fogs. And yet We must hasten, before Fogfinger devises a Way to raise his Beastly Army,' she frowned.

Tockle said, 'What about the Winder Uppers? If we could persuade them to join us and stop winding, then all the automata would stop. And if Fogfinger's automata weren't working – then *he* wouldn't seem so wonderful any more.'

'Or so invincible,' added Amneris.

'Yes,' said Tockle, 'and the Venetians would start to think about the bad things he's done.'

'What a Clever Boy It is!' rejoiced Lussa. 'I did not think of the Winder Uppers because They seem the most Trampled upon of all the Venetians, forced to work their Fingers to the Bone & to never see the Sun. Temistocle, You have shed a New Light here. We shall commence Negotiations with the Winder Uppers this very Night. Some of Them are still Children, so can see & hear Us. We know their Routes and shall intercept Them!'

'Aye, aye!' said Chissa. 'We'd better take them a snack too, ye know, to get their danders up.'

Lussa turned to Biri. 'Child, I would like You to speak to your Friends the Moths & Beetles & Jointed Insects. Will You ask Them to attend their Unfortunate Friends at the Natural History Museum? Tell Them We are preparing a Spell to release Them from their Living Deaths, and that They shall be called upon to support our Cause. And have your Moths whisper the same Message in the Ears of all those Furred & Feathered Beasts who are trapped in that Terrible Place. Every Creature must be ready to do his Duty and avenge his own Wrongs besides.'

'Reckon,' said Biri. 'But what is *they* gonna eat, to get *their* danders up? There's lions and all sorts in there.'

'That could be a problem,' admitted Chissa.

'It's not the lions you need to worry about,' said a quiet voice. All heads turned to Latenia, as she mumbled, 'It's the baboons.'

That afternoon the mermaids busied themselves creating Seaweed Familiars in a submerged garden in the cavern. The boys and girls were supplied with pretty glass masks so they could press their faces against the water and watch. Amneris tried not to be distracted by the two Sea-Saurs who were napping in a nearby nook of the cavern.

On the sea-floor, the mermaids were digging holes in the golden sand. Around each hole they placed a circle of eight black stones, with one gap. Draped over their shoulders like cloaks were long strands of seaweed with delicate white roots.

'This will bind each Familiar's Spirit once It commences to grow,' explained Lussa. She alone did not dirty her hands with the gardening, but directed operations from her throne, with a basket of red coral branches on her lap.

'The Weeds!' she ordered.

Her mermaids now took plants from their shoulders and planted them carefully in the holes. The stones were polished with delicate fingertips and their circles adjusted to perfection. Lussa held up her basket of coral. Each gardener mermaid approached her queen, took one red branch, bowed and returned to her planting.

'Now, charge the Familiar!' said Lussa.

Each mermaid pressed her piece of coral into the gap in the circle of stones.

'Crystals!' said Lussa. This time Chissa made the rounds of the gardeners with a net full of glistening wedges.

'One at each of the Four Elemental Quarters of the Planting,' urged Lussa.

When this was done, she ordered, 'Now the Kissing & the Whispering!'

The seaweed rose from between the crystals and undulated like wheat in a windy field. Amneris was amazed to see how the mermaids now kissed, stroked and whispered to the plants.

'They are encouraging the Weeds to become their Helpers,' explained Lussa. 'We cannot take their Aid for granted unless They are conscious of our Needs, and of our Affection for Them.'

'Now the Blood.'

'Ugh!' moaned Latenia, who nevertheless looked on, fascinated.

Each mermaid reached down and snapped one of the scales from her tail. She used the translucent chip to make a swift incision in her thumb.

'Precisely Three Drops!' Lussa reminded them. 'No More, no Less.'

Having smeared their blood onto the seaweed, the mermaids then folded their hands and gazed at the plants. Their eyes glazed and their minds were clearly far away.

'They await a Message from their new Familiar. They must continue to stare until the Contact is made.'

One by one, each mermaid returned to the everyday world, smiling. They curved their arms around their plants, touching the leaves of their Familiars the way a human mother might pat her beloved baby.

'Soon,' said Lussa, 'the Familiars shall be ready to help.'

'How?' asked Amneris, voicing the concern of every child in the cavern. 'How can seaweed help in a revolution?'

Chissa rushed into the cavern in a plume of foam.

'Sea-shell message from the Adriatic! The Ark's gone down, all hands!' she gasped.

'Blood for breakfast!' cried a young mermaid.

In moments all the mermaids were gliding through the water in the direction of the entrance to the lagoon. Lussa alone remained in the cavern, talking to the Sea-Saurs, who then departed in the same direction as the mermaids.

'They too will try to save the Humanfolk,' Lussa told the children.

'We were going to sail on that Ark,' said Amneris.

'We only missed it by a cat's whisker,' said Biri. 'It was my fault, akshally.'

'Shhh!' said Amneris. 'Remember Tockle!'

Tockle had sagged against the wall of the cavern, his eyes flittering around in panic. He whispered, 'My mother and my sisters are … were … on that boat.'

The Skull-cure had not worked. Maffeo despaired. Pain continued to search out every cranny of his mouth.

Perhaps the child's skull had been too small?

He crept back to the Campo dei Morti at Santo Stefano. The pile of bones was still there. He raked through it with his foot until he found a fine big skull.

Again, he did not see the Fogs who patrolled the graveyard. And he did not notice them follow him home, or realize when they let themselves into the courtyard garden of the palace and climbed a tree that gave them a view into his room.

They were watching when he filled the new skull with water, stirred the lumpy mixture and threw back his head to gulp down the contents.

'Interesting?' said one Fog.

'And not in a good way,' replied his companion.

'But in a good way for us. When we tell the Finger, we'll get a fine reward for catching such a depraved criminal. We might even score the first new poxing. You know, the one announced at the Redentore Lambing.'

'He's so full of himself, that boy! I'd love to see him shrink to the size of a cat!'

'It will cheer the Finger up too. He's in a right foul mood since all those insects invaded the museum, crawling all over, even in his nasty Irish tea!'

While Maffeo retched and tried to keep the skull juice down, the Fogs slid off the branch and disappeared through the garden to rejoin the party that had been going on for a few days now at their headquarters.

Not a single child or cousin or mother of a Fog officer had been on the Ark when it went down.

44
A shipful of demons

Friday July 25th–Sunday July 27th, 1783

The sinking of the Ark was reported in a heartless way. Instead of obituaries for the drowned, the *Postiglione* wrote:

Shall we miss them?
Shall we mourn them?
These people who chose out of the bitterness of their hearts
to leave us?
These people who turned their backs on Venice.
Well rid of them!
Fate has intervened and made sure that they got nowhere.
A TRAITOR ARK, that's what it was,
full of TRAITORS.
Its sinking has purified the city of taint.

The mermaids returned from their mission empty-handed and grim-faced. There was no sign of the ship. But a few days later, the bodies of two old men and a woman floated into Venice: three bodies and two brown bottles, one containing a new letter. Once more, the bottle rolled in to the Rialto Market along with the dawn deliveries of vegetables from Sant'Erasmo. Since the first letter, everyone had been looking out for another. So it was not long before a fisherman pulled it out of the water. San Giacometo's parish clerk was interrupted at his desk. A crowd assembled to hear him read.

Stained with smoke and splashed with what looked like blood, the letter's contents were short and horrifying.

In a sheltered bay, late at night, we were ambushed by a boat full of devils, horned, with forked tails, and, strangely, carrying muskets. The Fogs greeted them with cries of 'Welcome!' The devils threw some of the old men and a woman overboard. They are rounding up the younger women and children. They have a list of all their names, and they're reading them out. They are up to 'D'. They say we shall be sold as slaves in Alexandria. Now they are up to 'L'. I cast this letter into the water and hope that someone may read it, and tell the world what happened to this ship. They are calling my letter. God save us all.

Of all the people in Venice, only twenty-six girls knew what to make of those fork-tailed devils – Melchior Dubbini's twenty-four pale slaves, who had sewn their costumes, Amneris D'Ago, who had glimpsed those girls at work, and Latenia Malipiero, who had seen the devil costumes dancing through an open door in Fogfinger's palace. And when news of the letter was brought to the cavern, Latenia stood up and told the truth, speaking in a clear voice, so that no one had any doubt who had sent men dressed as devils to destroy the Venetians on the Ark.

'We can delay no more,' said Chissa. 'Assemble all snotties! There is things to be done. And to be said. And to be summoned up.'

'Summoned up?' asked Amneris.

'Our Rehearsals are at an End,' Lussa told the grave-faced children an hour later. 'And the First Thing We require is a little Privacy. Venice must be as mysterious as possible. The Venetians must feel a Sense of Enchantment. It shall make Them more Absorbent of the Strange Things They are about to see and become a Part thereof. So ... let us use Fog against the Fogs! I call upon all the Spirits of Nebulous & Misty Whiteness to come to our Aid!'

'Look into the turtle's shell!' urged Chissa.

The shell of a large turtle dangled from the gilded ceiling of the cavern. Its flat belly shone like a pool of silvery water, which churned and then cleared to a mirrored surface upon which a miniature image of Venice was conjured.

The turtle shell showed extravagant plumes and fat pillows of fog rolling in from the lagoon.

It showed the mist winding between the palaces, sidling up the canals.

It showed people pulling up their collars and hurrying home, feeling their way along the walls.

It showed Fogfinger pensive at the window of his palace, stroking his thin tooth of a face. Suddenly his mouth curved into a cruel sneer as a servant presented him with a new automaton – a stuffed baby seal that waggled its flippers and whimpered piteously for its mother.

A mermaid cried out, 'Not a flea's fingernail of conscience, dat one!'

Another muttered, 'A human face and a snake's heart!'

Lussa said solemnly, 'From this Moment, All Those who died before their Time, at that Man's Cruel Hand, shall be Entitled to another Slice of Life. And He who took their Lives shall Himself know the quaking Fear of Death! To work, Pretty Ladies!'

The mermaids crouched over their Seaweed Familiars, singing and humming. The boys and girls put on their glass masks and pressed their faces into the water to watch. Amneris felt the hairs on the back of her neck prickle as the fronds of the seaweed rose high above their earthy nests and the air filled with a deep chanting, like music but more ancient, a sound that throbbed directly from the deepest parts of the ocean.

The voices of the Seaweed Familiars mingled with those of the mermaids, chanting 'Life! Life where there was cruel death! Death to him who dealt in death.'

'Listen!' urged Lussa.

From down the Cannaregio Canal and along the Misericordia came the faint sound of the jungle, of the cries and growls of animals who belonged not in a Venetian palace but in the wilds of Africa. There came the distant whisper of glass splintering and the groan of torn wood and the pattering of paws: some light, some heavy.

The turtle shell showed the guards fleeing the Natural History Museum, only to be enveloped in the mist. It hovered over dark four-legged figures flitting through the windows and slithering into the canal. Momentarily it rested on an awkward human figure with an outsize head slipping into a gondola and two lumpier, larger silhouettes covering that figure with a black cape.

'Fögfinger escapes with his minions,' shouted Chissa.

Lussa said serenely, 'He cannot go Far. And 'Tis of little Matter now, when the Beastly Cohort is fully raised. And Raised not for Him, but for the Forces of Good! Now … let

249

the Mist thicken, churn, wrap and blind our City a While!'

The eye of the turtle shell roamed over Venice, following the tendrils and pulsing snakes of fog. Mist lay so close upon Venice that it seemed that the wooden poles in the water held up tented parts of a heavy veil.

Chissa watched with satisfaction. 'That mist is thick and oozy enough to confound a cat! It'll fog up your Fogs a treat.'

'Confound a cat!' cawed Biri's Scarlet Loory, and all the mermaids' parrots whistled with admiration.

For a few hours the fog hid everything that was happening in the lagoon and along the length of the Grand Canal. Out on the streets, the mist sagged down and sucked on the very breaths of the Venetians. When sunset came, the mist hung about the city like lace dipped in molten gold. The night sky churned grey and moody, swallowing the stars.

It was almost impossible to make out anything.

Almost.

People said, 'Did you see that?'

'What?' came the answer.

'I thought I saw a … no, never mind, I must have imagined it. It's just the mist.'

45
Flayed deer flying and dead apes walking

But soon half of Venice had 'imagined' seeing a procession of flayed deer, lions, zebras and one flat-bellied gorilla flying over the city like magic carpets with heads. They were joined by the legless front halves of ostriches, flapping their beautiful wings.

The Natural History Museum was emptying. The hole that the Primaeval Crocodile had left in the wall was now thick with escaping animals. Others broke windows or crawled away, depending on their mode of locomotion. First the big animals, and then the small, made their way out.

A billiard table mounted on rhinoceros legs walked carefully down the steps and then charged off through the misty streets. Doge Morosini's mummified cat knelt, stretched and then bowed to the rat who had spent several centuries between its paws. The two of them trotted down the stairs together and went off in the direction of Rialto, their noses twitching at the smell of fish and cheese.

The mounted heads of elephants, hippos and gnus stayed where they were, as they had no bodies or wings to carry them away from their hated prison. But they now talked freely among themselves.

And their talk was of war.

War on the man who had killed them, who had trapped them in eternal misery and who had wanted to use them to hunt and murder innocent Venetians.

Biri used a lantern to lead the moths and cockroaches and huge jointed insects out of the museum. She alone had realized she would need to stop them killing themselves by throwing themselves against the glass. And she knew she'd need to negotiate with the poisonous violin spiders to make sure that the little brown creatures knew not to bite anyone who was not a Fog.

'Let me go!' she'd pleaded to Lussa. 'In the confusion, no one'll notice me.'

That was true. The Natural History Museum had been abandoned by the Fogs and their master. Biri marched in unmolested.

She set to work training the insects. In a few hours, she had her personal team of wasps – a squadron, and biting beetles. She taught the butterflies to dance in formation, so they would distract the enemy and allow the archers to attack them.

Negotiations were proceeding with the Winder Uppers, Lussa reported.

'They are willing, if afraid. But We are in Need of Human Money to equip Them fittingly, to take over from the Soon-to-be-Vanquished Fogs. It shall take Human Money too to feed the Reanimated Beasts and win their Confidence. They already hate Fogfinger, but They must be taught to trust Venetians.'

It was true – the animals were starving. The herbivores had stripped every tree and garden in Venice and some of the carnivores had eaten some of the smaller herbivores, and mounted a dawn attack on the Rialto Market where they devoured every dead and living thing on the fish stalls.

After watching all these developments in the turtle shell, Lussa made a surprising declaration. 'Amneris and Latenia. You are to go Home tomorrow. Your Return to the City will undermine Belief in Fogfinger's Works and the Evil He pretends of the dear Sea-Saurs. But Temistocle—'

Tockle said dully, 'I know. No point in my going home. There's no one there. They went down with the ship.'

Amneris patted his hand, but he shook her off gently. 'I'm trying not to cry,' he admitted. 'Just let me be sad.'

Latenia said, 'At last, clean clothes and cake! I hope a suitable conveyance will be provided for my return. I'm not travelling by Sea-Saur again.'

'That girl is such a peach,' said Chissa sarcastically.

'Never had much use for a peach,' said the chef-mermaid. 'They squish so easily and they're only ever any good for five minutes before they rot.'

'A kick in the corybungus would do her an amazin' amount of good,' said Chissa. 'I lie awake nights thinking just how much good it would do her.'

46
Maffeo's moment

Sunday July 27th, 1783

Maffeo despaired of his fellow Fellows of the Fancy Stockings, he really did.

They were completely hysterical about the bats and flying ocelot skins and refused to come outside and enjoy the fun. Venice had become a living zoo! Maffeo wanted to take a trip down the Grand Canal to see all the strange stuffed beasts who had come to life and were now perching in trees and niches and on balconies all over town. The striped awning over their own balcony now acted as a hammock for a family of lemurs. On the other side of the canal the awnings were weighed down and wriggling with squirrels, snakes and lion cubs deposited there by parents who'd gone hunting. The rhino-legged billiard table had halted its charge in San Giacomo dell'Orio and it was so very amusing to watch how it threw off all the balls when anyone tried to play on it, and kicked their legs too. It was the jolliest thing that had happened in ages, Maffeo thought, if a bit smelly from all the droppings.

And it almost distracted him from his toothache.

'Well,' harrumphed Maffeo, 'if the boys won't come, I'll just go out on my own. I'm not frightened of a few dumb beasts.'

He was annoyed to see that the usual footmen who waited by the gondola were missing. How was he supposed to get aboard without them to operate the moving walkway from the threshold to the jetty?

'Oh, bother it,' he snarled, after cooling his heels for five minutes. 'I guess I'll have to walk.'

He made the five steps to the jetty, frowning ferociously.

And what was this? A squad of emaciated people in black robes, all wearing bloodstained white gloves, approached his jetty in a shabby old *sandolo*. Each of them carried a large brass key in his or her hand.

Winder Uppers! Maffeo was flabbergasted to see them. Normally the Winder Uppers came discreetly in the dead of night to do their duties.

'You're late! I shall be reporting you,' he told the Winder Uppers. 'Now – this gondola needs winding. Do it properly,' he ordered. Then he busied himself wiping specks of dust off his magnificent costume.

'Your boat is ready, Sir,' came a respectful, quiet voice.

Maffeo did not thank them. Why should he? His father paid plenty of Winding Up Tax. The slaves hastened away in their shabby boat as he stepped into the gondola.

He called for the gondolier in vain. 'Outrageous!' he muttered.

How difficult was it to operate a gondola?

'Not at all for a boy of my brain,' thought Maffeo, pressing the button that activated the mechanical propellers.

And suddenly he was on a dizzying, terrifying ride, clinging to the sides of his boat and screaming, battering first the jetty of Ca' Rezzonico and then ricocheting back to Ca' Falier-Canossa.

Dimly, Maffeo understood that the Winder Uppers had overwound his gondola. It continued to fly about all over the canal, spinning in circles, crashing into poles. Maffeo's teeth rattled painfully inside his head.

Finally, the gondola smashed into a Fog boat at Accademia, at such a speed that it cleaved the grey vessel in two. Fogs at both ends of the boat yelled for reinforcements. In minutes, Maffeo was in chains.

'Do you know who I am?' he yelled scornfully.

'You are a boy in deep trouble for vandalizing the boat of the officers of the law,' the captain informed him.

Another officer whispered something in his captain's ear.

'Maffeo Malipiero?' said the captain. 'Well, well, by coincidence we were just coming to get you.'

'Fogfinger requests the pleasure of my company at dinner, I suppose,' drawled Maffeo. 'It must be nice for him to have intelligent company *for a change*.' He looked directly at the captain.

Keeping his temper with visible difficulty, the captain said, 'Dinner with the Finger is not on the menu for you. You'll be dreaming of any kind of dinner soon.'

'Take him to the *Pozzi*!' he ordered his men.

Maffeo stood up in the boat. 'The dungeons? In the Doge's Palace? Wait a minute there. You'll be sorry for this.'

'Not as sorry as you, Master Malipiero. You stand accused of rifling the bones of graveyards and indulging in cannibalism.'

It was clearly a terrible mistake. He, Maffeo Malipiero, was Fogfinger's trusted *confidente*. Any minute now a new squad of Fogs would intervene, and the rude captain would be disciplined severely.

But instead of an apology and a great deal of grovelling, he was bundled into a boat by rough hands and shouted at in rougher voices.

'I am looking at you,' he told his captors. 'Oh ho, I shall remember your faces when the time comes to point you out for punishment. My excellent memory never lets go of a face.'

The captain mocked him. 'Oh ho to you, young Sir. You are the son of a man who appears to be falling out of favour as fast as a drop of water goes over a waterfall.'

At the Doge's Palace, the Fogs dragged Maffeo to a trapdoor in the floor, lifted it and threw him down the stairs. Round and down he tumbled, striking his knees and elbows on the sharp promontories of the stone steps. He landed in a crumple on a stone-flagged floor in time to see the trapdoor slam shut above him.

'Good afternoon and welcome,' said a quiet male voice.

47
Annibale's story

Sunday July 27th – Monday July 28th, 1783

Maffeo rolled painfully onto one side and levered himself upright. A stain of watery light stirred the darkness through some dusty strips of glass high up in the wall. The smell was of wetness: wet stone, wet moss, wet clothes.

The dirty light revealed a very old, bald man manacled to a stone throne. Tide marks on the walls showed where the high water came in. And so did the stains of the floodwater on the man's throne.

'I am Annibale D'Ago, prisoner of the usurper Fogfinger,' the old man said with dignity. 'Come closer and let me look at you. I haven't seen a living human being apart from Fogs in some decades. Hurry up! When the light goes, we shall be in total darkness for some hours.'

'I don't feel like coming closer. You look as if you might smell horridly,' said Maffeo. 'How long have you been here?'

'For nearly nineteen years I have been down here, chained

258

to this cold stone privy. I have come to know fifty generations of rats, and two hundred thousand of flies.'

As if in agreement, a large fly buzzed loudly in Maffeo's ear. He hit at it irritably, but to no avail.

'However,' continued the old man, 'your fastidious fears about my sanitary habits are unfounded. I am allowed out of these chains for a time each day. I'm taken under guard to a room where I may wash and change into clean robes, and then I'm conducted to the most secret workshop where I invent all the incredible and intricate automata that you see in Venice now. At least, I assume that they are seen there, for I know nothing of my city any more.'

This old man? An inventor of automata? A cynical smile curled Maffeo's lip. The stupid dodderer must have gone mad down here. So now he had delusions of grandeur, like so many lunatics.

'You doubt me?' The man's voice was rich with indignation. 'Well, then, here are a few of my inventions: the page-turner, the revolving cake stand, the wind-up gondola …' He named several more automata that had appeared only in the last month.

'Could this be remotely true?' Maffeo asked himself. Otherwise how would the man know all of those things, hidden away down here? Maffeo supposed he should say thank you to this man who had made the lives of the rich so much pleasanter. But it was a faulty automaton that had got him into this horrible place, with no chance to explain the misunderstanding and who he was.

So he stayed silent, ignoring his companion, a tactic that made him feel powerful.

'Do you not talk, boy?' asked the old man sorrowfully. 'I would love some pleasant company. But perhaps Fogfinger has tortured you? Perhaps your tongue is mutilated so it pains you to speak?'

His voice changed to suspicion. 'Perhaps you are a Fogfinger spy?'

'I say,' Maffeo crackled with anger, 'I am not a filthy spy. How dare you?'

'One can tell a lot by a voice,' said the old man. He sounded disappointed.

And he said no more. Gradually the light dimmed and soon they were sitting in total darkness, apart from a single shaft of moonlight that fell on the old man, making him look, Maffeo thought uncomfortably, like some kind of god, or ghost. A basket dropped from the ceiling into the old man's lap and he was able to lift his chained hands high enough to convey some artichokes and raw potatoes to his mouth. He began to eat ravenously.

There was no food for Maffeo.

'I say,' he began, 'I think that food is intended for both of us. Give it over.'

'How?' asked the old man, looking at his chained ankles and Maffeo's bound wrists.

It was late into the night and the old man's voice still droned on. Maffeo listened – it was better than thinking about his toothache, the extreme discomfort of the stone floor and his empty belly.

'Fogfinger heard of my talents, and of my amazing kaleidoscope, which I had made together with my dear friend Enrico, the greatest of all the kaleidoscope-makers in Venice. It was as wonderful as his own masterpiece, which went by the extraordinary name of Sweet-Nizzi-on-the-Mantelpiece, as I remember. But I digress. At that time I was a sea captain, and I had a little laboratory on my boat. During the long voyages, I amused myself with inventing things – such delicious things! Mechanical sailors, dancing musical anchors, fish fascinators, all manner of devices. I would sell them in foreign ports, and my fortune grew. In those days we sea folk did not really trust banks. So I turned all my wealth into precious gems, which I stored in an exceedingly cunning place—'

'Where?' demanded Maffeo. This might be useful – once the Fogs' stupid mistake was uncovered and he was allowed out, and handsomely apologized to.

'I can already see that you are not the kind of young man to whom I would wish to tell such a thing. I have learned the hard way that I must be discreet with people who are untrustworthy, greedy and ambitious. I'd say, from listening to you, that you are all three.'

Maffeo scowled.

'You see, once I was so innocent that I even trusted Fogfinger. When he said he was sending a ship with supplies of brass screws, with copper and silver wire in ten different widths, I believed him. I agreed to take his materials and fashion a dozen special automata for him. I did not realize that he would send a pirate ship to sink my beloved *Amneris* and to kidnap me.'

'Oho Amneris?' asked Maffeo, suddenly alert.

The old man took no notice. 'Fogfinger killed three dozen of my men, and scuttled the lovely *Amneris*, just so that he could make up a story that my ship had gone down in a storm. Fortunately, I had time to throw overboard that secret thing I mentioned, that cunning container in which I kept my gems. So he did not get his hands on it.

'But he got his hands on me. His men brought me back here. I was dragged before Fogfinger. I had thought we were friends. But I barely recognized the man I saw before me. The turban, earring, the Irish accent were all there – but all affection, indeed all humanity, had gone from his face.

'"I will slit your weasand," he said casually, "if you disobey me."

'The way he spoke was quite chilling. And I know I should have been frightened if there was slitting to be done, but I was preoccupied by looking at the smoke curling out of his fingers – that was new too. I said I would not help him. And he said that if I did not, then he would have my dear sister Margherita denounced as a traitor, and that he would slit *her* weasand.'

Maffeo yawned hugely. The old man did go on and on. But it was better than listening to the rats scratching, and it did stop him thinking about his teeth for seconds at a time.

'At this point,' the old man was saying, 'I began to take more interest in weasands. We bargained. He would leave my family alone if I would make his automata for him. And if I would consent to be detained as his guest down here in the *Pozzi*. After more mentions of my dear Margherita, I found that I would consent. As the years and decades passed, I realized I'd never have a wife or a child of my own. I could never have my sister or my family around me. I fell into a state of sad acceptance. It ceased to bother me that I never saw a newspaper, had no idea of what went on in the outside world. I drew into myself. The only thing that lifted my depression – at least by day – was to be able to use my talents in the workshop. And there I have worked, all these long years.

'But lately Fogfinger's been pushing me to create a deadly animal army from the corpses of his kills. That would be a crime! He has no respect for the soul – but I do! Nor did I like his ideas for making automata seeming to breathe. Clever machines – yes; living-dead animal – no! Where was that going to end? I told him it's impossible.'

Maffeo thought, 'Not impossible, actually. But of course

262

the old man's been locked up down here and hasn't seen what's going on in Venice just now!'

The old man was saying sadly, 'Yet I fear that I myself have been guilty of an unwitting evil. Energy and hard work were once the ancient virtues of this city. With my automata, I may have helped to let them waste away.

'But,' he suddenly sounded worried, 'why am I telling you this? You may well be a filthy spy after all.'

He fixed his fierce blue eyes on Maffeo. 'For better or worse, you know my story. If you have been thrown down here, I suppose it is because you have offended Fogfinger. So I *should* regard you as my friend. But there is something about you that I simply do not like.'

'Mutual,' muttered Maffeo. He wondered if he could be bothered to make up a lie, and decided that he could not. He decided to let the old man rave on.

'But at last, I hope, he will go too far. This is what I've been counting on for the last nineteen years. Fogfinger must surely have raised the ire of the ancient protectors of Venice. I feel in my bones that they shall soon come to her aid.'

The sound of marching feet interrupted his words and covered Maffeo's muttering, 'Ancient protectors? Ancient rot!'

'If they are coming for you,' the old man said quickly, 'if you get so much as a second outside before they kill you … tell everyone that you met me. Annibale D'Ago, the sea captain. Tell them that I am here! Get a message to my dear sister Margherita!'

The trapdoor creaked open and four Fogs came thundering down the stairs.

'Upsadaisy, my flower!' their leader said to Maffeo. 'You're out on your ear. Turns out it's not a crime to drink from a skull. Just a disgusting stupidity.'

'He's still got both ears?' laughed one of the other Fogs.

'They forgot to cut 'em off this time?' He pulled a knife out of his boot. 'Perhaps I'll do their homework for them.'

Maffeo cowered on the ground. His hands were chained so he could not protect his ears, which had never felt so delicate or so vulnerable before.

'Wait on!' said the leader. 'What it is, chaps, is we got to make this boy understand that if he ever talks about what happened to him today, *then* we cut his ears off and put 'em in his pocket.'

'Oh, *then* we cut his ears off—'

'If he says even *one weaselling word* about what he saw and whom he met down here. Otherwise, the ears can stay where they are.'

'I heard you,' said Maffeo faintly. 'I wouldn't dream of it.'

'There's a squeak in him yet!' joked a soldier.

The old man glared and shook his head as Maffeo was dragged upstairs.

48
Strange old codger

There was no one to row Maffeo home. The Fogs hadn't put a gondola at his disposal. Instead, they'd roughly emptied his pockets so he had no money to pay a boatman.

Maffeo faced an awful prospect: he might have to *walk*, on his own two legs, back to the Malipiero palace. But he did not know the way. Venice is as small as the palm of your hand, but Fogfinger's new generation of noble Venetians had no idea of her geography, as they were carried everywhere in boats. That suited Fogfinger, and it suited the spoilt young men of the *Compagnie della Calza*.

The idea of walking was repugnant to Maffeo, not just because of the effort and indignity of it. What if one of the other Fancy Stockings saw him looking like this – covered with the dust and filth of the prison, and without a gondola to row him home? The shame of it!

But Maffeo did not have a choice. In small, mincing steps, he began to walk.

In completely the wrong direction.

Hours later, Maffeo was in the northern part of Venice. He could hardly believe the humble sizes of the houses and the crumbling state of their walls.

He was also feeling two things he had never experienced in his life: hunger and thirst. A *bigolante* walked wearily past him, her buckets swinging from the yoke on her shoulders.

'I say, Poor Woman!' he croaked. 'Give me water. But from a clean cup, mind. I'm not swigging from those buckets where common people have put their dirty mouths.'

The woman's brows knitted under her top hat. Instead of kneeling to serve him, she spat so accurately that a glistening circle appeared just in front of his feet. Then she strode on, ignoring his protests and then his insults.

'What is going on?' Maffeo muttered. 'The poor don't know their place any more. They must be learning their manners from Fogfinger's baboons.'

At the next corner, Maffeo found himself face to face with Amneris D'Ago, who was rushing through the streets with a big smile on her lips.

Maffeo's bleary mind momentarily cleared. Something was wrong. This girl was supposed to be dead! He'd been in the church. He'd heard the trapdoor open, and her scream. How had she cheated the Fate in the Box? Surely there was a crime involved there! He'd always known there was something suspicious about this girl. He reached out a hand to grab her shoulder. She'd make a fine prize to deliver to Fogfinger. The Finger wouldn't want it known that a Lambing had failed. He'd want this one put away for good.

But the girl wriggled easily away from his languid touch and disappeared out of sight. Maffeo did not think he could walk another step, let alone run one. He'd have to rely on his brains rather than his muscles. Fortunately, he was much more intelligent than a seamstress. Wasn't this girl called D'Ago? Yes! He called out, 'Just met someone from your family. Your great-uncle Annibale. Strange old codger.'

Suddenly his ears were tingling with a memory of the Fogs' horrible threat to cut them off if he mentioned a word about what he'd seen and heard in the prison. He glanced around for the concealed ears of Anagrammaticulars in the walls. But it was too late now. The girl's footsteps had stopped. He told himself, 'She's an absolute no one. The Fogs only meant I should not tell someone *important*.'

He called reassuringly, 'There are no soldiers with me. I was looking for you out of the kindness of my heart because I supposed you'd like to know about the old chap. And then of course I thought you might find some little boatman to row me home, out of gratitude.'

From around the corner, Amneris sent her voice, disbelieving and quiet. 'You are lying, Maffeo Malipiero. You believed I was dead. You say my great-uncle Annibale is alive? I've news for you: he drowned nineteen years ago.'

'How would I even know who he is, if I hadn't just seen him? I don't habitually mix with commoners, you know.'

He heard the girl take two steps closer. A few curls, a cheekbone and one brown eye appeared at the corner.

'Alive? You swear it?'

'Alive and kicking. Well, not kicking much as he's in

chains. Told me some story about having a fortune in jewels that he threw overboard in a secret container when his ship was boarded by men dressed as pirates.'

'Fogfinger's men,' thought Amneris. 'Like on the Ark.'

She exclaimed, 'My granny will be overjoyed! My father and mother were young when he was taken, and I wasn't even born. But my granny is his twin sister. They were very close.'

'Yes, yes,' said Maffeo. 'Very sweet and all.'

'Where can I find him?' Amneris walked towards Maffeo, her eyes flickering right and left to check if he was telling the truth about being alone.

But there was no answer. Hunger, thirst, heat and pain had finally overcome Maffeo. He fainted in an undignified heap in front of her.

Mamma and Papà would not release Amneris from their arms. Granny's eyes were shining as she listened to the story of the saved Lambs, the *Piccolissimi Pochi*, the mermaids, and the true nature of the Saurs. When Mamma began to reproach Amneris for the deadly secrets she had kept, Granny clapped her hands.

'I will hear nothing bad! My granddaughter's just come back from the dead and Annibale is alive too! Of course he is. I never gave up hope. He was too good to die. There never was such a man. And truly original – the most wonderful mind of any man in Venice. He could think like a child, and create joy. He could think like an old man, and bring wisdom to any situation. But he was also a man who knew how to love. It would break his heart to see the poor state we live in.'

'That reminds me – the Malipiero boy also said something

about a secret container of jewels,' said Amneris. 'That Annibale threw overboard at the last minute, before he was captured. I suppose they were intended for us.'

'It was too kind of you to find a boatman to take that horrid creature home, Amneris!' grumbled Mamma. 'Most people would have left him where he dropped.'

'Then I'd be just like him, wouldn't I? And he had given me news of Great-Uncle Annibale – that alone deserved some thanks.'

'Harrumph,' said Granny. 'Poor Annibale, throwing his jewels overboard … he would rather lose it than let his fortune fall into Fogfinger's greedy hands. All those beautiful jewels lying at the bottom of the Adriatic Sea. What a waste. Still, who cares about jewels? My granddaughter is safe! My darling Annibale is alive!' She rose from her chair and danced a few steps of the *Furlana*.

Amneris's mother said anxiously, 'Mamma, don't set your hopes too high. That Malipiero boy is a bad seed and a known liar. What if he was just trying to trap Amneris?'

Granny said simply, 'I have faith.'

Amneris's father said quietly, 'There's a difference between faith and hope.'

Granny's eye fell on the 'dear creature' and the words written on the side. She said them aloud.

'If desperation strikes, turn the eye of the world on its head, tap three times, and empty.'

Granny turned to Amneris. 'Child, would you say that desperation has struck?'

'I would absolutely say it has.' Amneris's eyes opened wide. 'Do it, Granny!'

Granny picked up the kaleidoscope, chuckling, 'The eye of the world! That's a good one. Typical of Annibale!'

She turned the battered black tube on its head and rapped it three times on the table, sharply. The little disc of its glass eye flew off.

And a generous handful of priceless emeralds, diamonds and rubies lay on the table.

49
Rich and poor

Monday July 28th – Thursday August 7th, 1783

So many times in Latenia's company, Amneris had thought, 'If this is being rich, I'd rather be poor.'

Manners Make Ladies, not Ermine Tippets, she repeated to herself. She realized that she did not even want an ermine tippet. Fur looked so much better on the animals who grew it naturally than on rich spoilt humans. The escaped monkeys and baboons seemed to agree with her, for they had rifled the wardrobes of all the noble ladies, ripping their fur coats to fluff and dust. And there was almost nothing left of the little building of the Scuola dei Varoteri: the furriers' guild would never be able to meet there again after a whole army of animals chose it for their latrine.

But now, running her fingers through the glistening jewels on the table, Amneris was starting to understand that money had some use after all.

'The first thing we will do with this,' said Granny briskly, 'is bribe the Fogs at the prison to let Annibale out.'

For a little old lady with delicate skin, Granny was sounding more like a sea captain than a seamstress who had married her cousin the tailor and spent her life sewing.

'Then,' she said briskly, 'we can rely on Annibale to have an idea about finding the survivors of the Ark. Yes, I have *faith* that there *are* survivors. While that is happening, we can use the rest of the money to feed and equip the army that you, my girl, are going to lead against that criminal who imprisoned my brother and tried to Lamb you. And we'll start with those poor chaps with the bleeding fingers.'

'The Winder Uppers? Actually, I think they may be on our side already.' Amneris explained the mermaids' plans to recruit them. 'They just need money for food, wages and equipment,' she concluded.

'How,' asked Mamma, 'can we get this money to the Winder Uppers themselves? They come in the middle of the night. We'd have to break the curfew.'

'So we would,' Granny replied casually. 'Amneris, how soon can you organize the *Piccolissimi Pochi* to recruit? Three children each for Castello, San Marco, Dorsoduro, San Polo, Santa Croce, Cannaregio and Giudecca?'

'Tonight!' said Amneris.

They lay in wait for the pale wraiths, their speeches prepared. They finished with, 'Do not be afraid, gentle people. We want to give you your lives back. We want you to see the light again. And, if you'll join us, you'll never wear gloves again.'

A weak cheer went up, followed by a slithering noise – the sound of a thousand people pulling off their hated gloves and whirling them in the air before throwing them away.

'There's something else,' Amneris whispered. 'The Fogs

are nearly finished. We need a new force, of Civic Custodes, to look after the new Venice.'

'It would be an honour but we are so tired,' the Winder Uppers told them. 'We would like to help but we are starving and weak.'

'Food and wages will be supplied,' they were told. 'All we need is your willingness and your old boats.'

'With all our hearts!' agreed the Winder Uppers. 'We don't even need wages. We'll do it out of love. But you must put something in our bellies if we are to work. Goodness! What's that amazing smell?'

'Spiced pumpkin fritters in honey-tarragon sauce, I believe,' said Amneris, lifting the lid on one of the picnic baskets provided by the mermaids. 'Chilli-pea ravioli and coconut buns. Cumin biscuits with date chutney. Berry cordial.'

The Winder Uppers fell on the food with cries of delight.

'Now,' Amneris asked the Winder Uppers, when the baskets were empty, 'how about a night's sleep?'

'A night's sleep?' The Winder Uppers wept tears of joy.

By next morning, Venice was completely quiet. (Except, if you listened carefully, for the faint sound of snoring from many rooms in humble dwellings where Winder Uppers had finally returned home.) The automata had fallen silent.

Without the clacking and clicking of automata, Venetians could, for the first time in decades, hear themselves think.

What they thought was this: 'Time for a change.'

Time for a change in the way things were run in Venice.

Time for denouncing spies and bullies. Time to close down the lying *Postiglione* newspaper. Time to challenge the bullying Fogs and welcome back the exiled *Piccoli Pochi* and let them lead Venice back to the path of right.

Time to find the man who had changed Venice from a quiet, beautiful place into a cruel city as noisy as a small war. The man who had turned Venice into a town that Lambed her children and put mechanical monkeys in the place of priests.

Time to find him, and to deal with him.

In less than a day, Fogfinger's empire was dismantled. He and his cronies were now wanted men.

Latenia's homecoming had been nothing like Amneris's. When she tapped on the door of the Malipiero palace, her father sent down a scrawled note smelling of brandy: *Leave my doorstep, Imposter! My unworthy daughter is dead, slain by a Primaeval Crocodile. And Fogfinger insists on her dowry anyway. So I am ruined. Imposters need not apply – there is no money for them.*

The maid who used to fawn over her pretended not to know her, even when Latenia performed one of her best and most characteristic tantrums. The maid slammed the door in Latenia's face. A minute later, when Latenia was at the hiccuping and sniffing stage, the door opened again and all her cake stands – horribly mangled as if someone had jumped on them – were thrown out into the square.

After wandering the streets for a day, Latenia had been picked up by some of the brand-new Civic Custodes. The Fogs had quickly become too frightened to come out on the streets because baboons attacked their uniforms on sight.

Latenia was escorted, not unkindly but without ceremony, to an orphanage on Giudecca, a draughty one with long corridors and nuns dressed in grey. The only white Latenia wore now was a stiff little cap on her head.

There were no cakes and no cake stands. The gruels and the stale bread were not to her refined taste. But the nuns had no sympathy: their sugar ration had been abolished by Fogfinger and there was not one sweet thing to be had in the whole convent. Spoilt little girls were not to be tolerated.

Latenia shared a bleak dormitory with twenty-four pale girls, who fell on any food, no matter how hard, dry or tasteless, with delight and gratitude. They too were locked up, but they seemed to be happy about it.

The poor girls who'd sewed the pirate and demon costumes were now homeless, and the nuns were entrusted with keeping them safe from harm. Their master, Melchior Dubbini, was wanted for his part in the Redentore Lambing. The girls loved the convent – they smiled and chattered and sang all day long and into the night until the nuns shushed them.

'It's so much better than being at Signor Dubbini's,' they told Latenia.

'I know Dubbini!' she said. 'He used to come to our—'

Then she stopped herself. She did not want these girls to know who she was. They had been kind to her, trying to make her join in with their songs and storytelling sessions in the dormitory when the candles were blown out. Each one of them insisted on kissing her goodnight before they went to bed. She would have liked to kiss them back, but she felt too shy and too uncertain. Would they want her kiss if they knew who she really was?

Latenia was also being hunted.

'Bride of Fogfinger,' the animals called her. They had watched her receiving Fogfinger's gifts on the day her father signed the betrothal documents. They knew her brother. The animals had judged the entire Malipiero family, and had judged them poor specimens.

Turtles came to haunt Latenia at the convent, real, living turtles, who reminded her of her collection of tortoiseshell combs for which Amneris had reproached her.

When she looked outside the window, she saw the turtles' little faces gaping at her from the water.

'Where is Fogfinger?' they demanded with their beaky little lips.

'Dead, I hope!' she wept.

'We don't believe so,' they chanted. 'Not yet.'

50
A guttersnipe with a ruby

Thursday August 7th, 1783

The prison at the Doge's Palace was one of the last places in Venice still controlled by the Fogs. The new Civic Custodes were unwilling to storm it, fearing loss of life among the prisoners.

So an armed truce existed between the new Civic Custodes and the frightened Fogs who had barricaded themselves inside the stout walls of the prison. Huddling behind bars, like prisoners themselves, they listened to the animals snarling and barking outside. Food was passed through a slot in the gates, on the condition that the prisoners were fed too.

The Fogs at the prison were suspicious of the little girl with the old-fashioned features and the wavy chestnut hair who came tapping at the door. They did not trust an innocent face.

'Haven't I seen that face somewhere before?' asked one of them.

'Like on a WANTED poster?' said his companion,

lifting his lantern to peer at Amneris.

Before they could take a better look at her, she pulled the ruby out of her shawl, holding it up so that the lantern awoke the fire at its red heart.

'What's a guttersnipe like you doing with a thing like that?'

Amneris pulled the ruby out of the light. The men's faces fell.

One wheedled, 'Oh, we're not accusing you of anything, sweetie! I guess you've just come to report a theft. That's what it is, right?'

Amneris thought, 'Yes, the theft and imprisonment of my great-uncle! For nearly twenty years!'

She nodded encouragingly.

'So if you're a good girl and give us the stone, then you think we might arrange a little reward for you, is that it?'

Amneris lifted the stone in the light again. The ruby sent rich sparks into the eyes of the soldiers.

The men whistled.

'There's an old man locked away in here,' Amneris began.

'Oh, no, sweetie, more than our lives are worth to let a prisoner free—'

The man's jaw dropped, and his eyes narrowed with greed, when Amneris pulled out a second ruby, bigger and more lustrous than the first.

It felt strange to be walking hand in hand with a man who was part of her family but whom she'd never met until ten minutes before.

Yet there was something comforting and familiar about that age-speckled hand, as if Amneris had known it all her life. And of course she had – for Great-Uncle Annibale was

Granny's twin brother. Their hands, and their faces, were identical – except that Granny's was topped by ladylike grey curls mustered in a chignon at her neck, and Annibale was now resplendently bald.

As Amneris and Great-Uncle Annibale walked over the bridges and down the alleys that led away from the Doge's Palace, she explained what had been happening in Venice, about the exiled priests, the Lambing and the Fate in the Box itself.

Annibale stopped dead as she described the garish little toy and horrifying skull that popped out of it. 'That,' he thundered, 'is one automaton I *never* designed. Of course the mechanism is centuries old and very simple. Fogfinger had only to copy it from any German toymaker, and then attach a hinge to the trapdoor in the floor to make it deadly. My poor child, how you have suffered from that gruesome toy!'

'There is good news too, Great-Uncle.' Amneris tugged his sleeve. He smiled when she, somewhat hesitantly, told him about the mermaids, saying, 'I always suspected as much! Of *course* Venice would have mermaids to protect her. It makes fine and perfect sense. I look forward to meeting them. I suppose they are mouth-smackingly beautiful and sing songs to make a sailor lose his heart?'

'I am afraid,' Amneris said regretfully, 'they are visible only to children up to the age of fourteen. And their songs are, well, rough as guts.'

'Well, if they learned Humantongue from sailors and pirates, I suppose one shouldn't be shocked about a bit of gadzookery,' he smiled. 'We're a colourful lot, we sea folk, Niece.'

'And the food!' Amneris spoke of the radish-rolled samphire hotcakes, washed down with *acqua sgnanfa*, a rich orange-flower water, and other mermaidly treats until his stomach gurgled and they had to stop to buy some zucchini fritters.

Over those, Amneris told the tale of 'the dear creature' that had floated back to Venice, and of the white designs, and how its riddle had at last been unravelled. Annibale said, 'Well, Margherita took her time to work that out. Nineteen years! I wouldn't put it past that kaleidoscope to have brought about your meeting with that nice boy Temistocle, dear Enrico's grandson. There's magic in that creature, indeed!'

These were almost the only happy parts of the story Amneris recounted. For the rest, Annibale growled, shook his pale bald head, and sometimes brandished his fist at the sky. He stopped dead entirely when she told him about the shipful of demons that had sunk the 'Traitors' Ark'.

'Though of course the ship should never have been called that!' Amneris said passionately. 'Those were good and true Venetians, including Tockle's mother and sisters.'

'And you don't know *where* the poor souls went down?' Annibale asked.

'Even the mermaids couldn't find them. I suppose you'd have to take a fleet of boats and search every cove between here and Greece,' she said despairingly. 'We can only hope they've swum to shore and are sheltering somewhere.'

'There is, of course, a quicker way to survey an ocean,' said Annibale thoughtfully. 'I made some models in secret, when Fogfinger believed I was working on a project to fly white rabbits around the San Samuele theatre ... I believe that ... it would work on a larger scale. Of course, it'd need to be manned by someone with knowledge of the sea, and of charts.'

'It?' asked Amneris. There was no doubt about the 'someone' to whom he was referring, when he spoke of 'someone with a knowledge of the sea, and of charts'.

'So the family trade of sewing has continued in my absence. How much silk have you at home, Niece?'

'Sacks of it. But all in tiny pieces, leftovers from our commissions.'

'And how good are you at sewing, Niece? And how fast?'

'Good and fast. But I also know where there are plenty of girls who are good and fast too. They've been locked up and kept cruelly, like slaves. I've just realized that at last I can help them. Do you mind if we take a quick detour to Giudecca, Great-Uncle?'

'If it involves freeing some girls who have been locked up and kept cruelly, then I insist upon it.'

The members of the *Compagnie della Calza* were rounded up and imprisoned in one of the grimmer monasteries. Being so very garishly dressed, they were easy to find. The Fancy Stockings were now held accountable for their cruel pranks against animals and humans. Individual punishments were devised for them by *Piccoli Pochi* who now ran their Council of War from their new headquarters by the Rialto Market. Annibale D'Ago had joined the Council immediately.

In exchange for a profound apology to all cats he had ever offended, Maffeo was granted a cure for the dental curse. The process was not particularly pleasant for him.

Baffi had to stand on a stool in front of him, and lick his face in the shape of a cross – first downwards from the nose and then across the eyes. The cat had made sure of getting his teeth into an old fish supper before doing it. He could not, of course, make his tongue any rougher than it was. But he was satisfied that its natural rasp left a painful trail across Maffeo's face.

Maffeo shouted with disgust.

Baffi paused in his work to hiss. 'Conssssssider yourself lucky it's just my tongue. My paw is itching to ssscratch you. *Deeply* itching for a *deep* ssscratch.'

He flexed his claws to their full extent.

'You talk?' Maffeo gasped.

'Sssurely the most intelligent boy in Venice knew that alrrready?' sneered Shaveling, who had come to watch proceedings.

At the thought of having his face scarred in the shape of a cross, Maffeo fell silent, and submitted to his licking with eyes downcast.

Some of the Fancy Stockings were put in work clothes and made to repaint buildings they had defaced with rude words. They were taught to refit panes of glass to windows they had broken. They walked patients around the hospital courtyard where they had once held belching competitions.

'Not again!' shouted Maffeo, when the Custodes came for him the day after his licking. 'Don't you realize I am special?'

'Very special, Sir,' said a Custode. 'As one of Fogfinger's special favourites, we have some special tasks for you.'

And Maffeo was equipped with a sponge and some soap, and sent to scrub the litter trays of all the cats in every quarter of Venice.

'Of course,' Maffeo was told, 'there would be leniency for you if you would tell us the whereabouts of your old friend Fogfinger. As the most intelligent person in Venice, surely you are privy to that confidential information?'

Maffeo scowled and dipped the sponge in water. Beside him, Melchior Dubbini scrubbed a cat bowl stubbornly crusted with dried gravy.

51
Hunt for a shipwreck, hunt for a villain

Saturday August 9th–Friday August 15th, 1783

Great-Uncle Annibale surveyed the work of his niece, his sister and the pale girls they had rescued from the convent on Giudecca. The nuns had quickly unlocked the cells when he barked with an air of absolute authority, 'I have come to requisition labour for a civic project. Orders, you know. And speaking of orders, your sugar ration shall be restored immediately. I'll see to it personally.'

In less than two days, Annibale D'Ago and the *Piccoli Pochi* Council had put right a great many things in the city (including the nuns' sugar rations). Meanwhile, those talented girls had sewed together every scrap of silk in the D'Ago household, even unravelling the rag rugs, even using pieces of trimming from the cushion where the cat Grillo liked to sleep. He did not find the girls' thin laps an adequate substitute, and went back to the apothecary's for a few days. The girls slept in bedrooms offered by all the D'Agos' neighbours, but arrived, smiling, for work every morning at six. For her own safety, it was decided, Latenia

283

was to remain at the convent a little longer: her face had been seen at the Redentore Lambing, when she had been presented as Fogfinger's bride.

Every cloth-dyer on the Rio dei Mendicanti had handed over whatever scraps of fabric they could spare. Amneris calculated that one million, seven hundred thousand and forty-two stitches had gone into the strange silk masterpiece Great-Uncle Annibale had designed. Over ten thousand buttons – donated by every household in Cannaregio and Castello – fastened various flaps and bands together. Biri had contributed her entire collection of safety pins and pegs.

The masterpiece – which someone ignorant or rude might have called 'a patchwork rag-sack' – was more than twenty metres long. At its widest point, it was fifteen metres. At the insistence of Annibale's twin sister, it had been varnished with a coat of alum, to prevent fire. And at the suggestion of Tockle, there was a delicate fishnet spun over the entire sack, in case of any seams giving.

While work proceeded on the silk sack, Annibale had set up a workshop in the garden of the D'Ago house. He slept in a boat moored outside, insisting that he needed to 'feel the waves under my old bones again'.

Tockle and Ugo – now walking on his own – were sent to search through all the files and papers in every one of the Fogs' offices and hideouts, looking for information about the Ark. A picture was built up of a secret diversion towards Trieste. Biri was entrusted with the work of distributing Fogfinger's collection of turbans to the leaders of all the different packs of animals. The baboons, lions and leopards tied the strips of fabric around their necks, constantly refreshing their memory of his scent.

By the third day, everything was as ready as it could possibly be for the embarkation of Annibale's mysterious silk device. The sea charts were stowed in a huge lobster pot, as were supplies of firewood, water and dried fruits, a musket, a large yellow flag and a blue china chamber pot. There were sponges soaked in more alum, a rope ladder and a telescope.

'Light the fire!' ordered Annibale. One of the much-less-pale girls, now blooming on milk and polenta, brought her lantern to the lobster pot, where a miniature grate was already piled with kindling.

He shook hands with the members of the *Piccoli Pochi* Council, all gathered to wish him farewell. He hugged the woman in breeches. 'Soon you will be with your daughter, Lucia!' he whispered.

'Annibale! Are you sure this is wise?' His sister clung to his side. 'I've only just found you again after all these years.'

'After all these years in prison, a man needs to stretch his wings,' said Annibale. 'And Venice needs her Ark full of people back.'

He kissed his sister and his great-niece. They watched the hot air from the fire swell the long silk sack into a towering dome of brilliant colours. Soon the dome was tugging impatiently at its tethers.

'Don't want it to leave without me, do we?' Annibale vaulted nimbly into the lobster pot, saluted the assembled crowd and cut the ropes with the knife tied to his belt. He smiled and lifted the yellow flag. 'You'll be seeing this old man again, and he'll be waving this flag if the news is good.'

Amneris and her granny clung to one another as the swollen sack lurched up into the air. Beneath the silken dome, Great-Uncle Annibale's own bald dome shone in the sunlight.

'All alone,' moaned Granny. 'I should have gone with him. If he is to die again, this time I want to die too.'

'But he's not alone. Look! He has an escort! Isn't that … Grillo up there? And Baffi!'

285

'Did you know that they had wings?'

The balloon and its escort of flying cats flew gracefully over the roofs of Venice, dextrously avoiding the bell-towers.

Annibale's voice floated down to them. 'And while I'm away, find Fogfinger! Let the animals help you. Where in the world would you find better hunters than them?'

Fogfinger's last remaining turban was wet. It had shrunk and clung around his head with the ruby nodding loosely at the front. He'd had to escape very quickly, with no time to pack a trunk. Now he was living like a fugitive. He, Fogfinger, a fugitive? Someone would pay for this outrage! And painfully, too.

The only person he trusted with his whereabouts was Lardo Drossi.

The animals from his palace all had his scent. He had seen a lion with one of his own silk turbans tied around its neck in a great floppy bow. Lardo Drossi did not know how that happened.

As soon as he saw that lion, Fogfinger knew that the animals were hunting him, just as he had once hunted them.

The beasts had an advantage over him: they had excellent hearing. His ear trumpet was too clumsy to carry around with him, and would identify him instantly. So the animals were alert to his every step and every breath, but *he* could barely hear their growls and chirrups.

Fogfinger could not understand it. He'd taken flight under the confusion of the great migration of reanimated beasts, laughing as he watched them stream out of the Natural History Museum. He was sure that they were going to their deaths: he imagined a great cull. But the people of Venice were not hunting or killing the animals, even though it turned out that the Venetians were, strangely, equipped with muskets and bows and arrows. He'd seen the new Civic Custodes marching past, well armed, in perfect formation. *Who were they?*

But not a single bow or musket had been fired at a single beast. Instead, ridiculously, the Venetians were feeding those animals, cutting them out of their fancy costumes and giving them fresh water to drink in those bowls at the bases of the wells that were mysteriously running freely again. (How had *that* happened? And why hadn't he been told?)

And the animals, while not tame, were responding well to the Venetians' kindness. The foxes desisted from killing the domestic chickens and accepted butchers' sausages instead. The birds of prey left the cats and dogs alone. The lions sunned themselves quietly in the squares, bothering no one, and eating politely at the troughs of food put out for them twice a day. The snakes busied themselves decimating the rat population. Doge Morosini's mummified cat curled up on top of his former owner's magnificent grave in the church of Santo Stefano and purred loudly all through mass. In fact, the only creatures – apart from the rats – who were in difficulty with the animals were Fogfinger's own men.

Not a single bow or musket had been fired at a Fog by a human.

Instead it was the animals who had declared war on the Fogs, easily identified by their grey uniforms, and also by their well-fed bodies. Many of the Fogs had attended Fogfinger on his hunting expeditions in Africa. Each animal sought out the Fog who had shot it. When they recognized a hunter, they fell on him. And now the former hunters were the hunted: Fogfinger himself most of all.

So he was in disguise as well as in hiding. In fact, Fogfinger had no need to hide his face as it bore little resemblance those days to the handsome image on the frescoes and flags.

But his vanity did not allow him to admit that fact. So he had adopted a Pantalon mask – that of an old man with a furrowed brow and a long pointed nose. It was so long since he'd banned masks in Venice that there were some children who had never seen one. They screamed and ran away when they saw him coming, which suited him nicely.

Fogfinger still wore his famous turban above the mask, also for reasons of vanity. Even though it made him easier to identify, he refused to remove it, because then he would expose the long thin head that was now as hairless as a baby's but considerably more nobbly.

Some of the rich had adapted to an automata-less life in Venice. Those who could not stomach it had fled to their country estates, where their automata sat motionless and rusting with no slaves to wind them up.

Of course those who stayed could have ordered their servants to do the winding-up, but more and more of them were letting their automata simply wind down. The rich were finding some amusement in the primitive life without their machines. It had, in fact, been quite boring to never lift a finger, they confessed to one another. It had made them feel like machines themselves – useless ones.

They started hiring people again. The poor people who had jobs shared their wages with those who were still out of work.

The parishioners were busy restoring order in their churches. The masks were ripped off the statues of saints, and the dust carefully brushed from their noble faces. The mechanical lamb in the Frari was put away in the black coffin that hung on the wall in the right nave. Everything was ready for the return of the priests, but an expedition to the Fog-patrolled island monastery where they were held was still deemed too dangerous.

The glass-blowers, led by Signor Castrauro of the *Piccoli Pochi*, were creating hundreds of blue glass seahorses, one for every Venetian, to mark the end of oppression and the beginning of good times in Venice.

Those whose families had been on the Ark waited, but now – at last – with hope. News of Annibale D'Ago's expedition had spread around the city. There were lookouts on all the towers, waiting for any sign of his return.

And on the ground, everyone was looking for one thing – Fogfinger.

Fogfinger opened his long velvet cloak. Inside were sewn a hundred pockets, each with a different perfume. He selected a new bottle, and extracted its cork. Then he poured it all over himself, disguising his smell. Lardo Drossi had provided the coat, the perfume and the idea. So far, it had worked.

He waited on the street corner, like a beggar, for Lardo Drossi's square wife to come with his food and the address of the empty house where he'd stay that night. Sometimes he had to resort to one of the stuffy *cofanetti*, the little detention rooms that had formerly housed the shabbiest of criminals.

He was shaking with anger under his Pantalon mask, and the smoke was curling out of his fingers. Earlier that day, he had crept around to the warehouse in Santa Croce that stored his 'Wild Water'. The green bottles, and the brown bottles of 'Ordinary', were piled up to the ceiling – untouched.

From the volume of bottles, Fogfinger realized that the 'Wild Water' trick had been failing for some time: almost from the moment he instituted it. Someone had betrayed him, and kept this vital information from him. Someone in his inner circle.

'Things might be gloomy,' brooded Fogfinger, 'but I still have a few choice means of revenge. When I find out who the perpetrator is.'

At least Lardo Drossi had remained loyal, Fogfinger smiled, when everyone else had abandoned him. There he was now, with a packet of wafer biscuits and whipped cream from the *pestrini*. Good man!

The Fogs were in hiding, terrified after watching several of their company attacked and killed by animals. It was suspected that the soldiers were lurking in their boats, covering themselves with canvas and emerging only at night. There were hundreds of Fog vessels in Venice. Any one of them could be holding a squad of armed Fogs. They had even abandoned the prisons, chased out by Biri's army of jointed insects who mounted a miniature plague when they were all sleeping in their bunks, and bit them raw.

To approach the Fog boats would mean death for any brave soul who tried – several lemurs had already been shot as they lifted the canvas on a *peata*. It was too sad for these brave beasts to die a second time: although they were willing, Lussa decreed there would be no more sacrifices of this kind. Biri's moths were despatched to identify which boats held Fogs. They hovered in clouds above them until *Piccoli Pochi* armed with knives arrived to cut the vessels adrift. Then the mermaids dragged the boats out into the centre of the lagoon where they set their Seaweed Familiars to guard them.

'As soon as them finkle-swotted Fogs gets a bit peckish,

and try to swim for the shore to get some vittles,' Chissa explained, 'the Seaweed Familiars shall surround 'em, tangling their nasty toes and enveloping their arms so they cannot swim.'

'You mean to drown them?' Amneris asked.

'No,' said Lussa. 'That would be Murder, and Mermaids do not murder. They wage Honourable War. When each Mermaid hears, deep inside her Soul, that her Particular Familiar is engaged with a Fog, then She shall swim to the *Bacino* and present Herself to the Fog.'

Biri interrupted, 'But them Fogs is growned men. None of 'em will see a Mermaid.'

'Yar, but He shall feel her Presence and grow Bewildered.'

'Bewildered, mammering mad, froth-brained and measle-headed,' pronounced Chissa happily.

'Whereupon,' continued Lussa, 'each Mermaid will sing to Him so that She Unlocks the Tenderness in his Heart. She will explain that He has been under a Kind of Evil Enchantment. She will sing & explain until each Fog is weeping with Shame for what He has done to the Poor Citizens of Venice. Every Fog will vow to atone for his Crimes, Each in a Different Way.'

'What kind of ways?' asked Tockle.

'Some shall go to the Wretched Island where the Priests are shut up. They shall rescue those Good Men & bring Them back to Venice. The Venetians have great Need of Them now, as with Salvation there often comes a Burning Sense of Guilt. People have also lost Loved Ones, and the Living shall need Comfort.'

'Meanwhile,' said Chissa, 'the rest of those lubbery scoundrels will be set to feeding the animals—'

'And shovelling their—' began a young mermaid, but Lussa's eye fell on her with a dreadful sternness.

Amneris clapped her hands. 'And the Winder Uppers are

already freed from slavery. And the animals are free. And the Fate in the Box?' She shuddered at the memory of the brightly coloured little toy that once had the power of life or death over her – and had chosen death.

'Shall be destroyed. Just as soon as We can obtain the Key to the Tower.'

'Poetic justice!' said Amneris. But privately she felt that she would not feel quite happy again until she had seen the Fate in the Box reduced to a thousand irreparable pieces.

'Yar, highly Poetical,' smiled Lussa. 'And look! The very first Mermaid has received a Message from her Familiar!'

Chissa, a distracted expression on her face, was swimming out of the cavern at speed, shouting, 'Rouse out! Shake a leg!'

Lussa asked Amneris, 'Is there News of your Great-Uncle?'

'Not yet,' said Amneris in an artificially bright voice. 'Not yet.'

52
A small symbol of hope

Saturday August 16th, 1783

It was the lookout at San Sebastiano – a fisherman – who saw it first, in the dim light of dawn.

The multicoloured dome dipped and swooped over the ocean currents, but its direction was clear. And so was the yellow flag that waved from the lobster pot. And so, even though the fisherman rubbed his eyes, was the escort of winged cats.

A yellow flag!

'It's going to land in San Marco!' cried the fisherman, who had traced the trajectory according to the wind. And he scrambled down the ninety-eight steps of his tower to alert the next lookout in the next tower. He was halfway down the steps when he remembered what he was supposed to do, and ran back up. He used the pot of black ink to paint a message on the white sheet, and then hung it out of the belfry, tying it securely to two hooks. Then he jangled the bells with a hammer to make sure everyone looked up to see what he had written.

293

GOOD NEWS ABOUT THE ARK. EVERYONE TO SAN MARCO!

When the lookout on the next tower saw this sign, he reached for his own ink pot and unrolled his own sheet.

The dome of silk coasted into San Marco just as the sun was rising. The soft light gilded the bald pate of Annibale D'Ago and his huge smile. The Civic Custodes had carefully roped off a large space in the centre of the square so that no one would be hurt when the vessel landed.

Everyone was there – summoned from every parish in Venice by the sheet-messages on the bell-towers. The men and women of the *Piccoli Pochi* were there in force, including the chestnut-haired woman in breeches. The returned priests were there, ready to say prayers for whatever the news might be. Biri and Tockle were there, with the entire D'Ago family. The nuns were there, offering cakes all round. The twenty-four pale girls were there, no longer pale and now full of smiles. Only Latenia Malipiero remained closed up in the convent, away from the anger of the crowds.

Annibale leapt gracefully from the lobster basket. Amneris and her granny took him into their arms.

Over the tops of their heads, he shouted, 'Soon all of you shall be hugging your own loved ones. They are safe and well, on an island near Trieste. There are no more dead than those poor souls who already floated into the city.'

He pulled a marked chart out of his breeches. 'Every able-bodied seaman to his boat. You can be there in a day and a half.'

A serious fisherman, one of the *Pochi*, took the map. 'We'll have it copied immediately, and set out within the hour. The boats are ready, Sir.'

'I only regret that I could not bring them all back with me. However,' he smiled, gently disengaging himself from his great-niece and sister, 'I did manage to bring a small symbol of hope.'

The crowd surged forward to see what he had brought out of the lobster pot.

'Is there a Temistocle Molin in the square?'

Tockle pushed forward. Annibale reached into the lobster pot and brought out a wicker basket in which a tiny girl lay sleeping, her thumb pressed between her lips.

'My sister!' Tockle cried. 'It must be true! They are safe!'

Granny took the basket in her arms. 'As if that great galumphing boy could look after a little treasure like you!' she cooed to the little one. 'I'm taking you home. In the meantime, here are twenty-four young nursemaids just panting to give you a cuddle. So why the red nose, boy?'

'I wish the captain had brought my mamma and sister Stella too,' gulped Tockle. 'Though I never thought I'd say that about Stella.'

Amneris felt a tug at her skirt. It was Grillo, looking somewhat windswept.

'You're wanted in the mermaid cavern. You, Biri and the boy.'

'Great-Uncle Annibale!' Amneris tried to attract his attention, but he was surrounded by eager faces and strong arms wanting to embrace him.

'Down with Fogfinger! Annibale D'Ago for Doge!' someone cried. And soon the whole square had taken up the cry.

53
'For once in his reeky spleeny snipy life'

Saturday August 16th, 1783

The baboons were hunting him. They were too intelligent. It was terrifying. They had got his scent, despite the perfume. The last batch had seemed strangely watery, Fogfinger recalled.

It was just before dawn, and the air was rent with the baboons' bloodthirsty cries.

It was like a single lion being chased by a mob of hyenas, or a pack of hunters with guns and dogs.

So cruel! So unfair! So undignified! He could not stop the incriminating fog from curling out of his fingertips and up into the air like an exclamation mark that said, 'Look! I'm here!'

He heard the baboons skittering on the roofs behind him. He saw their shadows leaping on the ground ahead of him. He could see what they were planning: to trap him in a narrow *calle*, and to seal it at both ends, with more of their number on the roofs. Then they would move in for the kill. Baboons were untidy killers. He'd seen and admired their work in Africa, where he had destroyed so many of their kind himself. And he was aware that baboons were known to start eating before their victims were even dead.

He hurried to the *fondamenta* in front of the Frari church.

He bent over the water, looking into its green depths with fear. If only he could swim!

And that was when the She Sea-Saur surged up in front of him.

Images played across the turtle shell's smooth inner surface, creating flickering blazes of light on the gold mosaics of the cavern.

Inside the curve was a scene of Venetian rooftops, crowded with chattering baboons.

'They're hunting, aren't they?' said Tockle, looking at their glittering eyes and hunched shoulders, their snouts thrust forward, sniffing.

'Reckon it would be more like proper hunting if they gave them monkeys some muskets,' said Biri.

The turtle shell clouded over and began to clear, revealing a new scene.

'You may wish to shade your Eyes now, Children,' said Lussa. 'Or You may choose to witness, but It is right that You are here, Biri, Temistocle and Amneris. We shall require You to inform the Venetians of the Event that is about to take Place.' Her voice was grim and quiet. 'They shall need to know when their long Nightmare is over.'

Such a horror of roaring and dragonly weeping was being played out on the turtle shell. Fogfinger, his mask hanging off one ear, crouched on the *fondamenta*, his head down. His hands were clasped as if in prayer.

'It's the She Sea-Saur,' whispered Tockle. 'She's telling him what he did to her.'

'As if he didn't know!' said Amneris.

Chissa told them, 'That suck-egg skink Fogfinger's been made to listen for once in his reeky spleeny snipy life. That poor Saur has surely got plenty to get off her chest.'

Lussa translated, '*You killed and flayed my Husband. You kept us apart all these Years. I was so lonely in the Sea. Even the Humans hated Me …*'

A second, larger Sea-Saur hove into view. His scales were patchy but they had nearly all regrown. He joined his wife berating Fogfinger, who took each roar with a wince as if it was a blow.

Chissa said, 'Yoiks! Now the old man's blowing his scaly top! He's saying, "*You took me from my lady wife, before we had even hatched a single egg. We could have become extinct. For years you have set me up as a dead horror for the humans to gawk at in the museum. Yet all the time, my spirit was alive, and suffering. And you knew it.*" Oh! Now *he's* givin' Fogfinger the glad eye. Look how close he's leaning in. Saur breath ain't the sweetest.'

A young mermaid observed, 'Smelled sweeter tings under da heads o' pirate ships after a raid on a beer-boat. That gorbellied pantaloon, he's getting a noseful!'

'Somefing fierce!' agreed Biri.

Amneris whispered, 'What will they do to him? You said that they were kind and loving creatures, Lussa.'

'Even Kind & Loving Creatures have a Limit to their Compassion.'

The She Sea-Saur bent over to rip off Fogfinger's mask.

Chissa cried, 'They're goin' for him now. He'll be – Oh! Bless my old soul!'

Whimpering, Fogfinger threw himself backwards against the wall, and then slid around the corner into the alley that led to the Campiello Zen, where the baboons were waiting for him. They'd been joined by the flat-bellied gorilla, who towered above them. The creatures surrounded Fogfinger in an instant, reaching out with their long fingers, poking at his chest. The gorilla tugged at his turban, unwinding the fringed end of it. A baboon leapt at the ruby brooch above his forehead. The stone tumbled to the ground. A smaller baboon tucked it into his navel and folded his belly skin over it. He strutted about on his short legs, while the other baboons screamed excited approval.

For a moment, they had forgotten about their prey.

Fogfinger sidled back onto the *fondamenta* by the canal. The Saurs had submerged again, but he had no doubt they were waiting for the baboons to deliver him.

Was there nowhere safe in Venice?

Yes! There was!

Fogfinger's hand closed around the key inside his frock-coat. He calculated that if he made it across the bridge and then the square, he could be inside the Frari church in one minute. He'd slam the great doors behind him to gain some time, and then he could run through the left nave and unlock the door to the tower, and bolt himself in.

Of course there was no one to wheel him up to the top in his bath chair this time.

But once he was inside his tower, no one could touch him.

54
The last Lamb

Saturday August 16th, 1783

'He's getting away!' cried Biri.

'I think not,' said Lussa. 'The Apes give Chase.'

'But now he's shut the baboons out of the church,' said Tockle. 'Oh look, the turtle shell can see inside the nave. He's gone to the tower, of course!'

The apes battered angrily at the great doors of the Frari. The gorilla flung himself at a stained-glass window.

'Even if they get in, they'll never break the lock to the tower – it's like a little fortress in itself.' Amneris remembered that door and its stout bolts all too well.

'Where are them baboons off to?' asked Biri. 'Are they giving up? Shame on them! Ah! They's talking to them Saurs at the edge of the canal.'

Both lizards disappeared under the water.

'Where have the Saurs gone?' asked Tockle. 'Why has the turtle shell gone so dark? Oh, I see, it's showing us *inside* the tower now. Look at Fogfinger. He thinks he's safe.'

Then the green snout of the He Sea-Saur burst through

the water at the bottom of the ramp. He clambered out, followed by his wife.

'Griddled goats!' shouted the mermaids. 'Watch 'em waddle!'

With his right hand, Fogfinger was scrabbling at the cold rough bricks of the tower – just like all the Lambs he had sent stumbling up that ramp before him.

The difference was that there was no little mechanical lamb in front of Fogfinger. Instead, the two Sea-Saurs lumbered behind him at a shockingly fast pace, despite the fact that their muscular bodies almost filled the space between the inner and outer towers.

Fogfinger could hear the Sea-Saurs' rhythmic grunts and their eager breath. He reeled at its sourness: he could even feel the damp warmth of it on the back of his neck. He was only one half-turn of the ramp ahead of them, and he was starting to feel a weakness in his knees and the dizziness of exhaustion. The Saurs, however, kept plodding tirelessly. The tall arches of the inner tower offered him terrifying glimpses of the She Sea-Saur's grim grin and flickering tongue as she trudged behind her husband, her legs angled out from her body, her tail thrashing eagerly.

For one terrible moment, Fogfinger lost his footing and slid back a few metres. The male Saur's jaw grasped the tails of his silk frock-coat. With all the energy still left in him, Fogfinger wrenched himself free of the delicate fabric, leaving his coat tails in the monster's mouth. He staggered forward, and around the next bend.

Around and around went Fogfinger and his pursuers. The little glimpses of Venice through the hooded arched windows seemed to wink mockingly at him.

'Surely,' he thought, 'I shall lose the creatures at the belfry. They shall not be able to climb up those last steep steps into the roof space. It's more of a ladder. I shall be safe.'

Bursting into the belfry, he was dazzled by daylight glimmering like mother-of-pearl. He tripped, falling headlong, narrowly missing the hole in the centre of the floor down which all the condemned Lambs had plunged. This time the Saur's teeth closed on his high-heeled satin shoe.

Shaking it off, Fogfinger slithered to the steps on his belly and then leapt straight up to the third step, gaining the roof space in a moment. Inside, he paused panting in front of the fluted stone pedestal on which the Fate in the Box stood. Below him the belfry filled up with the two lizards. He could hear their heavy steps and their heads smiting the stairs, the bronze bells, the marble arches. The male roared and lashed his tail, so that the bells shuddered out deafening, discordant notes.

'They cannot get up here!' Fogfinger allowed himself to smile, just for a moment, as he lit the red-paned lanterns.

Even as he spoke, a bell began to toll in a regular, powerful rhythm.

'How—?' he started to ask as the wood splintered beneath his feet, and the male Saur's head thrust into the chamber, questing and snapping among the velvet curtains while its body swung from the bronze bell around which it had wrapped itself.

Fogfinger clung to the column that held the Fate in the Box, using it as a shield. The Saur lunged. Jolted, the gaudy little machine began to tinkle its sweet, childlike tune.

A penny for a spool of thread,
A penny for a needle ...

Fogfinger tried to grab the machine, to stop the handle from revolving. If the grinning skull popped out of the garish little box then the trapdoor beneath his feet would drop.

But the handle kept turning, as if of its own volition, releasing its cascade of delicate notes as fast as the throbbing of Fogfinger's own pulse.

That's the way the money goes,

Pop! Goes the ...

The skull with its strings of hair surged up, the trapdoor opened, and Fogfinger dropped into the well of the tower, still grasping the Fate in the Box.

'I can't sw-i-i-i-m,' he cried, plummeting, as the Fate in the Box crumbled to sawdust and springs in his hands.

55
The way of Humanfolk

The atmosphere inside the cavern was not at all triumphant. Some of the younger children were sobbing or trembling. The chef-mermaid rushed to the edge of the pool, distributing spiced sea cocoa and sugar-dipped chilli shortbread fingers.

Lussa explained gently, 'What started with Blood – the Blood of Innocent Human Children like Yourselves – must end in Blood. That is the Way of Humanfolk.'

'There, there, snotties. That maggot of machinery is smashed now. It cannot kill again,' said Chissa.

Tockle had been quietly sick in a corner. He tried to cover his embarrassment by joking to Amneris, 'At least your friend Latenia's not getting married now.'

'By the way, how did them baboons find the Finger in the end?' asked Biri.

'Annibale D'Ago's last Emerald paid for the Information,' said Lussa. 'Ugo traded It. A Signor Lardo Drossi – a Singularly Unpleasant Specimen of Your Race – now has that Traitorous Jewel in his Possession.'

Chissa said complacently, 'And he is one who shall shortly be meeting a hyena in a dark alley in Cannaregio.'

'And his wife?' Amneris remembered the hard hands and cruel voice of Maschaccia at her Lambing.

''Twas she who told us where to find her goaty husband,' said Chissa. 'And the bears have been told to get that nice emerald back off yon lumpy lady before they finish with her. And by the way, Master Temistocle, the baboons found *this* in her pocket.'

She held out the old kaleidoscope known as Sweet-Nizzi-on-the-Mantelpiece.

'Food!' called the chef-mermaid. A flotilla of silver salvers appeared in the water. There was a Cremonese cow-pea soup fragrant with coriander and coconut topped by crisp shavings of river horseradish tossed in chilli oil. There were scallop shell-shaped biscuits heaped with toadstool-and-truffle pâté and generous portions of minced mayflower roulade stuffed with ginger and cashew nuts, followed by Trembly Pudding – a soft, wobbling jelly made of cream, sugar and the spicy berries of the Fear-Bush.

After that, they nibbled on caramelized baby-pea popcorn and talked far into the night about what to do about a Venice that was now free from Fogfinger but was also a rather dangerous zoo.

It was only when Amneris recalled the scuttled Ark the Venetian fishermen had just dredged from its shallow grave and towed back to Venice that she exclaimed, 'But of course! Great-Uncle Annibale can take the animals back to Africa in the Ark, when it's repaired. He must be dying for a sea voyage after nineteen years cooped up in prison!'

Tockle said, 'I'll go with him – we shall find my father and bring him home.'

56
The beginning of a mother

Wednesday August 20th, 1783

Latenia did not want to raise her eyes, even when the silhouette of a tall woman interrupted the light from the window.

She knew she should be eager to see her visitor.

But she did not know how to address this woman even when she did finally allow herself to look up, taking in the sunburned skin, the rich hair, the full mouth so like her own, though not turned down at the corners like hers.

In the chilly little parlour of the convent, a fire had been lit. Woman and girl stared at the flames.

'I have not been a good mother to you,' the woman said in a deep, beautiful voice.

'You have been a better mother than Papà has been a father,' said Latenia bitterly. 'At least you didn't try to sell me to Fogfinger.'

'I had no idea that he would sacrifice you like that.'

'He said he needed the money,' said Latenia dully.

'It might also have been to spite me,' said Lucia Malipiero.

'Or to compete with me, even. He wanted to be even less caring than I seemed – that was his mission, I realize now. I have been so wrong! I did not take you away with me because I believed your life would be better in the palace. How could I take you away from the comfort and safety of home to make you live a feral existence as a warrior's child in a cave on an island in the lagoon? Yet it was the hardest thing I ever did, to leave you.'

'How could you do it? Did you never truly love me?'

'Of course I loved you, both of you. I even attempted to love your father once.'

There was a silence. Latenia said, 'Once.'

'It was an arranged marriage, you see. Neither of us had any say in the matter. I tried hard at the beginning to be a good wife. But he never made the slightest effort to be a good husband. I was discouraged, and then grew bitter. I began to assert myself. We stopped agreeing on anything at all. At first, it was little things. He preferred hot chocolate. I liked coffee. Then he started not to like my hair. Then he criticized my laugh. I stopped laughing.'

Latenia thought back. Did she remember her mother's laughter? There was nothing at all that seemed familiar about this woman.

Lucia Malipiero continued. 'It was not just on your father's part. I started not to like his eyes. His voice grated on my ears. And then I began to find his obsession with money rather distasteful.

'I started overhearing what people said about us. Both of us! They supposed that because I was married to him, I was like him: greedy, cold-hearted and a devoted toady of Fogfinger. I realized that I did not want to be one half of that couple. So I started to do things with our money that were the opposite of your father's desire to pile it up in a selfish mountain. At first, it was to prove that I was different from him. But then, as I began to really know the poorer people I met, I did it because it was the right thing to do.

'And he did not like it when I began to give money to the poor. I organized some of the other noblewomen to give up part of their housekeeping every month to help the poor pay the Winding Up Tax, which was crippling them. Each of us took responsibility for one poor family. Of course, by that time I was already spending far less on clothes. Your father hated my new, simple dresses. I wonder what he would have made of the breeches I eventually wore!'

Latenia pondered aloud, 'No one ever helped Tockle's family, or Biri's, or Amneris's. I guess there were not enough noblewomen to go around. Or perhaps they were afraid of their husbands finding out.'

She was astonished to see her mother weeping. Lucia Malipiero said softly, 'It all came to a head when the daughter of my beloved family was chosen to be Lambed. She had been like a daughter – another daughter – to me. Such a clever, sweet-natured girl. Many was the time I sat in her parents' kitchen with the child on my knee, drawing pictures. I taught little Maddalena to read.'

'Where was I?' Latenia regretted her jealousy as soon as the words were out of her mouth.

'At home in your crib, asleep, surrounded by the best automata in Venice and maids in uniform. I thought you could spare me for a few hours. I came and whispered to you sometimes, but you rarely seemed to wake. You were a remarkably sleepy baby. I suppose by that time Fogfinger had seen to it that Venetians really *were* born tired.'

'Maddalena's parents had to go out to work, so sometimes I would look after her. When she was Lambed, something turned inside my heart. She was the very first Lamb, you know. I always wondered if your father contrived it so, to hurt me.'

'But the Lambs—'

'The first two Lambs really did plunge to their deaths. It was a little while before the mermaids knew to save them, as I am sure you've been told. My little Maddalena drowned. I tried not to think of my own grief. Her parents had so little. And now their little daughter was taken from them. Fogfinger had exiled the priests by then – they could not even hold a funeral. The image of the Lamb was disgusting to me – I could not bear the way that Fogfinger had perverted everything good and innocent. I was young, healthy and I wanted to fight. After Maddalena's Lambing, I never lived at home again. First, I stayed with her parents, sleeping on the kitchen table. Then I made contact with the *Piccoli Pochi*. And they took me in.'

'Did Papà not send for you?'

'No. I think he was relieved that I was gone from his house. By this time, we could hardly bear to look at one another. Though I am sure he began to regret that I was out of his control. I put out rumours that I had run away to Paris and was living a high life, as I did not wish to draw attention and danger to my new comrades in the *Pochi*.'

'Did you not miss us?'

'Of course I did. But your father had forbidden me to come to the house unless it was on his terms. And for several years I found a way to come and watch you sleeping. There was a servants' passageway leading from the coal store and I would creep through it at the dead of night. I left a blue glass seahorse on your pillow every time I did.'

'I found them! But why did you stop?'

'Maffeo stopped me. Coming home late from one of his nasty revels, he caught me creeping across the passageway.

He shouted for help and I fled. I was masked and veiled, so I shall never know if he realized who I was. But the next time I came to see you I found the wall bricked up. That was why I had to resort to the secret notes in the handkerchiefs embroidered by your friend Amneris. So your father never knew that I was with the *Pochi*?'

'He told us nothing about you. Maffeo and I thought you were dead. Then I heard from Fogfinger that you were disgraced. And if I married him, he said, it would be a way to clean the dirt from our family's reputation. But—' Latenia struggled for the right words, 'I think you were brave. And kind.'

'May I hug you?'

Latenia did not hold out her arms. Stiff and uncomfortable inside her mother's embrace, she heard the words, 'That dreadful marriage might have happened, because I was not there to protect you. I am sorry. I am sorry. I cannot even ask you to forgive me.'

'You don't have to ask my pardon,' Latenia said politely. 'I am sure I am grateful to you. Venice is grateful to you and the *Piccoli Pochi*. I'm not upset. And I was so young when you left, I did not even know that I was separate from you. Maffeo perhaps felt it more than I did.'

'Frankly – and here I show myself for the poor mother they say I am – it was not such a wrench to leave Maffeo. He was already a bad sort. And sadly, never very bright. I had no influence over him, right from the start. He rejected me. He was a little lord, and he did not respect anyone, particularly not his mother.'

'And why my terrible nickname? The she-tapeworm?'

'I named you "Natalia". It was your father who went to the Daughters' Magistrate to change your name after I left. He knew I would hear. It was another act of revenge.'

'Well, I suppose he's sorry now.'

Signor Malipiero was among a dozen of Fogfinger's former cronies now awaiting trial. By coincidence, he was chained to the same throne where Annibale D'Ago had lived and slept for nineteen years. But Signor Malipiero had been used to much softer living and therefore found the cold stone that much harder on his hindquarters.

'He's asked me to plead on his behalf,' said Lucia Malipiero.

Latenia gave a short, bitter laugh. 'He wanted you dead so he could marry a Golden Book dowry. I suppose you'll be telling Doge Annibale to give him the death penalty?'

'No,' said Lucia Malipiero. 'The hatred and the revenge have to stop. And, after all, he is your father.'

'Don't mind me,' said Latenia, 'if you want to destroy him. And Maffeo.'

'I hate to hear this hardness in your voice, Lat—, no I shall call you "Natalia", as you were christened. You need to learn to trust, to be a child again. Like your friends – Amneris and Biri and Temistocle.'

'Do you think they are really children? They were Lambed! They saw terrible things. They were forced to do terrible things. But at least they always knew their parents loved them. Of course, you'll know Tockle's father already – he was in the *Piccoli Pochi* with you, wasn't he? Rizardo Molin and the friars and Signor Castrauro the glass-blower and Thadeo Fava: they were your real family these last years, were they not? It was with them that you did those very risky, important and glamorous missions. Which you loved.'

Latenia's voice did not rise above a monotone. 'Still, I suppose I had my jewels and my silks – glamorous too – and I have them back now.'

'Daughter,' said Lucia, rising abruptly, 'you've been accustomed to luxury instead of love. You still consider luxury more important. I recognize this is my fault.'

'Don't go!' The words slipped from Latenia's mouth.

'I have no intention of it.' Lucia Malipiero took her hand. 'It's also a very risky, important and glamorous mission to be the mother of a daughter.'

EPILOGUE
Boon or Bust?

In the cavern under the House of the Spirits, Lussa had called a meeting. Attending were Amneris, Biri, Ugo and all the members of the *Piccolissimi Pochi*, including the former Lambs. The adults of the *Piccoli Pochi* were of course obliged to wait for news of proceedings from their colleagues who were not yet fourteen years old. Tockle was on his way back from Cairo with his father aboard Annibale D'Ago's Ark. Any day now the ship would pull into Zadar harbour, where Biri's parents were waiting to board.

Chissa offered steaming sea-cocoa all round. 'The mouth dries up when ye's chewing the rag. I brung ye some appley-toffee too. Has a powerful alleviatin' effect on the tied tongue.'

Lussa said, 'Before He set off for Africa, Doge Annibale asked for our Advice. What is to be done about the Automata of Venice? What is the Just Fate for all those Ingenious Devices that presently lie idle and a-rusting in Venetian Palaces? Doge Annibale has supplied an Inventory.' She showed them a thick scroll. 'There are fully Three Hundred and Fifty Thousand Automata in this City.'

'Burn 'em all!' growled Biri. 'I'll dance on the embers, me.'

'Me too!' cried Amneris and Ugo.

'I can understand your Bitterness, Children. But You must divide your Anger and your Good Sense. Not *all* Mechanical Devices are Evil.'

'Show me a good 'un,' muttered Biri.

Lussa smiled. 'We Ourselves have contemplated taking up the Art of Printing, so that, in Times of Peril, We may spread our Messages to Adult Venetians, who cannot see Us … yet. We have hung back, worried.'

'Why?' asked Ugo. 'That seems an excellent idea.'

'Yar. But We watched how Machines robbed the working Venetians of their Trades & turned Half the City into Lazy & Luxurious Parasites—'

'Floppin' around loik dying goldfish!' said Chissa scornfully. 'There's more muscle in my earlobe than in the whole Golden Book of Venetian nobles.'

'… With the other Half Poor and Oppressed. The Automata created a Life of Misery for the Winder Uppers, as Slaves of the Machines Themselves.'

Everyone nodded.

'But the Machines are not Evil in Themselves – They are Clever, Surprising, Useful & even Beautiful. And Why should We rein in & subdue the Brilliant Creativity of Doge Annibale? That in Itself would be a Crime!'

Amneris said, 'Anyway, I don't believe even mermaid magic could stop him.'

Lussa nodded. 'So, are these Machines a Boon or a Bust? That is the Question.'

'Bust,' muttered Biri. 'Bust, Bad Luck and Botheration.'

Chissa said, 'Yoiks! I like yer style, little maid.'

'So what is your decision?' asked Amneris.

Lussa made a gesture with her hand towards a lumpy

314

outcrop at the edge of the cavern. Two mermaids tugged at a silk sheet, revealing a beautiful jewel box of a printing press, studded with oysters and pearls, with fish bones for levers.

'The Solution is that We shall proceed with Caution. And We ask You to advise Doge Annibale that Venice should not destroy the Beautiful & Ingenious Automata for 'Twould be a Wanton Waste. Yet 'Tis but Half an Answer, I fear.'

Amneris cried, 'There *is* a solution! It's simple! *Everyone in Venice shall wind their own automata.* So no one shall pay a tax for the service.'

Biri said, 'But in the Frari, the day we got Lambed, that Fog captain said there was one hundred and forty thousand Venetians—'

'So if you divide three hundred and fifty thousand automata by the number of people, then everyone will need to wind ...' Amneris quickly did the sum in her head 'Only ... two-and-a-half automata. Quite manageable!'

'Da beautiful brain on dat maid!' marvelled a young mermaid. 'Yoiks!'

'Indeed, a Sterling Notion.' Lussa clapped her hands.

'Food is served,' called the chef-mermaid.

'Fud!' 'Fud!' 'Fud!' cried the mermaids' parrots.

'Where in wibble did yon varminty birds get learned to *talk*?' demanded Chissa.

Biri smiled. 'My Scarlet Loory gave 'em a few lessons.'

'Not sure we'll be thanking ye for that,' grumbled Chissa. 'It's one thing to teach a parrot to speak, quite another to make him shut his babbling beak.'

'Babbling, babbling, babbling,' called the parrots happily.

'Parrot school for ye brutal ugly lot!' threatened Chissa. 'Floggings and no supper for shoddy squawking.'

'Brutal,' remarked one parrot in a small, dismal voice.

'Perhaps wind-up parrots would be better?' continued

Chissa. 'Then there'd be no dirty doings with the Parrot Particular.'

'Pooh!' agreed the parrots.

'Avast heaving there!' cried Lussa. 'I'll have No Dead Metal Carcass impersonating a Living Thing in my Kingdom.'

'Sp-speaking of living things,' stammered Amneris. 'Will … will the Sea-Saurs come … back into this cavern?'

What she really wanted to ask was, '*Now that they have killed, do they have a taste for human flesh?*'

'No,' Lussa read her thoughts, 'remember, the Saurs did not dine off our Enemy, Child. 'Tis not their Way. And They are already Far from Venice, en Route to their Ancestral Waters near Cappadocia. But They have left Us a Gift.'

A large straw basket was floated into the cavern by four mermaids. Seaweed Familiars clustered at its edges. In the middle rested a smooth oval object in stippled greens and blues.

'Behold,' said Lussa, 'a Sea-Saur Egg. They have entrusted It to Us. In precisely One Hundred and Eighteen Human Years – Two Sea-Saur Ones – It shall hatch.'

'Why did they leave it here?' asked Amneris. She could not quite find it in her heart to rejoice at the strange gift.

'Your Instinct to worry is Correct,' said Lussa. 'I fear that the Answer is not One to soothe. It means that when the Infant Sea-Saur is born, It will be Ready to protect this City against a New & Terrible Danger.'

'So in 1901, Venice will be threatened again?' Amneris calculated. 'At least we'll have a hundred and eighteen years of peace in between.'

'No, One cannot say even That,' said Lussa. 'A City like Venice shall always attract Fearsome Enemies. She is too Beautiful not to be Hated, Coveted, Desired, Punished. To every Age, There shall come a New Danger, a New Enemy who shall wish to make a Ghost Town of Her. This is what is Written in the Book of Venice's Destiny. This is Why there are Mermaids, and that is Why, in every Age, Brave & Clever Children are born into this Marvellous City.'

She raised a chalice to Amneris, Biri and Ugo. 'To You, and to Those Babies who shall be Born to You!'

Chissa echoed, 'And the babies born to them, and so on and so on, all the way to 1901.'

'And so on! And so on!' called the parrots.

Amneris blushed fiercely. She was glad Tockle wasn't there to hear about all these babies and so ons. It was the first time she'd been glad about his absence. Venice had seemed curiously quiet and empty these last few weeks, and not just because the automata were silent.

'Belly up!' cried Biri. Amneris noticed she was holding Ugo's hand.

What is true and what is made up

Fogfinger, his frightful Lambing ceremony, the Sea-Saurs and the mermaids are all invented, but Venice provided (and still provides) the watery, light-washed magical environment, the delicate architecture and the historical elements that combined to make this story possible. So there are historical facts and real place names embedded in every magical scene, and the descriptions of the clothes and food of the time are based on fact, as is the well-known (and risky) craving of Venetians for any kind of novelty.

Saint George and the Dragon

In some ways, this story is a retelling of the Saint George and the dragon legend – one quite sympathetic to the dragon's point of view.

The classic tale is of a dragon holding a pagan town hostage, extracting two young people as tribute every year. Saint George agreed to kill the dragon if the townspeople would convert to Christianity. It is generally accepted that the dragon is an allegory of evil, and that George represents the triumph of Christian goodness.

I have always been interested in the passivity with which the people of the Saint George legend allowed their children to be given up to the dragon. The Christian legend seems to indicate that it was their very paganism that allowed the townspeople to be so complicit in the sacrifice of their own sons and daughters.

318

Saint George was adopted as patron saint of England by Edward III, and was said to have helped the Christian crusaders at Antioch in 1098.

Venice also took on the cult of Saint George. Stone reliefs of the saint and his dragon can be found all over Venice – at *vaporetto* stops, on the front of churches, in quiet alleys. The most beautiful paintings of the story are, in my opinion, to be found at the Scuola Dalmata and were painted by Vittore Carpaccio at the turn of the sixteenth century.

And Venice added her own local side-story to the Saint George legend, as recorded by David Rosand in his *Myths of Venice*. A vicious storm approached Venice on the night of February 25th, 1341, bringing winds and waves that threatened to engulf the city. An old fisherman hoped to weather the tempest by crouching down under a bridge, from where he was approached by a man who appeared to have come out of the basilica of San Marco. The stranger ordered the fisherman to row him across the storm-tossed *bacino* to the island of San Giorgio Maggiore. There the boat was boarded by a second stranger. The fisherman was commanded to take the vessel to San Nicolò al Lido, where a third man joined them. Then all three revealed their true identities: Saint Mark, Saint George and Saint Nicholas. They asked the fisherman to row them out to sea. In the midst of the waves, they encountered a galley manned by demons determined to destroy Venice. But the three saints prayed hard. Saint Mark made the sign of the cross and the diabolical vessel finally sank to the depths. The story is commemorated in a vast painting by Jacopo Palma il Vecchio, commissioned by the Scuola di San Marco and completed after his death by Paris Bordon: *Venice saved from Demon by Saints Mark, George and Nicolas*. (Its alternative title is *La Burrasca, The Storm*.) The painting can be seen at the Accademia galleries today. I went to look at it when writing the scene about Fogfinger's devil-shop attacking the Traitors' Ark: the chilling image provided all the inspiration I needed.

Names

Amneris D'Artania was a witness in a murder trial in Venice in the 1920s, about which the historian Lucio Sponza has written a fascinating article. Amneris is also the name of the Pharaoh's daughter in Verdi's opera *Aida*. Other names were taken from Venetian history books, telephone directories and doorbells.

Rio dei Mendicanti – the cloth-dyers' quarter

Antonio Canaletto's large painting of this area shows it as it was in 1724 – a poor, crowded place with pennants of dyed cloth drying on racks on the roofs. 'Mendicanti' means 'beggars' in Italian. One of the city's poorhouses was on this canal, and it doubled as a famous musical academy for young orphan girls. This painting is one of the few Canaletto masterpieces left in Venice, and you can still see it at Ca' Rezzonico.

Compagnie (or 'Fraglie') della Calza

The Companies of the Stockings really did exist in late fifteenth- and sixteenth-century Venice. Maffeo's costume resembles a member of the Fraglia dei Zardinieri, as painted by Vittore Carpaccio in his cycle of paintings about Saint Ursula. Young noblemen joined together in these groups to play music, stage plays and banquets, recite poetry, play games and organize regattas and fancy-dress parties and masquerades. It was these young men who are thought to have started the Carnevale for which Venice became famous all over the world. There were dozens of companies, with names such as the *Belli*, the *Pigna*, the *Ziati*, the *Soprani*, the

320

Signorili, the *Piavoli*, the *Fraterni*, the *Potenti*, the *Perpetui*, the *Reali*, the *Floridi*, the *Sbragazadi*, the *Valorosi*, the *Zardinieri*, the *Ortolani*, the *Trionfanti*, the *Immortali*, the *Sempiterni*, the *Accesi* and the *Modesti*.

The Companies of the Stocking fell into decline at the end of the sixteenth century. Carnevale itself, which had become a six-month event that drew the world to Venice, was suppressed by Napoleon after the city surrendered to him in 1797. A revival took place in the late 1970s. And in the following years some of the old *Compagnie della Calza* were reborn as the *Nuovi Cortesi*, the *Accesi* and the *Antichi*.

The Natural History Museum in Venice and the Fondaco dei Turchi

Not many tourists seem to realize that Venice, perhaps unfairly stuffed with so many other attractions, also boasts an extremely splendid Museum of Natural History. Every child who comes to the city should nag and pester and carry on until their parents take them to the old Fondaco dei Turchi on the Grand Canal.

The collection is divided into several parts. First you climb to the second floor to see the skeletons of a wonderful ancient crocodile, *Sarcosuchus imperator*, and a crested dinosaur, *Ouranosaurus nigeriensis*, both from the Cretaceous period, 110 million years ago. *Sarcosaurus*, on whom my Sea-Saurs are based, was as long as a bus and weighed eight tons. Its jaw was a metre long. At the end was a bulbous protuberance, the size of a large watermelon. This was the cavity for its nostrils, allowing it to take in air and hide under water for its prey. The curators also think that this large chamber would have given the *Sarcosaurus* a wonderful sense of smell and also allowed it to make terrifying noises (in my book, of course, it allows them to sing). It had a hundred sharp teeth. Unlike my Saurs, it used them on fish and perhaps also other animals.

After the *Sarcosaurus*, the museum traces 'The Path of Life' from the Precambrian to the Cenozoic periods, spelled out in a rich collection of fossils, beautifully displayed.

This leads into the older parts of the museum, where things take on a completely different character. Suddenly, you are in the world of 'ethnographic collections' of tribal weapons, musical instruments, tools and dress, collected by the poet, musicologist and explorer Gianni Miani (1810–72), who adopted Venice as his home. His collection of 1,800 objects includes a priestess mummified with her two crocodiles, which he found on an expedition to trace the source of the Nile in 1859. His handwritten, illustrated journal of his expedition also belongs to the museum. Miani died in Africa on another safari, this time to look for rare and unknown animals.

The next two rooms are rather more disturbing. They are lined with stuffed 'trophies' (dead animals) killed by Giuseppe de Reali (1877–1937) a rich Venetian landowner, politician and financier, who undertook no less than twelve big-game hunting expeditions to Africa between 1898 and 1929. Many of Reali's victims – some now extinct – are decapitated or flayed with just their heads stuffed. Below the mounted giraffes, rhinos, lions and antelopes are photographs of the animals dying: Reali immortalized the moment of their death.

Even worse than the mounted heads, in my opinion, is the way in which Reali fused parts of animals together to make bizarre ornaments and home furnishings. Some of the descriptions in this story are taken from what you can see in the museum today. The gorilla with the flattened belly is there – his plaque says he was killed in the French Congo in

1925. (The curator Margherita Fusco told me that his belly is bald because too many Venetian children have stroked it over the decades.) The billiard table with rhinoceros legs is also there, and the snake lamp-stands.

The Reali rooms reflect an attitude of their time that now seems quite inappropriate: that the 'white man' was entitled, by virtue of his 'superiority', to colonize and 'civilize' the world. The process included the conquest of the great creatures of nature.

The curators have done what they can to show sensitivity in today's display. The walls are painted blood-red – a colour that seems like a comment. And Reali's photographs of the whole animals, dead, are arranged at eye level, so you can see just what it cost to decorate this room. And most affecting of all are the sounds that you hear in the room: recordings of live animals making their natural noises in the wild. Instead of being a monument to death, the rooms remind you very vividly of what was lost every time Reali added another trophy to his collection.

Beyond Reali's mounted massacre is a room devoted to Giancarlo Ligabue, a Venetian businessman and palaeontologist born in 1931. He established the Ligabue Centre of Research Studies, which undertakes expeditions and digs all over the world.

Next, the visitor finds a 'Wunderkammer' or 'Cabinet of Curiosities' – a little circular room containing such strange things as a four-legged chicken, a fake mermaid, consisting of half a monkey thrust into half a fish, a basilisk made out of shark skin, a real two-headed calf, and a mummified cat, which I believe once belonged to Doge Francesco Morosini. It is inspired by the famous Wunderkammer of Imperato Ferrante in Naples and shows the preference for the strange kinds of creatures described with wonder in mediaeval bestiaries or in fanciful travellers' tales. It was, in fact, little collections of curiosities like this, dating from the seventeenth century, which launched the concept of displays of natural specimens for education and pleasure, paving the way for the great public museums of the present.

Through this room you reach the collection of endearingly shabby stuffed animals – sharks with crossed eyes, mouldy egrets – not hunting trophies but part of a scientific collection donated by Alessandro Ninni (1837–92) and others. Penetrating deeper into the room, you find embryos and body parts mysteriously preserved by a plastination technique that was lost with its inventor, the museum's long-term curator, Enrico Filippo Trois. There you can also see the skeleton of the bell-ringer, Campanaro, who was a giant. The story is that Trois won the right to this skeleton when he took on the bell-ringer's gambling debts.

The newest part of the museum follows, a series of beautifully arranged and curated rooms illustrating 'Strategies of Life', including locomotion, feeding and migration.

In this story, I write as if the museum and all its exhibits already existed just as they are in the 1780s. But the truth is that the museum was not always at the Fondaco de Turchi, and it did not contain quite so much until very recent times. The Fondaco was originally built in the fourteenth century as a private warehouse and residence. It also hosted important foreign visitors. In 1621, it was allotted to the Turkish community, who traded oil, wax, wool, leather and later tobacco in Venice. They occupied it (dividing it into sections for the Bosnians and Albanians, and the Persians and the Armenians) until 1838, and the city acquired it in 1858, subjecting it to a drastic restoration that caused howls of protest among art and architectural historians.

Natural history in Venice was not always just a matter of

hunting, even historically. Some Venetian nobles like Carlo Ruzzini had been collecting natural history specimens since the late sixteenth century, though collections of antiquities were more popular. Teodoro Correr (1750–1830) left a vast collection to the city, including natural history specimens. His donations and endowment provided the resources for the Museo Civico and Raccolta Correr. Nicolò Contarini (1780–1849) also left the Museo Correr his collection of natural history drawings and specimens, as did Giandomenico Nardo (1802–77), a specialist in Venetian and Adriatic zoology, and the surgeon Giovanni Zanardini (1804–78) who studied the algae of the area, and Alessandro Pericle Ninni (1837–92) who studied and collected Venetian fish and fauna. Finally, Enrico Filippo Trois (1838–1918), a pupil of Nardo and a collector of fauna, became curator of all Venice's natural history collections in 1866, keeping the post until he died. His innovative anatomical preparations – both dry mounting and liquid storage – received many awards. Examples are on display in the museum today.

In 1866, some of the current natural history collection came to the Fondaco, and was exhibited on the ground floor in 1880, the year that the building became the first home of the Correr Museum. The artistic and historical materials were transferred to the current premises in the Piazza San Marco in 1922 leaving space at the Fondaco. Gradually, more of the private scientific collections found their way there, including that of Count Alessandro Pericle Ninni. From 1923, the Fondaco dei Turchi became the official Natural History Museum in Venice. In 1930, the older collection was put in the rooms it occupies now. Extensive refurbishment and the creation of new displays kept the museum closed for many years. But now it is open again, and provides one of the most interesting and unexpected experiences you can have in Venice.

One of the nicest features of the museum is the Tegnùe Aquarium. This five-metre tank holds 5,000 litres of water and contains a miniature section of the northern Adriatic Sea's living natural history. Several graceful seahorses constantly make their way across the tank. In Italian, a seahorse is called *un cavallucio marino*.

Santa Maria Gloriosa dei Frari

This is the brick-built Gothic church where the Lambing takes place in the book. It is a church of the Franciscans, who were given the land to construct it in 1250. Building took place in several stages and over several centuries. Venetians do not usually use the full title of the church, but call it simply 'the Frari'.

Of course the real church, one of the biggest and most beautiful in Venice, has never been the site of anything so barbaric as Lambings.

Its walls are vivid with works by Titian, Giovanni Bellini, Vivarini and other Venetian masters. There is also a magnificent collection of reliquaries containing the bones and hairs of various saints.

If you visit the church, you can see some of the things described in the book. The black tomb where the mechanical lamb is buried belongs to Alvise delle Torre, murdered in a family feud in 1549. On the left of the nave, you see the three steps descending to a small door that gives access to the ramp of the square bell-tower, which was started in 1361 by the Venetian architect Jacopo Celega and completed in 1396 by his son Pier Paolo. (Outside, a stone plaque at the base explains these facts.) Funds were raised by the Bishop of Trebizond, and the Viaro family. (I wonder if this was a way for the Viaro clan to 'clean' their family name, as they were implicated in the murderous Bajamonte Tiepolo conspiracy of 1310 that lies behind the events of my first two children's novels, *The Undrowned Child* and *The Mourning Emporium*.)

At 70 metres, only the bell-tower of San Marco is taller than the Frari's, which is built of terracotta with horizontal stripes of white stone to mark the three orders. White stone is also used for the arches of the belfry. A bolt of lightning struck the tower in 1490, which resulted in a partial reconstruction of the upper part. Once a lead pyramid (like San Marco's tower), it is now a polygonal tambour.

The Frari's was one of the four towers in Venice whose bells announced meetings of the Grand Council. (The others were San Marco, San Geremia and San Francesco della Vigna.)

The bell-tower is not open to the public. But because of the kindness of Father Apollonio Tottoli, I was able to climb it and see its unusual and fascinating construction for myself. As this story reveals, the Frari's *campanile* hides a secret – it is, in fact, a double tower. The inner tower has arched windows three times the height of a man. The outer tower has tiny arched windows, which are, of course, visible from the outside. A pale light fills the stairwell, which takes the form of a ramp – so designed for wheeling construction materials more easily to the top. The ramp winds up between the inner and outer towers. With each new circuit of the four walls, you see a different view – at first the back of a canvas hung on the left nave wall, then the inside of the church glowing through a little window, then the street, then the roof of the church, than some of its towers. The glimpses of Venice grow increasingly panoramic the higher up you walk.

Amneris's fall down through the central tower would these days be prevented by the planks of wood that have been placed at every few metres. And of course there is no water at the base of the tower. Or Sea-Saurs.

The Lamb

The lamb is a traditional symbol of innocence and meekness. In Chinese mythology, the lamb represents the loyalty of children towards their parents. In the Christian faith, 'the Lamb of God' is one description of Jesus, who is sacrificed to save mankind.

But this gentleness has its own strength: even sorcerers are said to be powerless against the purity of the lamb. The lamb is depicted in different ways to illustrate different aspects of the faith: sometimes Christ carries a lamb – as the Good Shepherd who cares for his flock; a lamb with the cross represents the crucifixion; with a flag, the lamb symbolizes Christ's resurrection after death; with the book of the seven seals – the Last Judgement. A painting of a lamb flanked by a row of sheep signifies Christ and the disciples. The following saints are often seen with a lamb: John the Baptist, Saint Agnes and Saint Catherine.

The idea for the 'Lambing' of this story came when I was looking at a life-size stone relief of a lamb in the Frari. The lamb, in the Corner Chapel off the left transept, wears a smile. His undocked tail is as bushy as a fox's. He bears a tall cross. He marches proudly in a ring of rope held by two angels. He looks as if he might easily step out of it and take a little trot around the nave. I scribbled down a sketch of the lamb in my notebook, and that was the start of this book. Another favourite lamb is in a picture of Saint John the Evangelist in the country, by Marco Palmezzano (1460–1539) at Ca' Rezzonico in Venice.

Kaleidoscopes

These fascinating toys were invented in the 1820s or 1830s,

but I have taken the liberty of bringing their invention forward a little. Given the number of fragments of glass that must have been lying around on the floors of the famous glass-blowers in Venice, and the Venetians' love of firework displays, I think it very likely that some clever Venetian might have come up with such a toy some time before that happened anywhere else in the world.

Blue glass seahorses

Glass (and dried) seahorses really were used as good-luck talismans in Venice. In 1902, the English folklore specialist Edward Lovett (1852–1933) went to Venice where he commissioned some examples, which can today be seen at London's Wellcome Collection. He wrote:

> I found that the wives of fishermen, nursing babies, kept a dried seahorse on their breasts to facilitate the flow of milk [...] I am very much inclined to believe that the curious white metal prow of this remarkable boat [the gondola] is evolved from the seahorse.

Lovett's own collection featured in a 2011–12 exhibition called *Charmed Life: the Solace of Objects*, curated by the artist Felicity Powell. Her undulating display of tiny charms and amulets included a Venetian gondola *ferro* as well as some of the other talismanic objects that, in this book, Fogfinger foists on the credulous public.

In the *Miracles and Charms* exhibition held at the same time, I saw that the statue of Saint Jude in the church of San Hippolito in Mexico City was given a cloth mask during the swine flu epidemic – which was what gave me the idea of the saints being masked in Venice during Fogfinger's reign.

The Golden Book

This was the list of Venice's noblest families – those who had been dominant since the beginning of Venice's rise to power. There was a Silver Book for slightly less blue blood.

The Feast of the Redentore

The Redentore, with its procession of decorated boats and fireworks, still takes place on the third weekend in July. As this story explains, it celebrates the end of a plague that claimed a large part of Venice's population – 50,000 people – in 1577. And the religious side of the festival is still marked by building a temporary bridge of boats across the Giudecca Canal from the Zattere to the church of the Redentore.

Bigolanti

Walking water-sellers operated in Venice for centuries. They took their name from the *bigolò*, the long arched yoke they balanced upon their shoulders, with a bucket at either end. Their cry was '*Aqua mo!*' In 1493, their prices are recorded as eight buckets for a '*soldo*', the lowest unit of currency. Many of them were women. They carried water directly to people's houses and to shops. It was said that their water was '*dolce e chiara co fâ un spechio*' – 'sweet and clear as a mirror'. By the eighteenth century there were around a hundred *bigolanti*, taking water from 157 public wells, or from water barges that came in from Fusina or the Brenta Canal. The rich, and the convents, had their own wells in their private courtyards. It was said that there were 6,000 such private wells in the city.

Cats in Venice

I have written about Venetian cats in all my novels for children. In *Talina in the Tower*, my heroine even turns into a cat. In *The Undrowned Child* and *The Mourning Emporium*, you will also meet the 'famous' winged cats, who originally came from Syria.

Hot-air balloons

The first hot-air balloon was flown in France in 1783 by the brothers Jacques-Étienne and Joseph-Michel Montgolfier. The first hydrogen-powered balloon was launched in the same year. So Annibale D'Ago's balloon was a technical possibility. Indeed, Count Zambeccari launched one in Venice in 1784.

Fire at San Marcuola

The area really was devastated by a fire that started in an oil warehouse on November 28th, 1789. The blaze is immortalized in a painting by Francesco Guardi.

Faces

I borrowed some of the faces of my characters from Venetian paintings. Signor and Signora Malipiero's faces are from Lorenzo Lotto's *Portrait of a Married Couple*. To me, the husband and wife in that picture look as different – and as ill-suited – as the couple in this story. Lucia could also be the woman in Bernardini Licinio's *Picture of a Noble Lady and her Son* at Ca' Rezzonico. Maffeo's face too comes courtesy of Lotto: his *Portrait of a Young Boy*. Fogfinger's face and turban are those of the effete and mysterious musician in Pietro Longhi's painting *The Little Concert* and the same artist's *A Girl Spinning* showed me how the pale girls would have been required to hide their hair inside a scarf. His painting *The Apothecary* shows a dignified man in a yellow robe pulling a girl's tooth. Meanwhile, you can see a beautiful re-creation of an old Venetian apothecary's shop on the third floor of Ca' Rezzonico.

Automata

The great age of automata started around sixty years after this story is set. But automata were already a phenomenon in the eighteenth century. The most famous early example was a duck that walked, quacked, ate and apparently excreted. Presented to the public in 1739, it caused a sensation, and made its inventor, Jacques de Vaucanson, famous. He also created a mechanical flute player and a donkey-operated loom that wove intricate silk designs. An 'automaton chess player' was built by Wolfgang von Kempelen in 1769. Although it looked like an automaton, the chess player in fact hid a man inside, operating a mechanical arm: a series of skilled chess players was hired for the job.

Venice has a famous pair of automata from the fifteenth century: mechanical Moors who still hammer the bells in the clock tower at San Marco.

The Fate in the Box

The idea of a grinning skull inside a jack-in-the-box came to me during a visit to the Museum of Childhood at Bethnal Green in London. A little jack-in-the-box in the upper gallery struck me as horribly sinister. I thought, 'This is not a jolly toy. Actually it's a nasty surprise!' And, being a writer, I naturally turned my thoughts to even nastier surprises.

Indeed, the history of this toy is darker and longer than most. These days a jester or a clown pops out of the box when the handle is cranked. But it was not always so. One explanation is that it was invented by a fourteenth-century English prelate, Sir John Schorne, who trapped a devil in a boot to protect the village of North Marston in Buckinghamshire. In French the toy is known as a *diable en boîte* (literally 'devil in a box').

A German clock-maker is credited with making the first

jack – featuring a leering devil – for a prince's fifth birthday. The toy became popular. However, during the Renaissance, the devilish figure was gradually replaced with a colourful jester.

The jack-in-the-box was particularly popular during the 1930s and 1940s. The usual tune of 'Pop Goes the Weasel' was sometimes changed to 'Mary Had a Little Lamb'. At the end of the song, a lamb would pop out of the box.

Sheet messages

This has become a way for Venetians to communicate their feelings about certain issues – such as the waves made by speeding motorboats that undermine the foundations of buildings and the presence of the huge cruise liners that distort the skyline of Venice almost daily.

The Anagrammaticular

This is invented but inspired by stone lions' heads affixed to walls in Venice after Bajamonte Tiepolo's conspiracy in 1310. Citizens could drop written denunciations into the mouths of these lions.

Children's houses

Amneris D'Ago: in Cannaregio, a house stretched over the Calle Berlendis. The sewing room is the one in the arch over the street, with one window facing the street and the other on the Mendicanti Canal, from where, today, you can see the walled garden with trees.

Temistocle Molin: Corte Giovanelli, Santa Croce, a little *calle* off the square of San Zan Degola, where the round marble well has a handsome square pediment, and three holes for the local animals' drinking water in the base.

Biri Fava: Ramo della Tagliapietra (Tagiapiera in Venetian) near San Marcuola.

Ugo Paolin: the corner of the Calle delle Balote on the Fondamenta Morosini where three canals converge – the Rio dei Bareteri, the Rio dei Scoacamini and the Rio dei Ferali. Today there is a workshop with old furniture there.

Melchior Dubbini's shop would have been in the Mercerie, near San Marco, because that was where Venice's haberdashery shops were concentrated.

The Palazzo Malipiero is on the Grand Canal at San Samuele.

Michelle Lovric, May 2013

For more information about Venice and other children's books by Michelle Lovric, see www.michellelovric.com.

Acknowledgements

I'd like to thank Margherita Fusco from the Natural History Museum in Venice for her wonderful private tour and for answering my often strange questions, such as '*Do the legs of the billiard table belong to a hippo or rhinoceros?*' I'm grateful to Padre Apollonio Tottoli for allowing me to climb the long and winding ramp to the top of the Frari's bell-tower, to Ross Frassanito and Elena Romano for their joyful company up there and for taking the photographs from which I conjured the scenes, to Ornella Tarantola for perfecting my Italian, and to Ross MacFarlane at the Wellcome Collection for sharing his knowledge about Lovett's Venetian seahorse amulets. Many thanks also to my publisher, Fiona Kennedy, for her acute help and endlessly kind support, to my wonderful children's book agent, Sarah Molloy, especially for her idea for spicing up Fogfinger's last scene, to Sophie Hutton-Squire for copyediting, to Stephen Barber and Kristina Blagojevitch for patiently helping with other corrections, to Sarah Salway and Jane Kirwan for reading the early manuscripts, and to Meredith Crosbie, for setting up Facebook pages for the books. Nothing would be possible in Venice for me without Tony Bird – simply nothing. Love and thanks to Mary Hoffman, Laurie Graham, Penny Dolan, Adèle Geras, Dianne Hofmeyr, Louise Berridge and all the other History Girls for the welcoming community and nourishing intellectual resource they provide. And, finally, special thanks to my precious and precocious young editorial team of Lily Linke and Meli Pinkerton, whose marked-up copies of the manuscript are among my favourite possessions. With all this excellent help, obviously any mistakes that I have made are solely of my own manufacture.

the
orion star

Sign up for
newsletter to get inside information
about your favourite children's authors
as well as exclusive competitions and
early reading copy giveaways.

www.orionbooks.co.uk/newsletters

Follow  on twitter

Orion
Children's Books